Franz Kafka

Stories 1904–1924

Translated from the German by
J. A. Underwood

With a foreword by Jorge Luis Borges

An *Abacus* Book

First published in Great Britain by Macdonald & Co 1981
First paperback edition published by Futura Publications 1983
This edition published by Abacus 1995
Reprinted 1995, 1996, 1997

A CIP catalogue record for this book
is available from the British Library.

ISBN 0 349 10659 2

Printed in England by Clays Ltd, St Ives plc

Abacus
A Division of
Little, Brown and Company (UK)
Brettenham House
Lancaster Place
London WC2E 7EN

Contents

Foreword

Virgil on his deathbed asked his friends to burn the unfinished manuscript of the *Aeneid*, fruit of eleven years' noble and intricate toil; Shakespeare never gathered into a single volume his many separate plays; Kafka implored Max Brod to destroy the novels and stories that were to bring him lasting fame. Any affinity between these illustrious episodes is, unless I am much mistaken, an illusion. Virgil was surely relying on the devout disobedience of his friends, Kafka on that of Brod. Shakespeare's case is different. De Quincey believed that, for Shakespeare, a reputation was something to be achieved on the stage rather than through the printed word. The fact is, a man who really wishes to see his work consigned to oblivion does not entrust the task to someone else. I believe that Kafka and Virgil did not truly want such destruction to take place; they merely longed to disburden themselves of the responsibility that a literary work imposes on its creator. Virgil, I think, made his request for aesthetic reasons: he might still have wanted to change this or that verse, this or that epithet.

The case of Franz Kafka seems to be more complex. His work could be defined as a parable or series of parables on the theme of the moral relationship of the individual with his God and with his God's incomprehensible universe. For all their contemporary setting, his stories are less close to what is conventionally called modern literature than they are to the Book of Job. They presuppose a religious conscience, specifically a Jewish conscience; formal imitation of Kafka in another context would be unintelligible. Kafka saw his work as an act of faith, and he did not want it to discourage other men. Because of this, he asked his friend to destroy it. However, I suspect further reasons. Kafka knew he could dream only nightmares and was aware that reality is a continuous sequence of melancholy

5

nightmares. Added to which, he appreciated the dramatic potential of delays and postponements; this is apparent throughout his work. But both these themes, melancholy and delay, undoubtedly wearied him in the end. He might perhaps have preferred to be the author of a few happy pages—such as his honesty would not allow him to write.

I shall never forget the first time I read Kafka in a certain self-consciously 'modern' publication around 1917. The editors, who were not wholly devoid of talent, had dedicated themselves to inventing texts that were notable for their lack of punctuation, capital letters, and rhyme as well as for their alarming simulation of metaphor, abuse of portmanteau words, and other experiments perhaps typical of all young people. Amidst all this boisterous print, a short text signed by Franz Kafka seemed to me—in spite of my youthful docility as a reader—extraordinarily insipid. Now, in my old age, I dare at last to own up to a case of unforgivable literary insensitivity; I was offered a revelation, and I passed it by.

We know of course that Kafka never ceased to feel a mysterious guilt in the presence of his father, as Israel did in the presence of its God; Kafka's Judaism, which set him apart from the rest of humanity, was clearly a torment to him. Furthermore, his awareness of the imminence of death, coupled with the feverish exaltation of his tubercular condition, must have sharpened all his faculties and senses.

These observations, however, are tangential; the truth is that, as Whistler said, 'art happens'. Two ideas—or rather two obsessions—pervade the work of Franz Kafka. The first is subordination, the second infinity. In almost all his stories we find hierarchies, and those hierarchies tend to be infinite. Karl Rossmann, the hero of his first novel *America,* a poor German youth making his way through the labyrinth of a continent, is finally admitted to the great 'Nature-Theatre of Oklahoma'; this infinite stage, no less populous than the world itself, is a prefiguration of Paradise (with a very personal touch, for not even in Kafka's image of heaven do men achieve total happiness;

there is still the odd slight but irksome delay).

The hero of his second novel, Joseph K., increasingly oppressed by an insane penal procedure, is able neither to find out what crime he is accused of nor to confront the tribunal that is supposed to be judging him; forgoing a trial, the invisible tribunal eventually orders his execution. K., the engineer hero of the third and last novel, is summoned to a castle that he never manages to enter; he must die outside the walls without ever having been recognized by the castle's governing authority.

Critics have complained that in Kafka's three novels many intermediate chapters are missing, though they acknowledge that those chapters are not indispensable. It seems to me that their complaint indicates a fundamental misunderstanding of Kafka's art. The pathos of these 'unfinished' works arises precisely out of the infinity of the obstacles that repeatedly hinder their identical heroes. Franz Kafka did not complete his novels because it was essential that they be incomplete. Zeno states that movement is impossible: in order to reach point B we must first pass the interjacent point C, but before we can reach C we must pass the interjacent point D, but before we get to D . . . Zeno does not list all the points any more than Kafka needs to enumerate all the vicissitudes. It is enough to know that they are as infinite as Hades.

Kafka's most striking talent was for inventing intolerable situations. A few lines (e.g. from his *Reflections on Sin, Suffering, Hope, and the True Way*) suffice to engrave them for ever on our minds: 'The animal wrenches the whip from his master's hands and whips himself in order to become the master, not knowing that this is a mere fancy generated by a new knot in the thongs of the master's whip.' Or this: 'Leopards break into the temple and drink the contents of the sacrificial vessels; this happens over and over again; eventually it can be reckoned with, and it becomes part of the ceremony.'

Kafka's craft is perhaps less admirable than his invention. Only one character appears in all his work: the *Homo domesticus,* so Jewish and so German, so eager to keep his

7

place, however humble and in whatever order—the universe, a ministry, a lunatic asylum, a gaol. Plot and atmosphere are the essential characteristics of Kafka's work, not the convolutions of the story nor the psychological portrait of the hero. This is what makes Kafka's stories superior to his novels; this is why we can assure the reader that the present volume gives us the full dimension of this unique writer.

Jorge Luis Borges

Translator's preface

Even had Brod felt obliged to comply with his friend's request (and he explained why he had not in his Afterword to the first edition of *The Trial*), he could not have burnt *all* of Kafka's work because, very largely at Brod's own instigation, some of it had already appeared in reviews and much of that had subsequently been published in volume form. The present collection brings together, for the first time in English, all the stories that Kafka allowed to appear in volume form during his lifetime (*A Fasting-artist* in fact came out after his death, but Kafka had read the proofs). From the very earliest pieces that the author included in his first book, *Looking to See,* to his last work, *Josephine,* written in March 1924, it spans the twenty years of Franz Kafka's writing life—a life wholly committed to a desperate adventure of the mind that, out of what might seem to have been the most circumscribed of experiences (Kafka was a member of a German-speaking Jewish literary clique in turn-of-the-century Prague), created a body of work that has become an international landmark in modern literature.

I am not a critic, and it is not for me to seek to place these stories in the context of Kafka's work as a whole (though I can hardly avoid mentioning Kafka's other, earlier testamentary directive to Max Brod, quoted in the Afterword to the first edition of *The Trial,* to the effect that, 'of everything I have written, only the Judgement, Stoker, Metamorphosis, Penal Colony, and Country Doctor books and the Fasting-artist story are valid'). For a lively introduction to Kafka's work the reader is referred to Ronald Gray, *Franz Kafka* (Cambridge University Press, 1973), and for evidence of the abiding significance of that work to Professor J. P. Stern's recent symposium, *The World of Franz Kafka* (Weidenfeld, 1981).

What I have to answer is the obvious question, 'Why a

9

new translation of Kafka (since all these stories are currently available in translations by Willa and Edwin Muir and some in translations by other people)?' The answer is quite simply, in this instance, 'Because a new translator was asked to do the job.' And to the obvious second question, 'Is this simply a rewritten Muir?' I must reply that I made my translations without reference to the Muirs or to any of the existing English versions. Having made them, however, and knowing that my work would inevitably invite comparison with the 'standard version', I looked at what the Muirs had written. I found this a stimulating exercise, not only so long as it satisfied me that I had been more faithful to Kafka's German than they had, but also on the occasions when what I saw in the Muirs showed me the way to something better than either they or I had originally hit upon; where they came off best, I resisted the temptation to steal.

I have begged the question of fidelity in translation. This is of course the ideal and as such only to be approached, never achieved. A translator's rule of thumb might be to seek to carry as much of the original across to the reader of the target language as is compatible with an equivalent level of readability. Try to carry too much and the vessel founders; jettison too much and you are cheating the consignee. Enough goes by the board in any case. To take one example, when the protagonist of *The Metamorphosis* wakes up to find himself changed into a 'giant bug', most of the cultural resonance of Kafka's *ungeheures Ungeziefer* in terms of social and religious exclusion has been lost, though I hope his paradoxical tone of matter-of-fact outrage still comes across. (Strictly speaking, 'monstrous vermin' would be more faithful, but the awkwardness of that noun in the singular might balk the reader in a way that is irrelevant to Kafka's purpose.) On the other hand I make no apology for Anglicizing the first names Georg, Gregor, Grete, Josef, and Josefine (they are people, not foreigners) or for retaining most of Kafka's occasionally idiosyncratic punctuation. One is continually trimming for a balance between content and equivalence, between the demands of fidelity and the requirements of readability. Yet these dualisms are over-simple and falsely imply a conflict. For if Kafka is readable with keen pleasure in German, fidelity itself will require that the English reader be given access to the same order of enjoyment. And much of Kafka's prose asks to be read aloud—indeed, we know from Max Brod how Kafka himself enjoyed declaiming it to his friends.

One other point needs to be made here. An English translation of Kafka made in 1980 must avoid anachronism, of course, but it must also take some account of what has happened to literary English in the half-century and more since Kafka wrote, and in this connection, while it is a truism to say that Kafka was ahead of his time, it does serve to remind one that the Muirs were at this great disadvantage, as it were: they translated *Die Verwandlung* and *In der Strafkolonie* before Samuel Beckett, for example, published his first novel.

It would be odd if I did not presume to have improved to some extent upon the way in which Willa and Edwin Muir rendered these stories, but no one will ever challenge the part they played in introducing Kafka's work to the English-speaking world—certainly not one who has them to thank for his own first encounter with Kafka.

Finally, without shirking any of the responsibility for what follows, may I thank Alberto Manguel, Marion Boyars, and Toby Roxburgh for their different, very valuable contributions to this publication?

J.A.U.

Looking to See

(*Betrachtung;* the individual pieces were written
between c. 1904 and 1912 and published in volume
form by Ernst Rowohlt in December 1912.)

Children in the lane

I could hear the carts driving by on the other side of the fence; I even caught occasional glimpses of them through the shifting gaps in the foliage. How their wooden spokes and shafts creaked in that hot summer! Workmen returning from the fields laughed outrageously.

I was sitting on our little swing, having a rest among the trees in my parents' garden.

The commotion beyond the fence went on and on. Running children passed in a flash; wheat-carts with men and women perched on top of and all around the sheaves threw shadows on the flower-beds; towards evening I saw a gentleman with a stick out for a stroll and two girls, coming arm-in-arm in the opposite direction, side-stepped into the grass with a greeting.

Then birds flew up like spray and I followed them with my gaze, watched how they rose with one breath till I no longer believed they were rising but that I was falling, and holding tightly to the ropes I began to swing a little from sheer faintness. Before long I was swinging more strongly as the breeze blew cooler and in place of the flying birds flickering stars appeared.

When the candle was lit I was given my supper. I often leant both arms on the wooden table-top as I bit sleepily into my bread and butter. The coarse openwork curtains billowed in the warm wind, and occasionally someone going past outside would catch hold of them, wanting to see me better and have a word with me. Usually the candle soon went out, and in the murky smoke the assembled mosquitoes would gad about for a while longer. If someone asked me a question from the window I would eye him as if staring at the mountains or off into space, and he would set no great store by an answer either.

If he then vaulted in over the sill and announced that the others were waiting in front of the house, I would of course rise to my feet with a sigh.

'Hey, why the sigh? What's happened? Some out-of-the-ordinary, irretrievable disaster? Will we never be the same again? Are you saying all is lost?'

Nothing was lost. We ran round to the front of the house. 'Thank God, there you are at last!'—'You're always late, you are!'—'Why pick on me?'—'Well, you are. Stay at home if you don't want to come.'—'No mercy!'—'What do you mean, no mercy? What are you talking about?'

We took the evening head-on. There was no day-time and no night-time. One minute our jacket buttons were gnashing like teeth; next minute we were running at even intervals apart, fire in our mouths, like beasts in the tropics. Like dragoons in old-time wars, pawing and rearing, we spurred one another on down the short street and let our legs carry us far up the lane out of the village. Some dropped into the ditches; hardly had they disappeared against the dark banks when they emerged to stand like strangers high up on the field path, looking down.

'Come back down!'—'No, you come up!'—'For you to throw us down again? Not likely—we've more sense.' —'You mean you're too scared. Come on up, come on!'—'Scared? Of you? Think you can throw us down, do you? You've got a hope!'

We attacked, were pushed in the chest, and lay down in the grassy ditch, falling of our own free will. The world was a mellow place; we were aware of neither warmth nor cold in the grass, only of a weariness.

If you turned onto your right side and put a hand under your ear, you felt like falling asleep. You may have wanted to push yourself up once more with your chin in the air, but only to fall into a deeper ditch. Then you wanted to hurl yourself, holding one arm out straight, legs awry, off into space, and know you would fall back into a still deeper ditch. And you wanted to go on and on doing this.

How you would really lie down to sleep in your last resting-place, stretched right out, especially the knees, is something you hardly gave a thought to as, on the brink of tears, you lay on your back like an invalid. You blinked whenever one of the boys, holding his elbows in and showing his dark soles, leapt over you from the bank back into the lane.

The moon was already some way up the sky; a mail coach drove by in its own light. A gentle wind got up; you felt it even in the ditch, and the nearby forest started to rustle. You were no longer so set on being alone.

'Where are you all?'—'This way!'—'Everyone over here!' —'What are you hiding for? That's enough of that.'— 'Don't you realize the mail coach has already gone past?'—'No, surely it hasn't yet?'—'Of course it has; went past while you were asleep.'—'Me? Asleep? Come off it!'—'Shut up and take a look at yourself.'—'Oh, really!' —'Let's go!'

We stayed closer as we ran, some of us holding hands, and we had to keep our heads up as high as we could because the going was downhill. One boy yelled an Indian war-cry; we worked up a gallop like nobody's business; the wind gave a lift to our hips as we leapt. Nothing could have stopped us; we had so much momentum that even when overtaking we were able to fold arms and look casually about us.

At the bridge over the torrent we halted, those who had run on coming back. Below us the water smashed against boulders and roots as if it had not been late evening already. There was no reason why none of us jumped up on the handrail of the bridge.

From a coppice in the distance a train emerged, lights on in every compartment, the windows undoubtedly lowered. One of us started to sing a popular song, but we all wanted to sing. We sang much faster than the train was moving; we linked arms and swayed, because singing was not enough; our voices welded us into a euphoric throng. When you blend your voice with others it is like being taken on a hook.

And so we sang, with the forest behind us and the sound of distant travel in our ears. The grown-ups were still awake in the village; our mothers were getting the beds

17

ready for the night.

It was time. I kissed the person standing nearest to me, shook hands nonchalantly with the next three, started walking back the way we had come; no one called after me. At the first crossroads, where they could no longer see me, I turned off and followed the paths that led back into the forest. I was heading for the city in the south, of which they used to say in our village:

'There are people for you! Just think—they never go to sleep!'

'And why don't they?'

'Because they don't get tired.'

'And why don't they?'

'Because they're fools.'

'Don't fools get tired, then?'

'How could fools get tired?'

Unmasking a confidence trickster

Eventually, around 10 p.m., accompanied by a man whom I had known only slightly from a previous meeting and who this time had unexpectedly fallen in with me again and had been dragging me round the streets for two hours, I arrived in front of the elegant residence where I had been invited to a party.

'Right!' I said, clapping my hands together [to indicate the absolute necessity of our now parting company.] Several less resolute attempts already lay behind me, and I had had enough.

'Are you going straight up?' he asked. From his mouth there came a <u>sound like that of teeth meeting</u>.

'Yes.'

I was invited, as I had told him at the outset. But the invitation was to go up to where I so much wanted to be, not to stand about down there outside the door and stare past my interlocutor's ears. And now lapse into silence with him into the bargain, as if we had made up our minds to spend some time standing there. [It was a silence, moreover, in which the surrounding houses immediately took part, as well as the darkness above them and on up to the stars.] And the footsteps of invisible strollers whose course one had no wish to guess at, the wind that repeatedly thrust against the other side of the street, a gramophone singing behind the closed window of someone's room—all emerged from that silence as if it had been theirs for ever and always would be.

And my companion acquiesced in all this on his own and—after a smile—on my behalf, stretched his right arm out and upwards along the wall, and leant his face against it, closing his eyes as he did so.

I did not see the smile through to the end, however,

19

because a feeling of shame suddenly swung me round. The fact was, it had taken that smile to make me see that the man was no more than a confidence trickster. And I had been living in the city for months; I'd thought I knew their every trick, the way they approach you out of side streets at night, arms outstretched like head waiters, the way they hang about near the poster pillar by which you're waiting as if they were playing a game of hide-and-seek and spy on you round the curve of the column with one eye at least, the way in which, at street corners, the moment you begin to feel nervous, there they are, hovering in front of you on the edge of your pavement! I understood them so well; they were the first people I had got to know in the city's little pubs and restaurants, and it was them I had to thank for my first glimpse of an obduracy that now formed so integral a part of my picture of the world that I was beginning to be aware of it in myself. The way they held their ground, still facing you when you had long made good your escape, when, in other words, all possibility of pulling off the trick was past and gone! The way they neither sat down nor fell down but stood looking at you with eyes that, if only from a distance, were still persuasive! And their methods were always the same: they planted themselves in front of you, taking up as much room as possible; attempted to keep you from where you were trying to get to; offered you instead a place in their own heart; and, if your accumulated feelings eventually burst out of you in rebellion, accepted it as an embrace into which they threw themselves face first.

And these hoary ruses I had recognised on this occasion only after spending so much time with the man! I rubbed my fingertips together vigorously to obliterate the disgrace.

My man, meanwhile, still leaning in the same position, still looked upon himself as a confidence trickster; contentment with his lot brought a blush to his exposed cheek.

'Spotted you!' I said, giving him a tap on the shoulder. Then I hurried up the steps, and the unreasoning good faith written on the faces of the servants in the ante-room came as a delightful surprise to me. I studied them all, one by one, as my coat was taken away and my boots dusted. Drawing myself up with a sigh of relief, I strode into the hall.

The spur-of-the-moment stroll

When one has apparently made up one's mind to spend the evening at home and has donned one's house-jacket and sat down at the lamplit table after supper to do the particular job or play the particular game on completion of which one is in the habit of going to bed, when the weather out is so unpleasant as to make staying in the obvious choice, when one has been sitting quietly at the table for so long already that one's leaving must inevitably provoke general astonishment, when the stairwell is in any case in darkness and the street door locked, and when in spite of all this one stands up, suddenly ill at ease, changes one's coat, reappears immediately in street clothes, announces that one has to go out and after a brief farewell does so, feeling that one has left behind one a degree of irritation commensurate with the abruptness with which one slammed the apartment door, when one then finds oneself in the street possessed of limbs that respond to the quite unexpected freedom one has procured for them with out-of-the-ordinary agility, when in the wake of this one decision one feels capable, deep down, of taking any decision, when one realizes with a greater sense of significance than usual that one has, after all, more ability than one has need easily to effect and endure the most rapid change, and when in this frame of mind one walks the long city streets—then for that evening one has stepped completely outside one's family, which veers into inessentiality, while one's own person, rock solid, dark with definition, thighs thrusting rhythmically, assumes its true form.

The whole experience is enhanced when at that late hour one looks up a friend to see how he is.

Decisions

Lifting oneself out of a state of misery must be an easy matter even by the deliberate exercise of energy. I wrench myself from my chair, pace round the table, flex my head and neck, inject fire into my eyes, tensing the muscles around them. Inhibit every feeling, give A. a tumultuous welcome, should he turn up at this point, amiably bear with B. in my room, and with C., ignoring the pain and effort, take in everything that is said in deep draughts.

But even so every mistake—and mistakes are inevitable—will bring the whole enterprise, the easy and the difficult, to a grinding halt, and I shall have to turn back through one hundred and eighty degrees.

So the best advice is still to accept everything, act like a heavy mass even when one can feel oneself being blown away, not be tempted into taking a single unnecessary step, look at other people with animal eyes, feel no remorse—in short, physically suppress any spectral remnants of life, i.e. augment the ultimate quiet of the grave and allow nothing else to exist any more.

A gesture that is typical of this kind of condition is the little finger run along the line of the eyebrows.

The excursion into the mountains

'I don't know,' I exclaimed tonelessly, 'I really don't. If no
one comes, then no one comes. I've done no one any
harm, no one's done me any harm, but no one wants to
help me. No one, no one, no one. That's not the way it is,
though. It's just that no one helps me—otherwise the idea
of a lot of no one appeals to me. I'd like very much—why
not?—to go on an excursion with a whole crowd of no one.
Into the mountains, of course—where else? How they
jostle one another! So many arms held out sideways and
interlinked, so many feet separated by tiny steps! It goes
without saying that we're all in evening dress. We swing
along with the wind weaving through the gaps we leave
between us and between our limbs. How free the throat
feels in the mountains! It's a wonder we aren't singing.'

The bachelor's lot

It seems so awful to remain a bachelor, to beg with what one can salvage of one's dignity to be included when, as an old man, one wishes to spend an evening among people, to be ill and for weeks on end look out from one's bed corner at the empty room, always to say goodbye at the street door, never pushing one's way up the stairs beside one's wife, to have only side doors in one's room that lead into other people's dwellings, to carry one's supper home in one hand, to be forced to admire other people's children and not be allowed endlessly to repeat, 'I have none myself', to model one's appearance and behaviour on one or two bachelors remembered from one's youth.

That's how it is, no doubt, except that, in addition, there one actually stands today and will in the days to come be standing with a body and an actual head, which means with a forehead one can clap one's hand to.

The businessman

Possibly some people feel sorry for me, though I am not aware of it. My small business fills me with worries, which make my brow and temples ache, but without holding out the prospect of satisfaction because of its smallness.

I have to make arrangements hours in advance, jog the errand boy's memory repeatedly, warn against mistakes I fear may be made, and in any given season guess what the next season's fashions will be, not among the people of my own circle but among remote rural populations.

My money is in the hands of strangers; I have no perception of their circumstances and no notion of what misfortune may befall them, so how could I avert it! Perhaps they have adopted extravagant ways and are throwing a party in some garden restaurant, with other people, *en route* to a new life in America, dropping in on the party for a while.

When on a weekday evening I shut up shop and suddenly find myself facing hours in which I can do no work to meet the unremitting demands of my business, the excitement I had projected far ahead of me in the morning flings itself back at me like an incoming tide; refusing to be contained, it sweeps me along on its aimless course.

And yet I am totally unable to exploit the mood; all I can do is go home, because my face and hands are soiled and sweaty, my clothes are stained and dusty, I am wearing my working cap, and my boots bear the scratches of packing-case nails. At such times I walk as if wave-borne, clicking the fingers of both hands and, as children pass, stroking their hair.

It's not far enough, though; I am home in no time, opening the lift door and stepping into the lift.

I realize that I am now, suddenly, alone. Other people, with stairs to climb, tire themselves somewhat in the pro-

cess before having to wait with heaving lungs for someone
to open the door of their flat, which provides them with
occasion for irritation and impatience; they then enter the
hall, where they hang up their hat, and it is not until they
have walked down the passage past several glass doors and
reached their own room that they are alone.

I am alone as soon as I enter the lift, where I prop
myself on my knees to look in the narrow mirror. As the
lift begins its ascent I say:

'Be still, all of you; step back, if you will, into the shade
of the trees, behind the curtains in the windows, into the
canopy of leaves.'

I speak with my teeth, and the landings slide down the
panes of frosted glass like waterfalls.

'Fly away; may your wings, which I have never seen,
carry you to the village in the valley or off to Paris, if that is
the way the whim takes you.

'But enjoy the view from the window when the proces-
sions emerge from all three streets, refuse to give way to
one another, pass through one another, and between their
last departing ranks recreate the open square. Wave your
handkerchiefs, be horrified, be moved, applaud the lovely
lady driving by.

'Cross the stream by the wooden bridge, nod to the
children bathing there, marvel at the cheer raised by a
thousand sailors on the distant ironclad.

'Go on, pursue the inconspicuous little man, and when
you have pushed him into a doorway rob him and then,
each with your hands in your pockets, watch him go sadly
on his way down the street to the left.

'The scattered police on their galloping horses rein the
animals in and thrust you back. Let them; the empty
streets will make them miserable, I know they will. And
already—what did I tell you?—they're riding off two by
two, slowly round the street corners, flying over the
squares.'

Then I have to get out, send the lift down again, ring the
doorbell, and the maid opens the door as I bid Good
evening.

Wool-gathering at the window

What are we going to do with these spring days that will soon be upon us? This morning the sky was grey, but stepping to the window now one is surprised and leans one's cheek against the window catch.

Down below one can see the light of the sun—setting now, of course—on the face of a child-like girl as she walks along, looking about her, and at the same time one can see the shadow of the man coming up behind her at a brisker pace.

Then the man has gone past, and the child's face is really bright.

The way home

The sheer persuasiveness of the air after a storm! My
merits become visible to me and overwhelm me, even if I
do put up no resistance.

I stride along and my speed is the speed of this side of
the street, of this street, of this part of town. I am rightly
responsible for all knocks on doors and blows on table-
tops, for all toasts, for the loving couples in their beds, in
the skeletons of houses under construction, up against the
walls of dark alleyways, on brothel sofas.

I weigh my past against my future but find both
excellent; I can give preference to neither; in fact I can
only cavil at the injustice of a fate that so favours me.

Only as I enter my room am I a little thoughtful, though
without having found anything worth thinking about as I
was climbing the stairs. It is no great help to me to open
the window wide and have the band still playing in one of
the gardens.

Passers-by

When you are walking along a street at night and a man visible from a long way off—because the street slopes up in front of you and the moon is full—comes running towards you, you don't go for him, even if he is a weakling dressed in rags, even if there is someone running after him and shouting; you let him run on.

Because it is night, and it is not your fault that the street slopes up in front of you, lit by the full moon, and anyway, perhaps the two of them have staged the chase for fun, perhaps they're both after a third man, perhaps the first is being pursued without cause, perhaps the second is out to kill and you would become an accessory to murder, perhaps the two men are ignorant of each other's existence and are simply running home to bed, each on his own initiative, perhaps they are sleep-walking, perhaps the first one is armed.

In any case, haven't you a right to be tired, didn't you drink all that wine? You're happy not to be able to see the second one any more, either.

The passenger

I am standing on the platform of the tram, utterly unsure of my place in this world, in this city, in my family. I could not even begin to suggest what claims I might justifiably advance in any regard whatever. I am quite unable to defend my standing on this platform, my holding on to this strap, my allowing myself to be conveyed by this tram, or the fact that people are avoiding the tram or walking along in silence or standing in front of shop windows. Not that anyone is asking me to, but that is immaterial.

The tram approaches a stop and a girl takes up a position near the steps, ready to alight. She is almost palpably visible to me. She is dressed in black, the pleats of her skirt hang almost motionless, her blouse is tight-fitting and has a collar of fine white lace, her left hand is laid flat against the side of the tram, the umbrella in her right hand rests on the second step down. Her face is brown; her nose, pinched in slightly at the sides, is broadly rounded at the tip. She has a mass of brown hair, with wisps of it blowing about at her right temple. Her small ear is close-set, but since I am standing near her I can see the whole of the back of it as well as the shadow at its root.

I wondered at the time: how come she is not astonished at herself but keeps her mouth shut and says nothing at all?

Dresses

Often when I see dresses with lots of pleats and ruffles and trimmings beautifully draping beautiful bodies it occurs to me that they do not stay that way for long but get creases in them that cannot be ironed out any more, with dust so engrained in the decoration it cannot be removed, and that no one will wish to appear so dreary and ridiculous as to put on the same expensive dress every morning and take it off every evening.

Nevertheless I see girls who are undoubtedly beautiful and have lots of delightful muscles and little bones and taut skin and masses of silky hair and yet daily appear in this one natural disguise, always laying the same face in the palms of the same hands and having it reflected in their mirrors.

Only occasionally, when they come in late from a party, do they see it in the mirror as threadbare, baggy, dusty, too familiar, and almost past wearing any more.

The rebuff

When I meet a beautiful girl and ask her, 'Please—come with me,' and she walks by without saying anything, what she means is:

'You are no duke with a flowing name, no broad American with the build of a Red Indian, with a still, level gaze and with skin brushed by the air of the grasslands and washed by the rivers running through them; you've never journeyed to the seven seas, wherever they may be, and sailed on them. So I ask you: why should a beautiful girl like me go with you?'

'You forget that no motor car bears you through the streets in long, rolling thrusts, nor do I see the gentlemen of your escort, moulded in their clothes, marching behind you in a strict semicircle, murmuring blessings on your head; your breasts are ranged neatly in your bodice but your hips and thighs more than make up for such restraint; you have on a taffeta dress with a pleated skirt of the kind that had us all cheering last autumn, yet at intervals—with this horror on your back—you smile.'

'Yes, we're both right, and if we're to avoid being made indelibly aware of the fact we'd better, don't you think, go our separate ways home.'

For jockeys to ponder

There is nothing, when you think about it, to tempt a person into wanting to come first in a race.

The glory of being proclaimed the best rider in the land is too heady a pleasure as the band strikes up for remorse not to be inevitable next morning.

The envy of your opponents, wily and quite influential people, cannot help causing you pain as you ride through the serried guard of honour to the open ground that soon lay empty before you but for a few lapped riders tinily charging the line of the horizon.

Many of your friends hurry to collect their winnings, and their cheers come to you shouted over their shoulders from the distant tote windows; your best friends, however, had put no money on your horse for fear that, if they lost it, they would be bound to feel annoyed with you, but now that your horse has come in first and they have not won anything they turn away as you pass, preferring to look along the stands.

Behind you your rivals, seated firmly in the saddle, trying to take in the misfortune that has befallen them and the injustice that is somehow being done them, assume a fresh appearance as if a new race ought to start now, a proper one after that kiddies' event.

Many ladies find the winner ridiculous because he puffs himself up yet has no idea how to cope with all the handshaking, saluting, bowing, and hallo-there-ing, while the losers, mouths shut, casually pat the necks of their mostly neighing mounts.

Finally, the sky having clouded over, it even begins to rain.

The window on the street

Anyone who lives on his own but would like to have some sort of contact now and then, anyone who, allowing for the different times of day, weather, working conditions and so on, merely wishes to see an arm—it can be any old arm—that he could hang on to, such a person will not get by for long without a window on the street. And be his mood such that he is not even looking for anything but simply steps over to his window, a tired man, his gaze alternating between people and sky, and does so unwillingly, his head tilted back slightly, even then the horses down below will sweep him along in their wake of carts and noise and so eventually into harmony with the human race.

Wanting to be a Red Indian

Ah, if one were a Red Indian, on the alert immediately, and if leaning into the wind on one's galloping horse one went quivering swiftly over the quavering ground, over and over again till one stopped using the spurs, there being no spurs, till one threw away the reins, there being no reins, and one scarcely saw the terrain out in front as a well-mown stretch of moorland without even a horse's neck now or a horse's head.

The trees

For we are as treetrunks in the snow. They appear to lie
flat on the surface, and with a little push one should be
able to shift them. No, one cannot, for they are fixed
firmly to the ground. But look, even that is mere appearance.

Unhappiness

When it had become really unbearable—one late afternoon in November—and I began pacing the narrow carpet in my room as if it had been a racetrack, turned in alarm at sight of the brightly-lit street, and at the back of the room, in the depths of the mirror, did in fact find a new objective, and screamed aloud, only to hear the scream that receives no answer and from which nothing removes the force so that it goes up and up, without anything to counterbalance it, and cannot cease even when it stops sounding—at that point the door opened inwards, in a great hurry because after all haste was called for and even the carthorses down in the street were rearing up like horses crazed in battle, throats exposed.

A small ghost in the shape of a child emerged from the pitch-dark corridor, where the lamp had not yet been lit, and came to a halt on tiptoe on a floorboard that rocked imperceptibly. Dazzled by the half-light in the room, he made as if to bury his face in his hands but all of a sudden relaxed on looking towards the window, where outside the crossed bars the rising mist of the street-lighting finally came to rest beneath a layer of darkness. Propping his right elbow against the wall of the room, he stood inside the open doorway and let the draught from outside caress his feet and ankles and flow round his neck and his temples.

I looked at him for a moment; then I said, 'Good afternoon,' and took my coat from the firescreen, not liking to stand there half naked. I held my mouth open for a while to allow the agitation to pass out of me. I had a nasty taste in my mouth, my eyelashes were all aquiver—in fact this visit, which incidentally I had been expecting, was all I needed.

The child was still standing in the same place by the wall; he had pressed his right hand to the wall, and he could not, with his bright-red cheeks, get over the fact that its whitewashed surface was rough and grazed his fingertips. I said, 'Did you really want me? No mistake, is there? Nothing easier than to make a mistake in this huge house. My name's Soandso, third floor. Was it in fact me you wanted to see?'

'Hush!' the child said over his shoulder, 'everything's all right.'

'Well, come on in, then; I'd like to shut the door.'

'I've just shut it myself. Don't bother. And calm down, will you.'

'It's no bother, I assure you. But a lot of people live off this corridor, naturally all acquaintances of mine; most of them get home from work around now; when they hear voices in a room they think they can simply walk in and see what's going on. That's the way it is. They have their day's work behind them; whom are they going to take orders from during their bit of freedom in the evening? You know that yourself, incidentally. So let me shut the door.'

'What is all this? What's the matter with you? I don't care if the whole house comes in. And anyway, as I said, I've already shut the door. Do you think you're the only one capable of shutting the door? I even locked it.'

'That's fine, then. That's all I wanted. You needn't even have locked it. Well, now that you're here, do make yourself at home. Be my guest. Have complete faith in me. Don't be afraid to spread yourself. I shall put no pressure on you either to stay or to go. Do I even need to say this? You know me well enough, surely?'

'No, you really needn't have said it. Furthermore, you shouldn't have said it. I'm a child; why make such a fuss on my account?'

'Oh, I'm not. Yes, of course—a child. But not such a little one, after all. You're already quite grown-up. If you were a girl you couldn't allow yourself to be locked in a room with me just like that.'

'We needn't worry about that. All I wanted to say was: knowing you so well doesn't afford me much protection; it merely saves you the trouble of trying to lie to me. Yet even so you start paying me compliments. Don't do it, please—that's an order. And then there's the fact that I do not know you always and everywhere, let alone in the dark like this. It would be much better if you lit a lamp. No, don't. But I'll remember that you threatened me.'

'I beg your pardon—I threatened you? Oh, really! I'm just so happy that you've come at last. I say "at last" because it's already so late. It's a mystery to me why you've been so long in coming. So I may in my excitement have spoken in a somewhat muddled fashion and this possibly confused you. That I did in fact so speak I am more than willing to admit. Say I threatened you with anything you like—let's not argue about it, for heaven's sake! But how could you have believed it? How could you hurt me so? Why do you insist at all costs on spoiling for me this little time I have you here for? A total stranger would be more accommodating than you're being!'

'I believe you; you're hardly being very original. No matter how closely a stranger may accommodate you, I'm as close to you as that by nature. *And* you know it—so why the wistfulness? If you want to play silly games just say so and I'll go.'

'I see. You dare to say even that to me. Aren't you being rather over-bold? Don't forget you're in my room. That's my wall you're rubbing your fingers on like a mad thing. My room, my wall! And in any case, what you're saying is absurd, not just cheeky. You say that your nature is such that you are compelled to speak to me in this way. Really? Your nature compels you? Nice of your nature. Well, your nature is mine too, and if it is my nature to behave towards you in a friendly fashion, you may do no less.'

'You call that friendly?'

'I'm talking about earlier.'

'Do you know what I will be like later?'

'I know nothing.'

And I walked over to the bedside table and lit the candle. At that time I had neither gas nor electricity in my room. I then sat at the table for a while until, tiring of that too, I donned my waterproof, picked up my hat from the couch, and extinguished the candle. I caught my foot on a chairleg on the way out.

On the stairs I met a tenant from the same floor.

'Going out again, you bounder?' he asked, pausing with his legs astride two steps.

'What can I do?' I said, 'I've just had a ghost in my room.'

'You say that with the same sort of distaste as if you'd found a hair in your soup.'

'You jest. Mark my words, though: a ghost is a ghost.'

'Very true. But what if one doesn't believe in ghosts in the first place?'

'You don't think I believe in ghosts, do you? But how does not believing in them help me?'

'Very simple. You no longer need be frightened when a ghost actually appears.'

'Yes, but that's only the incidental fear. The actual fear is fear of what causes the phenomenon. And that fear there's no getting rid of. I possess a really splendid example of the genre.' In sheer nervousness I started searching through all my pockets.

'But having no fear of the phenomenon itself you could safely have interrogated it as to its cause!'

'You've obviously never spoken to a ghost. You'll never get a straight answer out of one of them. Talk about vacillation! These ghosts seem to doubt their own existence even more than we do, which given their fragility is hardly surprising.'

'I've heard one can feed them up, though.'

'You heard correctly. One can. But who's going to?'

'Why not? If it's a female ghost, for example,' he said as he swung himself up to the top step.

'Aha,' I said. 'But even then there's no future in it.'

I thought. My acquaintance was now so high up that in order to see me he had to bend down below an arch of the stairwell. 'All the same,' I called out, 'if you take my ghost away from me up there, you and I are finished—for good.'

'Oh, I was only joking,' he said, pulling his head back.

'That's all right, then,' I said, and in fact I could at this point have gone for a walk without worrying. But because I felt so utterly desolate I went back upstairs and went to bed.

The Judgement

a story for Miss Felice B.

(*Das Urteil,* written during the night of 22-23
September 1912, some six weeks after Kafka's first
meeting with Felice Bauer and eighteen months
before he first became engaged to her, and published
in Max Brod's *Arkadia* yearbook, Kurt Wolff, 1913;
separate volume publication in Kurt Wolff's 'Der
Jüngste Tag' series, 1916.)

It was a Sunday morning at the height of spring. George Bendemann, a young businessman, was sitting in his room on the first floor of one of the low, flimsily built houses that stretched in a long row along the river bank, distinguished in little more than height and colour. He had just completed a letter to a boyhood friend now living abroad; he sealed it with frivolous deliberation and then, propping his elbows on the desk, looked out of the window at the river, the bridge, and the hills on the other side with their hint of green.

He was thinking about how the friend, not content with his progress at home, had years before quite literally escaped to Russia. He now ran a business in Petersburg that had started extremely well but had apparently been falling off for some time, as the friend complained on his less and less frequent visits. There he was, far from home, wearing himself out to no purpose, the foreign-looking full beard imperfectly concealing the face George had known so well since childhood, with the yellow skin that seemed to suggest some developing illness. By his own account he had no proper contact with his compatriots, who formed a colony in the city, and virtually no social intercourse with Russian families either, so that he was settling down to a life of permanent bachelordom.

What was one to write to such a man, who had obviously got stuck in a rut and whom one could pity but not help? Ought one perhaps to advise him to come home, to move back again, resuming all the old friendships—nothing stood in the way of that—and for the rest relying on his friends' assistance? But that would be tantamount to telling him at the same time—and the more solicitously one did it, the more offensive would be the effect—that his efforts up to now had been abortive, that he should desist from them once and for all, that he should come back and

have everyone stare open-mouthed at the man who had
come back for good, that only his friends knew what was
what, and that he was an overgrown baby who must simply
do as his successful friends, who had stayed at home,
instructed him. And was it even certain that all the bother
one would have to put him to was going to serve some
purpose? Perhaps there would be no getting him to come
home at all—he said himself that he no longer felt he had
the hang of things in his native land—and he would stay
there in spite of everything, still abroad and now, embit-
tered by all the advice he had received, alienated even
further from his friends. If on the other hand he took the
advice and, having come back, succumbed to depression
—not of course through any fault except that of circumstances—if he failed to get along with his friends and
failed to get along without them, suffered humiliation, and
in the end had no real home any more and no friends,
would it not have been much better for him to have stayed
abroad where he was? Was it in fact thinkable in such
circumstances that he would ever get anywhere back at
home?

For these reasons it was not possible, supposing one
wanted to keep up a correspondence with him in the first
place, actually to tell him things in the way that one would
have no hesitation in telling them to the most casual
acquaintance. The friend had not been back for over three
years now on the thoroughly makeshift pretext of the
unstable political situation in Russia, as if this would not
permit even the briefest absence on the part of a small
businessman when hundreds of thousands of Russians
happily travelled all over the globe. As it happened, in the
course of those three years many things had changed as
far as George was concerned. News of the death of
George's mother some two years previously, since when
George had been living with his aged father, had in fact
reached his friend's ears and the friend had expressed his
condolences in a letter of such dryness as could be
accounted for only by assuming that grief at that sort of
event is quite inconceivable to one living abroad. Since that

time, however, George had thrown himself into everything, including his business, with greater determination. Possibly while his mother was alive his father had blocked any genuinely autonomous activity on George's part by allowing only his own views to prevail in business matters; possibly since his mother's death his father, while continuing to work for the firm, had made his presence less felt; possibly—as was in fact very likely—a series of happy accidents had played a more important role; at any rate, the business had expanded quite unexpectedly in those two years, they had had to take on twice as many staff, turnover was five times what it had been, and further progress was undoubtedly just around the corner.

The friend, however, had no idea of this change. He had previously—the last occasion had perhaps been that letter of condolence—tried to persuade George to emigrate to Russia, outlining in detail the prospects that existed for George's particular line of business in Petersburg. The figures had been infinitesimal in relation to the size George's firm had since assumed. But George had not felt inclined to write to his friend about his business successes, and to have made good the omission now would have created a curious impression to say the least.

George therefore confined himself to writing to his friend about such insignificant events as come to mind in no particular order when one sits down to think on a quiet Sunday. His sole aim was to leave undisturbed the conception that his friend had presumably formed of his native city in the long time he had been away and to which he had presumably become reconciled. It had happened, for example, that George notified his friend of the engagement of a person of no consequence to a girl of equally little consequence three times in letters written at quite long intervals apart—so that eventually the friend, very much contrary to George's intention, had begun to show interest in this curious fact.

George, however, much preferred to write to him about things like that than admit that he had himself become engaged a month before to a Miss Frieda Brandenfeld, the daughter of a wealthy family. He often talked to his fiancée about this friend and the peculiar relationship in which he stood to him through his letters. 'Then he certainly won't come to our wedding,' she said, 'and I have the right to meet all your friends.' 'I don't want to bother him,' George replied. 'You see, he probably would come, at least I think he would, but he'd feel that I was getting at him, that I was putting him on the spot; he might envy me, and he'd certainly feel discontented and incapable of ever shaking off that discontentment and travelling back alone. Do you know what that means—alone?' 'Yes, but might he not hear about our getting married through some other channel?' 'I can't prevent that, of course, but it's unlikely in view of the kind of life he leads.' 'George, if you have friends like that you shouldn't have got engaged at all.' 'I know, we're both to blame there; but I wouldn't have it any different even now.' And when, panting between his kisses, she went on to say, 'No, I'm hurt, I really am,' there did indeed seem no harm at all in writing to tell his friend everything. 'That's the way I am, and that's the way he must accept me,' he said to himself. 'I can't carve another person out of myself who might be better suited for friendship with him than I am.'

So it was that in the long letter he wrote on that Sunday morning he informed his friend of his engagement in the following words: 'I've kept the best news till last. I've become engaged to a Miss Frieda Brandenfeld, the daughter of a wealthy family that came to live here long after you left, so you're hardly likely to know them. There will be other opportunities to tell you more about my fiancée; let me just say for now that I am very happy and that the only change this has made to our relationship is that, instead of having a perfectly ordinary friend in me, you will now have a happy friend. You will also have, in the person of my fiancée, who sends you her best wishes and who will be writing to you herself very shortly, a sincere friend of the opposite sex, which for a bachelor is not without importance. I know how many things stand in the way of your paying us a visit, but wouldn't my wedding provide just the occasion to sweep all obstacles aside for once? Well, be that as it may, make no allowances but do only as you think fit.'

With this letter in his hand and with his face turned to the window, George continued to sit at his desk for a long time. An acquaintance passing in the street who wished him good morning received no more acknowledgement than a vacant smile.

Eventually, putting the letter in his pocket, he went out of his room and straight across a small landing into his father's room, where he had not set foot for months. Not that there was any need for him to do so in the ordinary course of events since he was in constant contact with his father at the office, they lunched at the same time in a restaurant, and in the evenings, though each looked after himself, they usually—when George was not out with friends or visiting his fiancée, as most often happened—sat up for a while, each with his newspaper, in the sitting-room that they shared between them.

George was amazed at how dark his father's room was, even on that sunny morning. What a shadow it cast, that high wall beyond the narrow courtyard! His father was sitting by the window, in a corner of the room that was adorned with various mementoes of George's late mother; he was reading the newspaper, holding it up to his eyes at an angle in an attempt to compensate for some deficiency in his eyesight. On the table stood the remains of his breakfast, not much of which appeared to have been consumed.

'Ah, George!' his father said, coming across the room towards him. His heavy dressing-gown fell open as he walked, the flaps swirling about him—'He's still a giant, my father,' George said to himself.

Then he said, 'It's intolerably dark in here.'

'It's dark, all right,' his father replied.

'And you have the window shut?'

'I prefer it that way.'

'It's really warm outside,' said George, as if following up his earlier remark. He took a seat.

His father cleared the breakfast things away and put

49

them on top of a cupboard.

'I just wanted to tell you,' George went on, following the old man's movements with a forlorn look, 'that I've sent word of my engagement to Petersburg after all.' He pulled the letter out of his pocket a little way, then let it drop back.

'Why to Petersburg?' his father asked.

'To my friend, *you* know,' said George, looking his father in the eye. 'He's not at all like this in the office,' he was thinking, 'sitting there so four-square with his arms across his chest!'

'Quite. Your friend,' his father said with emphasis.

'But I told you, father, how I didn't want to tell him of my engagement at first. Purely out of consideration, for no other reason. You know yourself how difficult he is. What I said to myself was, he may hear about my engagement from someone else, though it's hardly likely in view of the solitary life he leads—I can't help that—but he's not going to hear about it from me.'

'And now you've changed your mind, is that it?' his father inquired, putting his huge newspaper down on the windowsill, placing his spectacles on top of it, and covering the spectacles with his hand.

'Yes, now I've changed my mind. If he's a good friend of mine, I said to myself, then my being happily engaged will make him happy too. That's why I no longer had any hesitation in notifying him of the fact. But before I posted the letter I wanted to tell you what I'd done.'

'George,' his father said, pulling his toothless mouth into a broad slit, 'listen to me! You've come to me with this thing because you want to talk it over with me. That does you credit, no doubt about it. But it's no good, in fact it's less than no good, if you're not going to tell me the whole truth. I don't want to stir up things that have no place here. Since the death of your beloved mother certain not very nice things have been happening. Maybe there's a time for them too, and maybe that time comes sooner than we expect. A great deal escapes me in the office, though perhaps not because it's kept from me—the last thing I'm trying to suggest is that things are being kept from me—but I haven't the strength any more, my memory is beginning to go, and I no longer have an eye for all the little details. This is simply nature taking its course for one thing, and for another, Mummy's death hit me much harder than it did you. But as long as we're on the subject of this letter, promise me one thing, George: don't try to hoodwink me. It's a trifle, it's not worth bothering about, so don't try to hoodwink me. Do you really have this friend in Petersburg?'

George stood up in embarrassment. 'Never mind about my friends. A thousand friends could never take the place of my father. Do you know what I think? You don't look after yourself enough. Old age is demanding its due. I can't do without you in the office, you know that as well as I do, but if the business should ever start undermining your health I'd shut up shop for good tomorrow. I'm not having that. No, we're going to have to start a new regimen for you. Radically new, I mean. Here you are, sitting in the dark, when in the living-room it would be lovely and light for you. You peck at your breakfast instead of building yourself up properly. You sit around with the window shut when fresh air would do you so much good. No, Father, no! I'll get the doctor round and we'll do exactly what he says. We'll swap rooms: you move into the front room and I'll come in here. There'll be no difference as far as you're concerned because we'll move all your things over too. But there's time enough for all that. You go back to bed for a bit now; you've got to take things easy. Here, I'll help you get undressed. I can, you know. Or would you like to go in the front room now? You can have my bed for the time being. In fact that would be a very sensible arrangement.'

George was standing right beside his father, whose head of shaggy white hair had sunk to his breast.

'George,' his father said softly, not moving.

George immediately knelt down beside his father; he looked into his father's weary face and into the huge pupils staring out at him from the corners of his father's eyes.

'You have no friend in Petersburg. You've always liked to have your little joke, even with me. How should you have a friend there, of all places! I find that too much to believe.'

'Think back for a moment, father,' George said, heaving the old man out of his chair and, as he stood there in a really extremely weak condition, pulling off his dressing-gown. 'Nearly three years ago now my friend came here to see us. You didn't particularly like him, I remember. On at least two occasions I disowned him in conversation with you, although he was sitting in my room at the time. I could understand your dislike of him perfectly well; my friend has his peculiarities. But then there was that other time when you got on with him very well. I was really proud of the fact that you listened to him, nodded at what he said, and asked questions. Think back—you must remember. He was telling us those incredible stories about the Russian Revolution. About how for example on a business trip to Kiev he had become involved in a disturbance and seen a priest up on a balcony cut a large, bleeding cross in the flat of his hand, hold the hand in the air, and shout to the crowd. You've even recounted the story yourself on occasion.'

In the meantime George had managed to lower his father into his chair again, carefully remove the woollen trousers he wore over his linen pants, and pull off his socks. Seeing the not particularly clean state of his father's underwear, he reproached himself for having neglected the old man. He should certainly have made it his business to ensure that his father changed his clothes whenever necessary. He and his fiancée had not yet discussed in so many words how they were going to arrange his father's future; they had tacitly assumed that he would stay on in the old flat by himself. Now, however, George resolved on the spur of the moment to take his father with him when he set up house. In fact, on second thoughts, it looked as if the care and attention he planned to give his father there might almost come too late.

He picked his father up and carried him into bed. An

awful feeling came over him as he became aware during the few steps to the bed that his father, curled up in his arms, was playing with the watch chain at his lapel. So firmly did his father grasp the watch chain that for a moment George was unable to put him to bed.

Once he was in bed, however, everything seemed to be fine. He arranged the bedclothes himself, pulling the quilt unusually high over his shoulders. He looked up at George in a not unfriendly fashion.

'You do remember him, don't you?' George asked, nodding encouragingly.

'Am I covered up now?' asked his father, as if he could not tell whether his feet were adequately covered.

'See, you like it in bed,' said George, tucking the quilt in around him.

'Am I covered up?' his father asked again. He seemed to be particularly interested in what the answer would be.

'Don't worry, you're well covered up.'

'No, I'm not!' his father shouted, slamming the answer down on the question, and he threw the quilt back with such force that for a moment it opened out completely in flight. He stood up in bed, one hand pressed lightly to the ceiling. 'You wanted to cover me up, you scoundrel, I know you did, but I'm not covered up yet. If it's my last ounce of strength it's enough for you—more than enough for you. I know your friend, all right. A son after my own heart, he'd have been. That's why you've been deceiving him all these years, isn't it? Why else? Do you think I haven't wept for him? That's why you shut yourself in your office—the boss is busy, no one's to disturb him —purely in order to write your lying notes to Russia. But luckily for your father he doesn't need anyone to teach him to see through his son. And now that you thought you'd got the better of him, so much so that you could plant your bottom down on him and he wouldn't move, what does my high and mighty son do but decide to get married!'

George looked up at this terrifying vision of his father. The friend in Petersburg, whom his father suddenly knew

so well, affected him as never before. He thought of him,
lost in the depths of Russia. He saw him at the door of his
empty, looted shop against a background of smashed-up
shelving, ransacked stock, and bent gas brackets, barely
able to stand. Why had he had to go so far away?

'Look at me, will you!' his father shouted, and George
almost distractedly ran over to the bed to take everything
in but came to a halt halfway there.

'Because she hauled up her skirts,' his father began in a
slimy falsetto, 'because she hauled up her skirts like this,
the filthy bitch,' and by way of illustration he lifted the
hem of his nightshirt so high that the war wound on his
thigh was exposed, 'because she hauled up her skirts like
this and like this and like this you had to have a go at her,
and to make sure you can have your way with her
undisturbed you defile your mother's memory, betray
your friend, and stick your father in bed where he can't
budge. Well, can he budge or can't he?'

And he stood without holding on at all and kicked his
legs in the air. His eyes blazed with insight.

George was now standing in a corner, as far away from
his father as possible. A long time ago he had made up his
mind to keep a really close watch on everything lest he
should ever, by some devious means, either from behind
or from above, be caught by surprise. He recalled his long-
forgotten resolution and promptly forgot it, like drawing a
short thread through the eye of a needle.

'But the friend isn't betrayed after all!' his father
shouted, and a wagging forefinger corroborated this. 'I
was his locum tenens here.'

'Playactor!' George could not refrain from shouting;
realizing his mistake he immediately, though too
late—there was a glazed look in his eyes—bit his tongue so
hard that he doubled up in pain.

'Of course I've been playacting! Hah, that's just the
word for it! What other consolation was left to your old
widowed father? Tell me—and for the space of your
answer be my living son still—what else was left to me in
my little back room, persecuted by disloyal staff, an old

54

man to the marrow of my bones? And my son went about rejoicing, clinching deals that I had set up, giddying himself with pleasure, and departing from his father's presence with the opaque face of a man of honour! Do you think I didn't love you—having fathered you?'

'Now he's going to lean forward,' George thought. 'If only he'd fall and smash to pieces!' The words went hissing through his head.

His father leant forward but did not fall. Since George did not approach as he had expected, he straightened up again.

'Stay where you are, I don't need you! You think you still have the strength to come over here and are just holding back because you want to. Well, don't delude yourself! I'm still the stronger by far. On my own I might have had to stand down, but mother has left me her strength. I'm in business with your friend in a big way; I've got your customer right here in my pocket!'

'He's even got pockets in his nightshirt!' George said to himself, thinking that he could make him look ridiculous in the eyes of the whole world by this remark. He only thought it for a moment, because he always forgot everything.

'Just you take your fancy woman on your arm and come up and see me! I'll swat her away from your side for you, you'll see if I don't!'

George made a face as if he did not believe it. His father simply nodded, driving home the truth of his words, in the direction of George's corner.

'You made me laugh today, coming to ask whether you should write to your friend about your engagement! He knows everything, stupid, he knows everything! I wrote to him myself, because you forgot to take my writing things away. That's why he hasn't been here for years. He knows everything a hundred times better than you do yourself. He screws your letters up unread in his left hand while holding up my letters to read in his right!'

He waved an arm about enthusiastically above his head. 'He knows everything a thousand times better!' he yelled.

'Ten thousand times!' George said to poke fun at his father, but even before the words had left his lips they had a deadly serious sound.

'For years I've been waiting for you to come along with that question! Do you think I care about anything else? Do you think I read the papers? Here!' And he threw George a sheet of newspaper that had somehow got carried into bed with him. An old newspaper with a name George did not begin to recognize.

'The time it's taken you to grow up! Your mother had to die, she was not to see the joyful day, your friend's going to rack and ruin in Russia, he looked as if he was on his last legs three years ago, and you can see for yourself the state I'm in! You've got eyes, haven't you?'

'So you've been trying to catch me out!' cried George.

Sympathetically his father observed, 'You wanted to say that before, probably. Now it's completely out of place.'

And in a louder voice: 'So now you know what else there was apart from you; up to now you only knew about yourself! You were an innocent child, to tell the truth—though to tell the whole truth you were the devil incarnate! Therefore know: I hereby sentence you to death by drowning!'

George felt himself thrust from the room, the thud with which his father fell on the bed behind him still echoing in his ears. On the stairs, which he took at a rush as if descending an inclined plane, he surprised his cleaning lady, who was going up to tidy the flat after the night. 'Jesus!' she cried, hiding her face in her apron, but he had already gone. Out of the door he shot, his momentum carrying him across the road to the water's edge. He clutched the railing as a hungry man will clutch at food. He vaulted over it, expert gymnast that he had been in his boyhood days, much to his parents' pride. Still holding on with weakening grip, he glimpsed a bus through the bars, knew it would easily cover the noise of his fall, called softly, 'Dear parents, I did love you, always,' and let himself drop.

Crossing the bridge at that moment was a simply endless stream of traffic.

The Stoker

a fragment

(*Der Heizer,* written c. 1911-12 as chapter 1 of *Der Verschollene*—Kafka's title, 'Missing, presumed dead'—or *Amerika*—the title Max Brod chose when he edited the incomplete novel for publication in 1927. *Der Heizer* was first published by Kurt Wolff in May 1913, with Kafka's approval although he had really wanted the work to form part, with *Die Verwandlung* and *Das Urteil,* of a volume to be entitled *Die Söhne,* 'The sons'.)

As the sixteen-year-old Karl Rossmann, whom his poor parents had packed off to America because a servant-girl had seduced him and had a child by him, sailed into New York harbour on the deck of the now slow-moving ship, he saw the Statue of Liberty, which he had been watching for some time, bathed as it were in suddenly intensified sunlight. The arm with the sword reached up as if the goddess had just raised it, and the wind blew about her body without constraint.

'So tall!' he said to himself as, with his thoughts not at all on leaving the ship, and with growing numbers of porters pushing past him, he was gradually forced over to the rail.

A young man with whom he had become superficially acquainted during the voyage said as he went by, 'Do you not feel like going ashore yet, then?' 'I'm all ready,' said Karl with a smile, and in his exuberance, and because he was a powerful youth, he swung his suitcase onto his shoulder. However, as he looked beyond where his acquaintance was already moving off with the others, executing little flourishes with his stick, Karl realized with dismay that he had left his own umbrella below. He quickly asked his acquaintance, who did not appear too pleased about it, to wait by his case for a moment, glanced about him in order to be sure of finding the place again, and went hurrying off. Once below, he discovered to his disappointment that a gangway that would have made his journey very much shorter was for the first time barred, no doubt in connection with the disembarkation of all the passengers, and he had to find his way with much difficulty through a great many tiny rooms, up and down short stairways, one after another, along corridors that twisted and turned, and across an empty room containing an abandoned desk until eventually, having been that way only once or twice before and then always with a crowd, he

was well and truly lost. In his confusion, and because he
had not come across a single person but was aware only of
the continuous shuffling of a thousand feet above his head
and now registered a far-off exhalation that was the last
sound made by the engines as they were shut down, he
unthinkingly began banging at random on a little door
outside which he had come to a bewildered halt.

'It's not locked,' came a shout from inside, and Karl
opened the door with a sigh of real relief. 'Why were you
banging on the door like a maniac?' asked a huge man
after no more than a glance at Karl. Through some sort of
aperture in the cabin ceiling a murky light—the dregs of
what illuminated the decks above—fell on the wretched
interior, where a bunk, a cupboard, a chair, and the man
stood packed together like goods in a warehouse. 'I've lost
my way,' said Karl. 'I didn't realise during the voyage but
this is an awfully big ship.' 'You're right there,' the man
said with a certain pride as he continued to fiddle with the
lock of a small suitcase, pressing it to repeatedly with both
hands and listening to the sound of the bolt snapping
home. 'Come in, then,' the man went on. 'You're not going
to hang about out there, are you?' 'Am I not disturbing
you?' Karl asked. 'Good Lord, no—what a question!' 'Are
you German?' Karl wanted to know, seeking this assurance
because of all he had heard about the perils facing new
arrivals in America, particularly from Irishmen. 'Right
first time,' said the man. Karl still wavered, whereupon the
man abruptly seized the doorhandle and shut the door,
pulling Karl towards him into the cabin. 'I can't stand
people peering in at me from the gangway,' said the man,
who had gone back to working on his suitcase. 'Every
Tom, Dick, and Harry on the ship walks past here and
peers in—I'd like to see them put up with it!' 'But the
gangway's quite empty,' said Karl, who was squashed
uncomfortably against the bedpost. 'Now it is,' said the
man. 'We're talking about now,' thought Karl. 'He's a hard
man to hold a conversation with.' 'Why don't you lie on the
bunk—you'll have more room,' said the man. Karl crawled
in as best he could, laughing aloud at his initial, futile

attempts to vault in. But hardly was he in bed when he exclaimed, 'Good grief, I'm forgetting all about my suitcase!' 'Where's that, then?' 'Up on deck. Someone I'd met is keeping an eye on it. What was his name?' And he felt in the secret pocket that his mother had sewn in the lining of his coat for the journey and pulled out a visiting-card. 'Butterbaum, Frank Butterbaum.' 'Do you need the suitcase badly?' 'Of course I do.' 'Why give it to a stranger then?' 'I'd left my umbrella down here. I ran to fetch it but didn't want to drag the case along with me. Then I lost my way.' 'Are you alone—no one travelling with you?' 'No, I'm alone,' said Karl, thinking to himself, 'Possibly I should stick to this fellow; I don't know where I'll find a better friend so soon.' 'And now you've lost the suitcase too, not to mention the umbrella.' And the man sat down in the chair, Karl's affairs having, it seemed, begun to assume a certain interest for him. 'But I don't think the suitcase is lost yet.' 'Think what you like,' said the man, giving his short, dark, thick hair a vigorous scratch, 'but on this ship the morals depend on the port. In Hamburg your Butterbaum might have kept an eye on the case; here there's very likely no sign of either of them by now.' 'Then I must go up and check straight away,' said Karl, looking round for the best way to get out. 'Stay here,' said the man, and he put a hand on Karl's chest and pushed him almost roughly back into bed. 'Why?' Karl asked crossly. 'Because there's no point,' said the man. 'I'm going myself in just a moment, so we'll go together. Either your suitcase has been stolen, in which case there's nothing to be done, or the man has left it there, in which case we'll find it much more easily when everyone's off the ship. Same with your umbrella.' 'Do you know your way around the ship?' Karl asked uneasily. It seemed to him that the outwardly plausible idea that his things would be easier to find on an empty ship concealed a snag. 'I ought to—I'm a stoker,' said the man. 'You're a stoker!' Karl exclaimed delightedly, as if this exceeded all his expectations, and propping himself on his elbows he took a closer look at the man. 'Just opposite the cabin I slept in with the Slovak there was a

hatch through which you could see into the engine-room.'
'Right, that's where I worked,' said the stoker. 'I've always
been keen on mechanical things,' said Karl, pursuing his
thoughts. 'In fact I'd definitely have gone in for engineer-
ing if I hadn't had to come to America.' 'Why did you have
to come here?' 'Oh, because!' Karl said, dismissing the
whole episode with a sweeping motion of his hand and
smiling at the stoker as if to ask his indulgence even for
what he would not admit to. 'Bound to have been a
reason,' the stoker said in such a way that it was not clear
whether he was demanding or declining an account of it. 'I
could become a stoker myself now,' said Karl. 'My parents
couldn't care less what I become.' 'My job's going,' the
stoker said as, in full awareness of that fact, he stuck his
hands into his trouser pockets and swung his legs, which
were sheathed in crumpled, iron-grey leathern trousers,
up onto the bunk to stretch them. Karl had to move over
towards the wall. 'Are you leaving the ship?' 'That's right.
Off today.' 'But why? Don't you like it?' 'Well, it depends
on the circumstances. It's not always a question of whether
one likes a thing or not. Actually you're right—I don't like
it. You're probably not thinking seriously of becoming a
stoker, but that's just when it's easiest to become one. I
most definitely advise against it. If you wanted to study
back in Europe, why don't you want to do it here?
American universities are infinitely better than European
ones.' 'So they may be,' said Karl, 'but I have almost no
money to pay for a course. I did read about someone who
worked in an office during the day and studied at night
until he had his doctorate and I think became mayor, but
that must take enormous stamina, don't you think? I'm
afraid I haven't got that kind of stamina. Anyway, I was
never particularly good at school so I wasn't at all sorry to
say goodbye to the place. The schools here may be even
stricter. And I have virtually no English. In any event
there's tremendous prejudice against foreigners here, I
believe.' 'You've found that too, have you? Right, then. In
that case, you're my man. Look, this is a German ship, isn't
it, it belongs to the Hamburg-America Line, so why aren't

we all Germans on board? Why is the chief engineer a Rumanian? He's called Schubal. It's incredible. And that swine bosses us Germans around on a German ship! Don't think'—he ran out of breath and waggled a hand—'that I'm complaining just for the sake of it. I know you have no influence, you're just another poor bugger yourself, but it's too bad!' And he banged his fist down on the table several times, staring at his fist as he did so. 'I've worked on any number of vessels'—he listed twenty names one after another as if they had been one word; Karl felt quite dizzy—'and I've stood out, I've been praised, I was a crewman after my captain's heart, I even served on the same merchantman for several years'—he rose to his feet as if this had been the highpoint of his career—'but here on this tub, where everything's done by the book and brains are not required, here I'm no good, here I'm always in Schubal's way, I'm a layabout, I deserve to be slung out on my ear and only get paid as a favour. Do you follow that? I don't.' 'You oughtn't to stand for it,' said Karl excitedly. He had all but lost the sense of being on the insecure ground of a ship moored off an unknown continent, so perfectly did he feel at home in the stoker's bunk. 'Have you seen the captain about it? Have you been to him to demand your rights?' 'Oh, go away, will you—just go away. I don't want you here. You don't listen to what I'm saying and you hand out advice. How can I go to the captain!' And the stoker sat down again wearily and laid his face in his hands.

'It's the best advice I can give him,' Karl said to himself, feeling in fact that he would have done better to go and fetch his suitcase than to stay and give advice that, in the event, was only regarded as stupid. His father, handing the case over for ever into his keeping, had asked jokingly, 'How long will it be yours, I wonder?' And now the precious object was quite possibly lost in earnest. The only consolation was that his father stood little chance of learning of his present predicament, even were he to make inquiries. All the shipping line would be able to say was that he had travelled to New York. But it distressed Karl that the things in the suitcase had hardly been used as yet, despite the fact that, for example, he ought long ago to have changed his shirt. That really had been a false economy, because now, at the start of his career, just when he needed to present a neat appearance, he would have to turn up in a dirty shirt. That apart, the loss of the suitcase would not be too disastrous, since the suit he had on was in fact better than the one in the case, which was actually only a spare suit that his mother had had to mend quickly just before he left. He remembered at this point that the suitcase also contained a piece of Veronese salami, which his mother had packed for him as extra rations but of which he had been able to eat only a tiny portion, having had no appetite at all during the voyage, when he had found the bowl of soup that was distributed to the steerage passengers quite sufficient. Now, however, he would have liked to be able to lay his hands on the sausage in order to offer it to the stoker. That such people were easily won over with trivial gifts was something Karl had learnt from his father, who won the hearts of all the humbler employees with whom he did business by handing out cigars. Now all Karl had to give away was his money, and with the suitcase possibly gone he was reluctant to touch that for the time being. Once again his thoughts returned to the suitcase, and he really could not see the point of having kept so close an eye on it during the voyage that the vigil had almost cost him his sleep if he now allowed himself to be relieved of it so easily. He recalled the five nights during which he had unremittingly suspected a small Slovak lying two places to his left of having designs on his suitcase. The Slovak had only been waiting for Karl finally to succumb to weakness and nod off for a while; he could then have used the long stick he spent all day playing with or practising with to pull the suitcase over to him. By day the Slovak looked innocent enough, but once darkness had fallen he would from time to time sit up in bed and throw soulful glances at Karl's suitcase. Karl had been able to see this quite clearly, because there was always someone here or there who with the restlessness of the emigrant lit a little lamp, though the ship's regulations forbade this, and tried to decipher one of the incomprehensible emigration-agency brochures. If such a lamp was burning in his vicinity Karl could doze off for a while, but if it was some way away or they were in darkness he had to keep his eyes open. The strain of doing this had completely exhausted him, and now it looked as if it might all have been in vain. Oh, if he ever bumped into that Butterbaum again!

At that moment the silence, hitherto total, was invaded from a long way off by a series of short, sharp taps sounding like children's footfalls; they came closer, grow-ing louder all the time, until they assumed the relaxed rhythm of men walking. The men were clearly proceeding in single file, as of course they would be in the narrow gangway, and one could hear what might have been the clink of weapons. Karl, who had been on the point of stretching out in bed and slipping into a sleep undisturbed by concern about either his suitcase or the Slovak, sat up with a start and nudged the stoker, who still seemed to be unaware that anything was happening, into attention, the vanguard of the procession having evidently just drawn level with the door. 'That's the ship's band,' the stoker said. 'They've been playing up on deck and now they're going to pack. It's all over now and we can go. Come on!' He took Karl's hand, at the last moment unhooked a framed Madonna picture from the wall above his bunk, stuffed it into his breast pocket, picked up his suitcase, and he and Karl hurriedly left the cabin.

'Now I'm going to the office to tell the bosses what I think. The passengers have all gone and I can speak my mind.' The stoker reiterated this several times with varia-tions and as he went along tried with a sideways movement of his foot to stamp on a rat that had run across their path, only to push it even faster into the hole it had managed to reach in time. His movements generally were rather slow, because although his legs were long this only made them unwieldy.

They passed through a part of the galley where a number of girls in dirty aprons—they splashed them deliberately—were washing dishes in huge tubs. The stoker called a girl named Lina over to him, put an arm round her hips, and, with her pressing flirtatiously against his arm the whole time, walked her along with him. 'It's pay day—you coming?' he asked. 'Why should I bother? Bring me my money here,' she replied, slipping under his arm and running off. 'Where did you pick up the pretty boy, then?' she called back, but without looking for an answer. The girls had all stopped work, and the galley rang with their laughter.

Karl and the stoker, however, went on and came to a door that was topped by a small pediment supported by miniature gilt caryatids. For a marine fitting it was decidedly extravagant. Karl realized that he had never set foot in this part of the ship before; probably it had been the preserve of first- and second-class passengers during the voyage, whereas now the dividing doors had been taken off their hinges for the great clean-up. They had in fact already come across several men with brooms over their shoulders who had said hullo to the stoker. Karl was amazed at the amount of activity; on his deck he had of course been aware of little of this. There were also electrical leads running along the gangways, and a little bell rang continuously.

The stoker knocked respectfully on the door, and when someone called, 'Come in!' he indicated with a wave of his hand that Karl should have no qualms about entering. This Karl duly did, but he stopped just inside the door. Through the room's three windows he could see the waves of the ocean, and as he watched their cheerful movement his heart skipped a beat, just as if he had not spent all of five long days looking at the sea. Great ships were cruising to and fro, making only such concession to the waves as their weight allowed. Seen through half-closed eyes, the vessels appeared to be staggering under that weight. At their mastheads flew long if narrow flags that, though drawn taut by the ships' way, nevertheless whipped from side to side. Probably from some warships came the sound of a gun salute; the gun-barrels of one such ship sailing past not far away gleamed with the reflection of its steel armour and were almost caressed by its steady, smooth, yet not quite horizontal progress through the water. The little ships and boats were, at least from the door, only visible in the distance, swarming in the gaps between the larger vessels. But beyond them all New York stood staring at Karl through the myriad windows of its skyscrapers. In this room there was certainly no mistaking where one was.

Three gentlemen sat at a circular table, one of them a ship's officer in a blue uniform, the other two officials of the port authority in black, American uniforms. The table was piled high with documents of various kinds, which the officer first glanced through, pen in hand, before passing them to the others, who either read them, made extracts from them, or put them into their briefcases, except when one of the two, who made little noises with his teeth almost continuously, dictated something that the other took down in a notebook.

At a desk by one window, his back to the door, sat a small gentleman who was busy with a number of enormous ledgers that stood in a row in front of him, ranged on a stout bookshelf at head height. Beside him stood an open and at least at first glance empty cash box.

The second window was empty and afforded the best view. Near the third window, however, two gentlemen stood in subdued conversation. One of them, leaning against the window, also wore the ship's uniform and was playing with the handle of his sword. The man he was talking to faced the window and from time to time made a movement that revealed a portion of the ribbons worn on the other's chest. He was in civilian dress and had a thin bamboo cane that, with both his hands on his hips, likewise stuck out like a sword.

Karl did not have much time to inspect everything before a steward came over to them and, glaring at the stoker as if he had no business there, asked what he wanted. The stoker replied in a voice as quiet as his questioner's that he wished to speak to the chief purser. The steward, having indicated his own disapproval of this request with a movement of his hand, nevertheless walked on tiptoe, taking a wide arc to avoid the circular table, over to the gentleman with the ledgers. He—one saw this clearly—went quite rigid at the steward's words but eventually turned to face the man who wished to speak with him and proceeded to gesticulate in a vigorously negative manner for the benefit of both the stoker and, for safety's sake, the steward as well. The steward then went back to the stoker and told him in the tone of one imparting confidential information, 'Get out of this room at once!'

The stoker, on receiving this reply, looked down at Karl as if the lad had been his heart to whom he was silently committing his lament. Without thinking twice Karl launched himself forward, straight across the room, even brushing against the officer's chair in passing; the steward advanced at a crouching run with arms held ready to grab him as if he had been some sort of vermin, but Karl reached the chief purser's table first and promptly clung to it in case the steward should try to pull him away.

The whole room of course immediately sprang to life. The officer at the table was already on his feet, the men from the port authority sat in attentive silence, the two gentlemen at the window had moved side by side, and the steward, now that the high-ups were taking such an interest, saw himself as out of place and retreated into the background. The stoker waited by the door, poised to intervene as soon as his help should be required. Finally the chief purser in his armchair turned all the way round to his right.

Karl plunged a hand into his secret pocket, which he had no misgivings about revealing in the presence of all these people, pulled out his passport, and laid it open on the table by way of introducing himself. The chief purser apparently regarded the document as immaterial because he flicked it aside with two fingers; Karl promptly returned it to his pocket as if a formality had been satisfactorily completed.

'I should like to say,' he began, 'that in my opinion the

gentleman here'—pointing to the stoker—'has been done an injustice. There is a man called Schubal who's been getting on his nerves. He himself has served on a great many ships—he can give you all their names—in an entirely satisfactory manner; he is a hard and well-intentioned worker, and it is quite incomprehensible that on this ship, where the work is really not over-arduous, as it is for example on sailing vessels, he should be found wanting. So it can only be slander that is hindering his progress and robbing him of the recognition that would otherwise undoubtedly be his. I have given you no more than the background to this affair; he will put his particular complaints to you himself.'

Karl had addressed his speech to all the gentlemen, because they were all in fact listening and the likelihood seemed far greater of there being one just man among their number than of that one happening to be the chief purser. Karl had also cunningly omitted to mention that he had known the stoker only for so short a time. For the rest, he would have spoken a great deal better had he not been put off by the red face of the gentleman with the bamboo cane, which from his present position he was seeing for the first time.

'That's right—every word of it,' the stoker said before anyone had asked for his opinion or indeed even looked in his direction. This precipitateness on the stoker's part would have been a big mistake had not the gentleman with the decorations—it suddenly dawned on Karl that this was of course the captain—evidently made up his mind in advance to listen to what the stoker had to say. He now reached out a hand and called over to the stoker, 'Come here!' in a voice so firm one could have hit it with a hammer. Everything now depended on how the stoker conducted himself, because as far as the justice of his cause was concerned Karl was not in any doubt.

Fortunately it became clear at this point that the stoker was very much a man of the world. With exemplary calm he reached into his little case and, finding what he wanted at the first attempt, drew out a sheaf of papers and a notebook; he then, acting as if this had been the obvious course, and completely ignoring the chief purser, took these over to the captain and spread his evidence out on the windowsill. The chief purser was obliged to make his own way over to join them. 'The man is a notorious grumbler,' he explained, 'and spends more time in my office than in the engine-room. He's driven Schubal, a normally even-tempered man, nearly to distraction. Listen to me!' he went on, turning to the stoker. 'You really take your impertinence too far. How many times have you been slung out of the wages office—quite rightly in view of your utterly and completely unjustified demands! How many times have you then come running to my office! How many times has it been explained to you in good faith that Schubal is your immediate superior and that you as his subordinate have to come to terms with him and him alone! And now you even come along when the captain is here, and not only do you shamelessly importune him but you have the affrontery to bring with you a tame mouth-piece for your fatuous accusations in the shape of this lad here, whom I have never seen on the ship before!'

It was with an effort that Karl prevented himself from leaping forward. But the captain had already intervened himself, saying, 'Let's hear what the man has to say. Schubal is in any case becoming much too independent for my liking, not that I mean to imply anything in your favour when I say that.' This last remark was addressed to the stoker; it was only natural that he could not immediately take his side, but everything seemed to be going well. The stoker embarked on a statement of his case, making a conscious effort right from the start in giving Schubal the title 'Mister'. How Karl rejoiced beside the chief purser's abandoned desk, where he kept pressing down a letter-balance in sheer delight.—Mr Schubal is unfair! Mr Schubal gives preferential treatment to foreigners! Mr Schubal ordered the stoker out of the engine-room and made him clean lavatories, which was most certainly not his job!—At one point doubt was even cast upon Mr Schubal's competence on the grounds that this

was more ostensible than actual. Here Karl looked at the
captain with all the intensity he could muster, his manner
that of a confiding colleague, purely in order to prevent
his being prejudiced against the stoker by the latter's
somewhat unfortunate choice of expression. It was true
that nothing precise emerged from all the stoker's talking,
and although the captain continued to stare straight ahead
of him, his eyes firm with a determination to hear the
stoker out this time, the other gentlemen began to lose
patience, and soon the stoker's voice no longer held
undisputed sway in the room, which certainly boded no
good. First the gentleman in civilian dress brought his
bamboo cane into play, tapping, if only lightly, on the
parquet floor. The others not unnaturally cast occasional
glances at him; the gentlemen from the port authority,
who were clearly in a hurry, took up the documents again
and started, if still somewhat distractedly, leafing through
them, the ship's officer pulled his chair up to the table
again, and the chief purser, believing his case to be as good
as won, heaved an ironic sigh. This general dissipation of
attention seemed to affect everyone but the steward, who
sympathized to some extent with the plight of the poor
man under the thumb of the great and powerful and
nodded earnestly to Karl as if seeking to make a point.

Meanwhile, outside the windows, the life of the port
went on: a flat freighter with a mountain of drums that
must have been miraculously well stowed for them not to
start rolling steamed past and plunged the room into near
darkness; small motor boats, which Karl could now, given
the time, have studied in detail, flew about as straight as
arrows under the tugging hands of men standing erect at
their helms; strange floating bodies occasionally emerged
from the restless waves, apparently of their own volition,
were immediately swamped again, and astonishingly sank;
boats belonging to the big steamers were pulled through
the water by perspiring matelots, full of passengers sitting
quietly and expectantly as they had been packed in, except
that some could not help swivelling their heads in response
to the shifting views. A ceaseless movement, a turbulence

transmitted from the turbulent element to helpless man-kind and its works!

All of it, though, urged haste, clarity, accuracy of description, but what was the stoker doing? He was admittedly talking himself into a lather, and his hands had for some time been trembling so much that he could no longer hold the papers on the windowsill; complaints against Schubal, each of them sufficient in his opinion to cook Schubal's goose completely, streamed into his mind from every point of the compass, but all he was able to produce for the captain was a pathetic hotch-potch of the whole lot. For some while now the gentleman with the bamboo cane had been whistling softly at the ceiling; the port authority gentlemen were actually holding on to the officer at their table and did not look like ever letting him go again; the only thing preventing the chief purser from intervening was clearly the captain's calmness; and the steward, standing at attention, expected momently to receive his captain's orders regarding the stoker.

Karl, able to remain inactive no longer, walked slowly over to the group, thinking fast, as he went, about how best to tackle the situation. It was really high time: much more of this and they could easily find themselves slung out of the office. The captain might be a good man, he might also at this point in time, as it seemed to Karl, have some special reason for showing himself to be a just superior, but he was not after all an instrument that one could go on playing until it wore out—which was exactly how the stoker was treating him, driven of course by the boundless indignation in his heart.

So Karl said to the stoker, 'You must tell it more simply and clearly; the captain can't do justice to it, the way you're telling it to him. Do you suppose he knows all the engine-room staff by their surnames, let alone their Christian names, so that when you just give that name he immediately knows whom you're talking about? Sort your complaints out a bit; say the main ones first and the others in descending order of importance; it may not be necessary then even to mention most of them. You've always explained it so clearly to me!' If one can steal suitcases in America one can also tell the occasional lie, he thought by way of an excuse.

If only it had done the trick! But perhaps it was too late in any case. The stoker did break off immediately on hearing the familiar voice, but his eyes, veiled as they were with tears of hurt male pride, appalling recollections, and deep present distress, were not even capable of recognizing Karl any more. And how was he at this stage—Karl must have appreciated this as he silently faced his now silent friend—how was he at this stage suddenly to change his way of speaking, for it seemed to him that he had already said everything there was to say without receiving the slightest acknowledgement, and that on the other hand he had said nothing as yet but could hardly expect the gentlemen to hear the whole thing through again. And at a time like this Karl, his sole ally, pipes up and, in seeking to give him some good advice, shows him instead that, yes, everything is lost.

'Oh, I wish I'd come sooner instead of staring out of the window!' Karl said to himself, dropping his eyes as he faced the stoker and slapping his hands against his trouser seams as a sign that all hope was gone.

The stoker, however, misunderstood this, probably sensing unspoken reproaches behind Karl's behaviour towards him, and with the honest intention of talking him out of these he now capped everything by picking a quarrel with Karl—at a time, that is, when the gentlemen at the circular table had long been irritated by the unnecessary noise, which interfered with their important transactions, when the chief purser was beginning to find the captain's patience incomprehensible and was on the verge of exploding, when the steward, restored completely to his masters' domain, was sizing up the stoker with wild looks, and when finally the gentleman with the bamboo cane, whom the captain himself favoured with a friendly glance now and then, having grown wholly indifferent to, indeed sick of the stoker, drew out a small notebook and, with his mind obviously on quite other matters, let his gaze wander from the notebook to Karl and back.

'Oh, I know, I know,' said Karl, who was having difficulty in withstanding the torrent of the stoker's words yet still managed to cut right across their quarrel with a smile of friendship for the other man. 'You're right, you're right, I never doubted the fact.' He was afraid that the stoker's flailing hands might land blows and would have liked to restrain them, though he would have liked even more to push him into a corner and whisper a few quiet, calming words in his ear, words that no one need have overheard. But the stoker was beside himself. Karl even began to draw consolation from the idea that, at a pinch, with the strength born of desperation, the stoker might have overpowered all seven men present. On the desk, however, as a glance in that direction revealed, lay an attachment with far too many push-buttons connected to electrical leads; one hand laid flat upon it and pressed down could have had the whole ship, with all its gangways packed with hostile elements, up in arms.

Here the thoroughly uninterested gentleman with the bamboo cane went up to Karl and asked in a voice that, while not over-loud, rose clearly above all the stoker's shouting, 'What is your name?' At that moment, as if someone had been waiting outside the door for the gentleman to say this, there came a knock. The steward looked across at the captain, who nodded. At this the steward went to the door and opened it. Outside, dressed in an old army frock coat, stood a man of medium build who, while he did not actually look cut out for engine-room work, was nevertheless—Schubal. Had Karl not known this from the look in everyone's eyes, where a certain satisfaction found expression from which not even the captain was immune, he would inevitably, and to his horror, have perceived it from the stoker, who clenched his fists at the ends of stiffened arms as if having them clenched had been the most important thing about him, the thing for which he was prepared to sacrifice every scrap of life in his body. That was where all his strength now resided, including that which was keeping him on his feet.

So there he was, the enemy, as free as air in his glad rags, under his arm an account book that no doubt contained the stoker's wages record and cards, his look frankly admitting, as it sought their eyes, that his first concern was to gauge the temper of each individual. The seven of them were in any case already his friends since, despite the fact that the captain had earlier found or perhaps only pretended to find fault with him, after the way the stoker had treated him it was unlikely that he had the least objection to Schubal any more. For a man like the stoker no discipline was too severe, and if Schubal could be reproached with anything it was with having failed to break the stoker's recalcitrant spirit sufficiently in the course of time to have prevented his daring to appear before the captain on this occasion.

There might none the less be grounds for assuming that this confrontation between the stoker and Schubal would have the same effect upon men as it would have had upon a higher forum, because however successfully Schubal might dissemble there was nothing to say that he would be able to keep it up to the end. One quick spark of his evil nature ought to kindle the gentlemen's appreciation of it; Karl intended to see to that. He already had an approximate idea of the perspicacity, weak points, and moods of the individual gentlemen, and in this respect the time he had so far spent in the room had not been wasted. If only the stoker had been in better shape, but he appeared to be completely *hors de combat.* Had someone held Schubal in front of him he would undoubtedly have managed to hammer open the hated skull with his fists. But even the few steps over to where Schubal was standing were probably more than he could achieve. Why on earth had Karl not foreseen what he might so easily have foreseen, namely that Schubal must in the end turn up, if not of his own volition then in response to a summons from the captain? Why on the way here with the stoker had he not discussed a precise plan of campaign instead of, as they had in fact done, simply walking in at the door, utterly

unprepared? Was the stoker even capable of speech in his
present state, of saying yes and no as, during cross-
examination—incidentally the most favourable eventuality
that they faced—he would be required to do? He was
standing there, legs apart, knees unsteady, head slightly
raised, air passing in and out through his open mouth as if
there had been no lungs inside to assimilate it any more.

Karl on the other hand felt more potent and alert than
he had perhaps ever been at home. If his parents could
only have seen how in a foreign country and in the
presence of distinguished persons he was fighting for what
was right and, though not yet victorious, nevertheless held
himself in complete readiness for the final offensive!
Would they have revised their ideas about him? Sat him
down between them and praised him? Looked just once,
just once into his oh so devoted eyes? Uncertain questions,
and what a time to ask them!

'I've come because I believe the stoker is accusing me of
some sort of underhandedness. A girl from the galley told
me she'd seen him on his way here. Sir,'—to the captain,
and to the others—'gentlemen, I am ready to refute every
charge with the help of my papers and if need be through
the testimony of impartial and unprejudiced witnesses,
who are waiting outside the door.' Thus Schubal. It was
certainly straight talking, and by a man, and from the
change that came over the listeners' faces one might have
thought they were hearing human sounds again for the
first time in ages. They failed, of course, to notice that
even this fine speech did not hold water. Why was the first
pertinent word that had occurred to him 'underhandedness'? Should the accusation perhaps have started at this
point rather than with his national prejudices? A girl from
the galley had seen the stoker on his way to the office and
Schubal had immediately understood, was that it? Was it
not that his wits had been sharpened by guilt? And he had
brought witnesses along straight away, had he, referring to
them as impartial and unprejudiced into the bargain?
What a swindler the man was! And the gentlemen put up
with it and even accepted it as proper conduct? Why had

he undoubtedly allowed a great deal of time to elapse
between the galley girl's announcement and his arrival
here? Clearly to no other purpose than that the stoker
should so weary the gentlemen as to rob them little by little
of their faculty of discrimination, from which Schubal had
most to fear. Had he not waited before knocking—because
he had surely been standing outside the door for some
time—had he not waited for the moment when, with that
gentleman asking his inconsequential question, he had
reason to hope that the stoker was done for?

The whole thing was clear and was even presented as
such by the unwitting Schubal, but for the gentlemen's
benefit it must be put differently, made more obvious.
They needed shaking up. Quick, Karl—at least take
advantage of the time available before the witnesses come
in and swamp everything!

The captain, however, put his hand up, and Schubal—
since his case appeared to have been deferred for a
while—promptly stepped to one side and began a muttered conversation with the steward, who had taken his
part immediately, a conversation that was accompanied by
many sidelong glances at the stoker and Karl as well as by
gestures of the most unreserved conviction. Schubal
appeared to be rehearsing his next major speech.

'Wasn't there something you wanted to ask the young
man, Mr Jacob?' the captain said amid the general silence
to the gentleman with the bamboo cane.

'Yes, indeed,' said the latter, acknowledging this courtesy with a little bow. And he asked Karl again, 'What is
your name?'

Karl, thinking that it would be to the advantage of the
main business to deal swiftly with this obstinate questioner's intervention, answered briefly and without following
his usual habit of introducing himself by showing his
passport, which he would first have had to look for, 'Karl
Rossmann.'

'But,' said the man who had been addressed as Jacob,
first stepping back with a smile almost of disbelief. The
captain, the chief purser, the other officer, and even the

77

steward likewise showed signs of inordinate surprise at the mention of Karl's name. Only the gentlemen from the port authority and Schubal reacted with indifference.

'But,' Mr Jacob reiterated, stepping somewhat stiffly over to where Karl stood, 'in that case I am your Uncle Jacob and you are my dear nephew. I suspected it all along!' he told the captain before taking Karl in his arms and kissing him, all of which Karl suffered in silence.

'What is your name?' Karl, the embrace over, put his question very politely but quite without emotion, trying hard to foresee the consequences this turn of events might have for the stoker. There was nothing at the moment to suggest that Schubal might profit by it in any way.

'You don't appreciate your good fortune, young man,' said the captain in the belief that Karl's question offended the dignity of Mr Jacob, who had moved over to the window, obviously in order to avoid having to show his discomposed face, which he was now dabbing at with a handkerchief, to the other persons in the room. 'The man who has made himself known to you as your uncle is Senator Edward Jacob. You can now, doubtless in stark contrast to your previous expectations, look forward to a brilliant career. Try to grasp the fact as best you can, having had it sprung upon you like this, and do pull yourself together!'

'I have got an Uncle Jacob in America,' Karl said, turning to the captain, 'but if I understand correctly Jacob is only the senator's surname.'

'That is so,' said the captain, expectantly.

'Well, my Uncle Jacob, my mother's brother, was christened Jacob, whereas his surname must of course be the same as my mother's, and her maiden name was Bendelmayer.'

'Gentlemen!' cried the senator, briskly returning from his retreat by the window to take up Karl's point. All present, with the exception of the port officials, broke into smiles, some as if sympathetic, others inscrutable.

Karl thought, 'It certainly wasn't as absurd as all that, what I said.'

'Gentlemen,' the senator repeated, 'you are involved against my wish and your own in a minor family scene. I therefore have no alternative but to offer you an explanation, since I believe only the captain'—reference to whom resulted in an exchange of bows—'is wholly in the picture.'

'Now I must really pay attention to every word,' Karl said to himself, happy to discover from a sideways glance that the stoker was beginning to show signs of life once more.

'I have during all the long years of my sojourn in America—though that word sojourn is hardly appropriate usage for an American citizen, which I am with heart and soul—during all those long years, I say, I have been without contact of any kind with my European relations, and this for reasons that firstly have no place here and secondly would be too painful for me to relate. I even dread the moment when I may be constrained to relate them to my dear nephew, for in doing so I shall unfortunately have to be quite frank about his parents and their circle.'

'He's my uncle—no doubt about it,' Karl said to himself as he listened. 'Probably he's changed his name.'

'My dear nephew has been—let us not be afraid to call a spade a spade—quite simply got rid of by his parents, rather as one might throw out a cat that was annoying one. I am certainly not trying to gloss over what my nephew did to be punished in this fashion, but his fault was such that the mere admission of it carries sufficient pardon.'

'Well said,' thought Karl, 'but I don't want him telling everyone about it. Anyway, he can't possibly know. How could he have heard?'

'The fact is,' his uncle went on, executing a series of little bows with the support of his bamboo cane, which he held pressed to the ground in front of him with both hands, and managing by this means actually to disencumber the matter of such unnecessary solemnity as it would otherwise inevitably have assumed, 'the fact is that he was seduced by one Johanna Brummer, a servant girl of some thirty-five years of age. In using the word seduced I have no wish to insult my nephew, but it is difficult to find another word as suitable.'

Karl, who by now had moved fairly close to his uncle, turned round at this point to examine the effect of his uncle's account on the faces of those present. No one was laughing; they were all listening patiently and earnestly. Not that one does laugh at the nephew of a senator on the first occasion that presents itself, though the stoker might have been said to be smiling at Karl, however faintly, which was in the first place encouraging as being a further sign of life and in the second place excusable by virtue of the fact that, back in the cabin, Karl had tried to make a particular secret of this matter that was now becoming so public.

'This Brummer,' Karl's uncle went on, 'subsequently had a child by my nephew, a healthy boy who was baptized Jacob, no doubt with my humble self in mind, the surely only passing references to me made by my nephew having even so, it would appear, produced a powerful impression on the girl. And a good thing too, I might add. Because in view of the fact that his parents, to get out of paying maintenance and to avoid any further scandal possibly implicating themselves—I must emphasize that I am familiar neither with the laws in force there nor with the parents' circumstances apart from this—rather, as I say, than pay maintenance or risk any scandal, had their son, my dear nephew, shipped off to America—shamefully ill-equipped, as we see—in view of that fact the young man, without the signs and miracles that are still a part of life in this country, left to his own devices, would probably have succumbed immediately to depravity in some alley in New York harbour had not that servant girl, in a letter to me, which after a long and complicated journey came into my possession the day before yesterday, told me the whole story and appended a personal description of my nephew as well as, very sensibly, giving the name of the ship. Were it my purpose to divert you, gentlemen, I could easily read one or two passages from that letter'—he pulled two enormous, closely written sheets of stationery from his pocket with a flourish—'aloud for your benefit. It would undoubtedly impress you, being written with somewhat simple if well-meaning guile and with a great deal of love for the child's father. But I look neither to divert you any more than is necessary to put all this across nor possibly to mar this reception by offending feelings my nephew may still entertain; the letter is his, if he wishes, to read in the silence of the room that already awaits him.'

Karl, however, entertained no feelings for the girl. In the press of a continually receding past she sat beside the dresser in her kitchen, elbows propped on the marble slab. She would look at him when, every now and then, he came into the kitchen to fetch a glass for his father's drink of water or on some errand for his mother. Sometimes she was writing a letter in that awkward position at the end of the dresser, and Karl's face would apparently provide her with ideas. Sometimes she had a hand over her eyes, and there was no getting through to her then. Sometimes she was kneeling in her little room off the kitchen, praying to a wooden crucifix; the door stood ajar and Karl, as he passed, peeped in at her very shyly. Sometimes she would be dashing about the kitchen and would shrink back, cackling like a witch, whenever Karl crossed her path. Sometimes she shut the kitchen door behind Karl when he came in and kept her hand on the handle until he begged to be allowed to leave. Sometimes she fetched things he did not want at all and wordlessly thrust them into his hands. On one occasion, however, she said, 'Karl,' and in his bewilderment at this unexpected use of his name she led him, with much sighing and grimacing, into her room and locked the door. Throwing a pair of choking arms round his neck, she begged him to undress her while in fact she undressed him and laid him in her bed as if she meant never to give him up to anyone but to go on caressing him and looking after him until the end of time. 'Oh, Karl, my Karl!' she cried as if seeing him and confirming her possession of him, while he, seeing nothing at all, simply felt uncomfortable in all the warm bedclothes that she seemed to have piled up especially for his benefit.

Then she joined him in bed and tried to get some secret or other out of him, but there was none he could tell her and she became angry either in jest or in earnest, shook him, listened to his heart-beat, offered her breast for Karl to do the same but could not persuade him to, pressed her naked belly to his body, fumbled—this was so repugnant that Karl shook his head and neck free of the pillows —with her hand between his legs, then thrust her belly against him a number of times—as if, he thought, she had been part of him, and it may have been for this reason that he was overcome by a feeling of terrible distress. Eventually, after many pleas on her part that they should see each other again, he made his way weeping to his own bed. That had been all, though his uncle had certainly managed to make a meal of it. So she had been thinking of him too and had notified his uncle of his arrival. That had been kind of her and he would doubtless find an opportunity to reward her.

'And now,' cried the senator, 'I want to hear you say straight out whether I am your uncle or not.'

'You are my uncle,' Karl said, and he kissed his hand and received in return a kiss on the forehead. 'I am very glad to have found you, yet you are wrong in thinking that my parents speak only ill of you. But even apart from that there were several errors in what you said, by which I mean that it did not all happen that way in reality. Still, you really cannot hope to see things so clearly from this distance, and in any case I think no particular harm will have been done if, regarding something that can really be of no great interest to them, these gentlemen have in matters of detail been to some small extent misinformed.'

'Excellently put,' the senator declared before leading Karl over to the obviously interested captain and asking, 'Haven't I got a splendid nephew?'

'Mr Senator,' said the captain with a bow of the kind that betrays a military training, 'I am delighted to have made your nephew's acquaintance. It is a particular honour that my ship should have been able to furnish the venue for such a meeting. The crossing in our steerage accommodation must I'm afraid have been an ordeal, but how is one to know who is down there? We do our best, of course, to make the crossing as painless as possible for our steerage passengers—we do much more than the American companies, for instance—but I must admit that we have yet to succeed in making it a pleasure.'

'I'm none the worse for it,' said Karl.

'He's none the worse for it!' the senator echoed with a shout of laughter.

'Only I'm afraid I may have lost my suitcase'—and with that it all came back to him, everything that had happened and that still remained to be done; he looked about him and found all the people present back in their original positions, silent with respect and astonishment, staring at him. Only the port-authority officials showed—in so far as their stern, self-satisfied faces showed anything—regret at having come at so inopportune a moment, and the pocket watch that now lay before them was probably of greater consequence to them than anything that was going on in the room and might yet occur there.

The first person after the captain to express a sympathetic interest was, curiously enough, the stoker. 'My sincere congratulations!' he said, and he shook Karl by the hand, seeking in the process to express something else that might have been gratitude. When he tried to say and do the same thing to the senator, the latter took a step backwards as if the stoker had been guilty of presumption, whereupon the stoker immediately desisted.

The others, however, understanding what was now required of them, immediately formed a knot of bodies around Karl and the senator. One consequence of this was that Karl even received congratulations from Schubal, accepted them, and thanked him for them. The last to come up, once calm had returned, were the port-authority officials, who said two words in English, creating a ridiculous impression.

The senator was very much in the mood to make the most of a pleasant occasion by recalling for his own and the others' benefit some of its more incidental aspects,

83

which everyone of course not only bore with but followed with interest. He pointed out, for example, that he had entered Karl's chief distinguishing characteristics, as mentioned in the cook's letter, in his notebook in case he should ever need to refer to them at short notice. With the stoker blathering on so intolerably he had happened, purely for something to do, to take out his notebook and play at trying to compare the cook's observations, which of course were hardly adequate as an instrument of detection, with Karl's appearance. 'How to find your nephew!' he concluded in a voice that sounded as if he might have been in search of fresh congratulations.

'What's going to happen to the stoker now?' Karl asked, ignoring his uncle's latest anecdote. In his new position he felt able to say everything that was on his mind.

'The stoker will get what he deserves,' said the senator, 'and what the captain considers to be right. I think we have all had more than enough of the stoker, and I am sure that every one of the gentlemen present will agree with me.'

'That's not the point when justice is at stake,' said Karl. He was standing between his uncle and the captain and believed, possibly under the influence of this position, that the decision was his.

And yet the stoker himself appeared to have given up all hope. His hands were half in his trouser belt, which together with a ring of patterned shirt had become exposed as a result of his excited movements. He could not have cared less about this; he had told his tale of woe—so let them see the few rags with which he was clothed before they carried him away. He had the notion of the steward and Schubal, as the two lowest-ranking persons present, rendering him the last honours. Schubal would have his peace and would no longer be driven to distraction, as the chief purser had put it. The captain could then take on a lot of Rumanians, Rumanian would be spoken all over the ship, and perhaps things really would be better like that. No stoker would come blathering to the chief purser's office any more, but his final blather would be quite kindly remembered as having, as the senator had expressly

declared, indirectly occasioned the recognition of the
nephew. Incidentally the nephew had tried several times
to make himself useful to him earlier and in so doing had
already rendered more than adequate thanks for his
contribution to the recognition scene; it did not occur to
the stoker to ask anything more of him now. Anyway,
senator's nephew or not, he was certainly not a captain, but
it was from the captain's mouth that the angry word would
eventually fall. In accordance with his belief, the stoker did
actually try to avoid looking at Karl, but unfortunately in
this room full of enemies there was nowhere else his gaze
could rest.

'Don't misunderstand the situation,' the senator said to
Karl. 'Justice may be at stake here, but so too is the
question of discipline. Both matters, and in particular the
second, fall in this instance within the jurisdiction of the
captain.'

'So they do,' murmured the stoker. Those who heard
and understood smiled strange smiles.

'Furthermore we have already so seriously hindered the
captain in the transaction of his official business, which is
bound to pile up incredibly with the ship's arrival in New
York, that it is high time we disembarked before, to make
matters worse, we contrive by quite uncalled-for meddling
to turn this petty squabble between two engineers into a
major incident. I perfectly understand, my dear nephew,
why you acted as you did, but for that very reason I feel
entitled to effect your speedy removal from here.'

'I'll have a boat lowered for you right away,' the captain
announced without—to Karl's astonishment—raising the
slightest objection to what his uncle had said, although this
was indubitably open to interpretation as a piece of self-
abasement on the latter's part. The chief purser scurried
over to his desk and phoned the captain's order through to
the boatswain.

'Time is running out,' Karl said to himself, 'but short of
offending everybody there's nothing I can do. I can't leave
my uncle now, when he's only just found me again. The
captain may be polite, but that is as far as it goes. When it's

a question of discipline, goodbye politeness, and Uncle was undoubtedly voicing the captain's own thoughts when he said what he did. I don't wish to speak to Schubal; I'm even sorry that I shook hands with him. And the rest of them here are so much chaff.'

With these thoughts passing through his mind he went over to the stoker, pulled the man's right hand out of his belt, and held it casually in his own. 'Why don't you say anything?' he asked. 'Why do you just take it all?'

The stoker merely furrowed his brow as if searching for a way to express what he had to say. He also looked down at Karl's and his hands.

'You have been wronged more than anyone else on the ship; I know that for a fact.' And Karl drew his finger back and forth between the stoker's fingers while the latter looked about him with shining eyes as if a bliss were his that, however, none should begrudge him.

'You must defend yourself, say yes and no—otherwise people will have no idea of the truth. You must promise me that you'll do as I say, because I have every reason to fear that I'll not be able to help you myself any more.' Whereupon Karl wept as he kissed the stoker's hand, and he took the chapped, almost lifeless hand and pressed it to his cheeks like some treasured possession that must be forgone. But already his senator uncle was at his side, drawing him, albeit with the most delicate coercion, away from there.

'The stoker seems to have you under his spell,' he said with a look of deep understanding directed over Karl's head at the captain. 'You felt lonely, you found the stoker, and now you're grateful to him—all very commendable. Don't, however, if only for my sake, take it too far, but learn to come to terms with your situation.'

There was a noise outside; shouts were heard, and it even sounded as if someone had been brutally thrust against the door. A sailor entered the room in some disorder, a woman's apron round his waist. 'There are these people outside,' he exclaimed, swinging his elbow round as if he were still being jostled in their midst. He got

himself under control eventually and was about to salute
the captain when, catching sight of the apron, he tore it
off, flung it to the floor, and exclaimed, 'What a sick thing
to do—they tied a woman's apron on me!' Then, however,
he did bring his heels together with a click and salute.
Someone tried to laugh, but the captain said sternly,
'That's what I call high spirits. Who is outside?'

'They're my witnesses,' said Schubal, stepping forward.
'Please accept my humble apologies for their ill-behaviour.
With the crossing behind them, people sometimes seem to
go mad.'

'Call them in immediately!' the captain ordered, and
turning to the senator he said courteously if rapidly,
'Would you, Mr Senator, and your nephew be so good as
to go with this sailor? He will escort you to the boat. I am
sure I need hardly say what a pleasure and indeed what an
honour it has been for me, Mr Senator, sir, to make your
acquaintance. My only wish, sir, is that I shall soon have an
opportunity to resume our interrupted discussion of
American naval affairs in order, it may be, once again to be
interrupted in so pleasant a fashion as today.'

'The one nephew will be enough for me for the time
being,' said Karl's uncle with a laugh. 'And now, sir, may I
offer you my most sincere thanks for your kindness and
bid you farewell? And it is of course by no means
impossible that on our next trip to Europe'—he hugged
Karl warmly—'we may perhaps be able to spend some time
with you.'

'I should be only too delighted,' said the captain. The
two men shook hands; Karl could do no more than offer
the captain his hand quickly in silence because the captain
was already preoccupied with the fifteen or so people who,
bewildered but still very noisy, were being ushered into the
room by Schubal. The sailor asked the senator if he might
go ahead and proceeded to part the crowd for him and
Karl, who then passed easily between the bowing figures
on either side. These essentially good-humoured people
appeared to regard Schubal's quarrel with the stoker as a
joke that could be treated as such even in the presence of

the captain. Among them Karl noticed the galley-girl Lina as, with a cheerful wink in his direction, she tied on the apron that the sailor had flung down, for it was hers.

They followed the sailor out of the office and along a little gangway that brought them after a few paces to a door, from which a short ladder descended to the waiting boat. The sailors in the boat, whom the one who had been leading them immediately joined with a single leap, stood up and saluted. The senator was just warning Karl to be careful how he climbed down when Karl, still on the top step, burst into tears. The senator put his right hand under Karl's chin, held him tightly to him, and used his left hand to stroke him. In this close embrace they slowly descended step by step and got into the boat, where the senator found a good seat for Karl right opposite him. At a signal from the senator the sailors pushed off from the ship and fell to rowing at full stretch. Before the boat had gone more than a few yards Karl made the unexpected discovery that they were on the side of the ship that the windows of the chief purser's office looked out on. All three windows were occupied by witnesses of Schubal's, who were waving to them in the friendliest manner imaginable; even Karl's uncle acknowledged their greetings, and one of the sailors somehow contrived, without breaking his stroke, to blow them a kiss. It was just as if the stoker had ceased to exist. Karl looked more closely at his uncle, whose knees his own were almost touching, and began to doubt whether this man could ever take the stoker's place as far as he was concerned. His uncle, moreover, avoided his gaze, looking instead at the waves that were tossing their boat about.

The Metamorphosis

(*Die Verwandlung,* written between 18 November and
6 December 1912 and first published in October 1913
in the review *Die Weissen Blätter*; separate volume
publication in November 1913 in Kurt Wolff's 'Der
Jüngste Tag' series.)

I

Gregory Samsa woke from uneasy dreams one morning to find himself changed into a giant bug. He was lying on his back, which was of a shell-like hardness, and when he lifted his head a little he could see his dome-shaped brown belly, banded with what looked like reinforcing arches, on top of which his quilt, while threatening to slip off completely at any moment, still maintained a precarious hold. His many legs, pitifully thin in relation to the rest of him, threshed ineffectually before his eyes.

'What's happened to me?' he thought. This was no dream. His room, a normal human room except that it was rather too small, lay peacefully between the four familiar walls. Above the table, which was littered with a collection of drapery samples—Samsa was a traveller—hung the picture that he had recently cut out of a magazine and mounted in an attractive gilt frame. It showed a lady in a fur hat and boa, sitting up straight and holding out an enormous fur muff that entirely concealed her forearms.

Gregory's gaze shifted to the window, and the murky weather—raindrops beat audibly on the zinc windowsill —made him feel quite melancholy. 'Why don't I go back to sleep for a bit and forget all the fooling about?' he thought, but this was impossible: he liked to sleep on his right side, and in his present state he was unable to assume that position. Try as he might to throw himself over to the right, he always rocked back into his previous position. He must have made a hundred attempts; he shut his eyes to keep out the sight of all those toiling legs; and he gave up only when he became aware of a faint, dull ache in his side of a kind he had never felt before.

'God,' he thought, 'what a gruelling job I chose! On the go day in and day out. The business side of it is much more hectic than in the office itself, and on top of that there's the wretched travelling, the worry about train connections, the awful meals eaten at all hours, and the constant chopping and changing as far as human relationships are concerned, never knowing anyone for long, never making friends. Oh, to hell with the whole thing!' He felt a slight itch high up on his belly; pushed himself, on his back, slowly closer to the bedpost, the better to lift his head; located the itchy place, which was covered with a lot of tiny white spots he did not know what to make of; and tried to touch the place with a leg, withdrawing it immediately, however, because the contact sent cold shivers through him.

He slid back into his original position. 'These early mornings,' he thought, 'are enough to drive one round the bend. A man needs his sleep. Other travellers live like kept women. I mean, when I go back to the hotel during the morning to write up my orders, some fellows are just sitting down to their breakfast. If I tried that on with my boss I'd be out on my ear immediately. Might not be a bad thing for me, at that. If it weren't for my parents I'd have handed in my notice long ago; I'd have gone to see the boss and given him a piece of my mind. Why, he'd have fallen off his desk! Funny habit, that, his sitting on the desk and talking down to his employees from a great height, especially since you have to step right up close because of his deafness. Ah well, there's still hope; once I've got the money together to pay off my parents' debt to him—that might take another five or six years—I'll definitely do it. I'll take the plunge. Meanwhile, though, I'd better get up; my train leaves at five.'

And he looked across at the alarm clock that stood ticking on the wardrobe. 'Heavens above!' he thought. It was half past six, and the hands were moving steadily onwards; in fact it was after half past, it was almost a quarter to. Had the alarm not rung? He could see from the bed that it had been set correctly for four o'clock; it must have rung. Yes, but—how could he have slept calmly through a ring so loud it shook the furniture? Well, not calmly, he hadn't slept calmly, but probably all the more soundly for that. What was he to do now, though? The next train left at seven; to catch that would have meant a frantic rush, and there were the samples to be packed, and he was not feeling particularly spry to start with, far from it. And even if he did catch the train he was in for a rocket from the boss because the office boy would have been at the station at five and would have reported his absence long ago, the office boy being a tool of the boss and a spineless, mindless creature. What if he were to report sick? No, that would be highly embarrassing as well as suspicious, Gregory not having had a day's illness in his five years with the firm. The boss would be sure to bring the health-insurance company's doctor round and blame his parents for having an idle son, cutting short all their protests by quoting the doctor's view that people were invariably in perfect health, just work-shy. And would he in fact be so wrong in this case? Aside from a certain drowsiness, quite superfluous after his long sleep, Gregory really felt very fit and was even aware of having an unusually robust appetite.

As he was rapidly considering all this, though without managing to make up his mind to get out of bed—the alarm clock was just striking a quarter to seven—there came a cautious knock on the door at the head of his bed. 'Gregory,'—it was his mother speaking—'it's a quarter to seven. Weren't you going off this morning?' That gentle voice! Gregory gave a start when he heard his own voice in reply; it was unmistakably his, but blended with it, as if welling up irrepressibly from below, was a distressing squeak that allowed the words to retain their clarity only for a moment, afterwards distorting their resonance to the point where one wondered whether one had heard correctly. Gregory had wanted to answer at length and explain everything, but in the circumstances he confined himself to saying, 'Yes, yes—thank you, mother, I'm just getting up.' Because of the wooden door the alteration in Gregory's voice was presumably not noticeable outside, for his mother, reassured by his words, went shuffling off. Their brief exchange, however, had alerted the other members of the family to the fact that Gregory, unexpectedly, was still at home, and soon his father was knocking at the door on one side, not hard, but with his fist. 'Gregory, Gregory,' he called, 'what is it?' And after a little while he repeated his admonishment in a deeper voice: 'Gregory! Gregory!' At the door on the other side his sister was quietly plaintive: 'Gregory? Are you all right? Can I get you anything?' 'Just coming,' Gregory replied to them both, trying by means of the most careful enunciation and by leaving long pauses between the words to remove any conspicuous quality from his voice. His father did indeed go back to his breakfast, but his sister whispered, 'Gregory, open the door, *please.*' Nothing was further from Gregory's mind, however; in fact he was congratulating himself on his cautious habit, adopted from his travels, of locking all the doors of his room at night even when he was at home.

He first wanted to get up in peace and quiet, dress, and above all have breakfast, and only then contemplate the future, because as he knew full well he would never think things through to a sensible conclusion as long as he remained in bed. He recalled having quite often felt some slight pain in bed, possibly as a result of having lain awkwardly, which had turned out to be purely imaginary once he was up, and he was curious to see how this morning's imaginings would gradually evaporate. Not for a moment did he doubt that the alteration in his voice was merely an early symptom of that occupational affliction of commercial travellers, the streaming cold.

Getting rid of the quilt was quite simple; all he needed to do was to puff himself up a little and it fell to the floor. After that, however, things became difficult, particularly since he was so extraordinarily broad. He would have needed arms and hands to lift himself up, but instead he had only a large number of legs that were in continuous, multifarious motion and in any case quite beyond his control. Whenever he tried to bend one it promptly stretched out straight; and if he did eventually manage to make the leg execute the desired movement all the others, left as it were to their own devices, went on working away in a state of the most acute and painful excitement. 'Right

—that's enough dawdling in bed!' Gregory told himself.

First he tried to get the lower part of his body out of bed, but this lower part, which incidentally he had not yet seen and of which he could form no very clear idea, proved too unwieldy; progress was so slow; and when finally, in a kind of rage, he summoned all his strength and recklessly thrust himself forward he had mistaken the direction, striking the lower bedpost a violent blow, and the sharp pain he felt informed him that it was this lower part of his body that was perhaps the most sensitive at the moment.

So he tried to get his upper body out of bed first, carefully twisting his head round towards the edge of the mattress. He managed this without difficulty, and despite its width and great weight his body did eventually begin to follow the movement of his head. But when at length he had his head out beyond the edge of the bed in mid air he suddenly thought better of continuing, afraid that if in the end he let himself fall like that it would take a miracle to prevent his sustaining a head injury. And the last thing he wanted to do just then was to lose consciousness; he would rather stay in bed.

But when after a similar struggle he lay back with a sigh in his first position and again saw his legs locked in what seemed if anything even fiercer combat than before, powerless to bring any kind of order into their chaos, he again told himself that he could not possibly stay where he was and that the only sensible thing was to risk all for even the faintest hope of somehow freeing himself from his bed. At the same time he was careful to remind himself at intervals that desperate decisions were no substitute for cool, calm thought. At such moments he focused as sharply as his eyes would allow on the window; unfortunately the sight of the morning mist, which even shrouded the other side of the narrow street, had little to offer in the way of brisk reassurance. 'Seven o'clock already,' he said to himself as the alarm clock struck again, 'seven o'clock and still such a mist.' And for a while he lay quiet, hardly breathing, hoping perhaps that total silence might bring about a return to normal, everyday reality.

But then he said to himself, 'Before a quarter past seven strikes I simply must be out of bed—right out. Anyway, someone will be here from the office by then to ask about me, because the office opens before seven o'clock.' And he set about rocking the whole length of his body evenly out of bed. If he allowed himself to fall out in this way his head, which he intended to lift smartly as he fell, would presumably remain unhurt. His back appeared to be hard; probably falling onto the carpet would do no damage to that. What worried him most was the thought of the loud crash that would inevitably accompany his fall and in all likelihood occasion if not alarm, at least concern beyond the various doors. But he would have to take that risk.

When Gregory was already leaning half out of bed—the new method was not so much work as play, since all he had to do was to keep rocking to and fro—it occurred to him how simple everything would be if someone were to come to his assistance. Two strong people—he had in mind his father and the maid—would have been quite sufficient; they need only have slid their arms under his arched back, eased him out of bed, bent down with him, and simply waited with patient vigilance until he had swung himself over onto the floor, where his legs would then, he hoped, acquire some purpose. So, quite apart from the fact that the doors were locked, should he really have called for help? In spite of his predicament he was unable to suppress a smile at the thought.

He had reached the stage where, if he rocked a little harder, he almost lost his balance, and he was very soon going to have to make up his mind once and for all because in five minutes it would be a quarter past seven—when the doorbell rang. 'That'll be someone from the office,' he said to himself and almost froze, except that his legs started dancing about all the more frantically. There was a moment's silence. 'They're not letting him in,' Gregory said to himself, caught up in some absurd hope. But then of course, as always, the maid strode purposefully to the door and opened it. The visitor's first word of greeting sufficed to tell Gregory who it was—the chief clerk himself. Why was Gregory of all people fated to work for a firm where the least little omission promptly aroused the greatest suspicion? Were all employees without exception knaves; was there not one single loyal and devoted person among them who, having failed to turn a mere couple of hours one morning to the firm's advantage, was driven so distracted by qualms of conscience as to become incapable of getting out of bed? Would it not have been enough to send an apprentice round to inquire, assuming this whole inquisition to be necessary in the first place? Did the chief clerk really have to come in person, so demonstrating to the entire, innocent family that the investigation of this suspicious affair could be entrusted only to a person of his discernment. And it was more in consequence of the state of agitation into which Gregory was thrown by these reflections than as a result of a genuine decision that he now swung himself out of bed with all his might. There was a loud thump, though not in fact a crash. To some extent his fall had been softened by the carpet, and also his back was more resilient than Gregory had thought—hence the muffled and really quite unremarkable sound. But he had not been careful enough about his head and had banged it; he twisted it round and rubbed it on the carpet in anger and pain.

'Something just fell down in there,' said the chief clerk in the room on the left. Gregory tried to imagine whether something similar might not happen to the chief clerk one day as had happened to him this morning. One had to admit it was possible. But as if in brusque reply to this question the chief clerk, in the next room, now took several resolute steps that made his patent-leather boots creak. From the room on the right Gregory's sister informed him in a whisper, 'Gregory, the chief clerk's here.' 'I know,' Gregory said under his breath, not daring to raise his voice to the point where his sister could have heard his reply.

'Gregory,' came his father's voice from the room on the left, 'the chief clerk has come round to ask why you didn't leave on the early train. We don't know what to tell him. In

97

any case he'd like a word with you personally. So please will you open the door. He'll have the goodness, I'm sure, to overlook the mess in your room.' Meanwhile the chief clerk put in a friendly, 'Good morning, Mr Samsa.' 'He's not well,' Gregory's mother told the chief clerk as his father was still talking through the door. 'He's not well, sir, you can take it from me. What else would make Gregory miss his train? Why, the boy thinks of nothing but his work! It makes me quite cross that he never goes out in the evening; now he's just had a whole week in town, but every evening he spent at home. He sits there with us at the table and quietly reads the paper or pores over timetables. His only amusement is when he does his fretwork. He made a little picture frame, for instance, which took him two or three evenings; you'll be surprised how pretty it is; it's hanging up in his room; you'll see it in a moment, when Gregory opens the door. I'm glad you're here, sir, by the way; we'd never have got Gregory to unlock the door by ourselves, he's so stubborn; and I'm sure he's unwell, although he said he wasn't this morning.' 'Won't be a moment,' Gregory said slowly and deliberately, keeping quite still in order not to miss a word of this exchange. 'I likewise, madam, can think of no other explanation,' said the chief clerk. 'Let us hope it's nothing serious. On the other hand I am bound to say that those of us who are in business are—unfortunately or if you like fortunately— very often obliged simply to shrug off minor indispositions for business reasons.' 'Can the chief clerk come in, then?' asked his father impatiently, knocking on the door again. 'No,' said Gregory. In the room on the left an embarrassed silence fell; in the room on the right his sister began to sob.

Why did his sister not go round and join the others? Probably she had only just got out of bed and had not even begun dressing yet. And whyever was she crying? Was it because he did not get up and let the chief clerk in, because he was in danger of losing his job and because the boss would then start pestering his parents again about those old debts? Worries of that kind were surely quite superfluous for the present. Gregory was still around and had not the slightest intention of abandoning his family. Just at the moment he happened to be lying on the carpet, and no one who was aware of his condition would seriously have expected him to let the chief clerk into the room. But this minor discourtesy, for which a suitable excuse could easily be found at a later stage, hardly constituted grounds for firing Gregory on the spot. And to Gregory's way of thinking it would have been far more sensible to leave him in peace now instead of plaguing him with tears and exhortations. But of course it was the uncertainty that was upsetting the others and that accounted for their behaviour.

'Mr Samsa,' the chief clerk now called out in a louder voice, 'what is going on? You barricade yourself in your room, answer in monosyllables, are causing your parents grave and unnecessary concern, and are in addition—this merely by the by—neglecting your professional duties in a quite outrageous manner. On behalf of your parents and your superior I ask you most earnestly for an immediate and unequivocal explanation. I am astonished, I really am. I knew and believed you to be a calm and reasonable person, and suddenly you seem bent on manifesting these freakish whims. Your superior in fact intimated to me this morning a possible explanation for your absences—it had to do with the cash-up recently entrusted to you—but I assure you I gave him virtually my word of honour that that could not possibly be the true explanation. Now, however, having witnessed your incredible obstinacy, I find myself losing all inclination to plead your cause in any way whatsoever. I would add that your position is very far from assured. It was my original intention to tell you all this in private but, since you choose to make me waste my time here in this fruitless fashion, I see no reason why your good parents should not hear it too. Your figures recently have been most unsatisfactory; this is not of course the season for doing a lot of business, we recognize that; but a season for doing no business at all does not exist and cannot, Mr Samsa, be allowed to exist.'

'But, sir,' cried Gregory, most upset and forgetting

99

everything else in his excitement, 'I'm just going to open the door, this very moment. A slight indisposition, a dizzy spell, prevented me from getting up. I'm still in bed. But I already feel perfectly fit again. I'm getting out of bed now. Just be patient for a moment. Things aren't going quite as well as I expected. I'm all right, though. Funny how something like that can hit you. Yesterday evening I was fine, my parents will tell you, or rather, I already had a sort of feeling then that something might be wrong. You'd think it would have shown on my face. Whyever didn't I send word to the office! One always thinks, doesn't one, that one can get over these things without staying at home. Sir, spare my parents this ordeal, please! All these reproaches you've levelled against me are quite unfounded; no one's ever said a word to me about any of this. You may not have seen the latest batch of orders I sent in. Incidentally I'll be on my way by the eight o'clock train; the few hours' rest has done me good. Don't let me keep you, sir; I'll be in the office myself directly; would you be so kind as to tell the boss so with my compliments?'

And while Gregory was blurting all this out, barely aware of what he was saying, he had managed to reach the wardrobe without difficulty, no doubt as a result of the practice already acquired in bed, and was now trying to use it to pull himself upright. He really did intend to open the door; he intended to let himself be seen and have a word with the chief clerk; he was eager to find out what the others, wanting him as they now did, would say when they saw him. If they panicked, Gregory would be absolved of responsibility and could relax. If on the other hand they reacted calmly, then he too would have no call to get excited and could indeed, if he hurried, be at the station by eight. At first he kept slipping on the wardrobe's smooth surface, but in the end, after one final heave, he was standing erect; he had completely forgotten about the pains in his lower region, acute though they were. Next he let himself fall against the back of a nearby chair, gripping it around the edge with his legs. Having got himself under control in this way, he stopped talking; now he could listen to what the chief clerk had to say.

'Did you understand a word of that?' the chief clerk was asking Gregory's parents. 'I suppose he's not trying to make complete fools of us?' 'Heavens,' cried his mother, already in tears, 'he may be seriously ill and here we are, tormenting him. Meg!' she shouted then, 'Meg!' 'Yes, Mother?' cried his sister from the other side. They were communicating through Gregory's room. 'You must go round to the doctor this minute. Gregory's ill. Quickly, now—fetch the doctor. Did you hear Gregory talking just then?' 'That sounded like an animal,' said the chief clerk in a quiet voice that contrasted sharply with the mother's yelling. 'Anna! Anna!' his father shouted down the hall in the direction of the kitchen, clapping his hands as he did so, 'fetch a locksmith immediately!' In a moment the two girls were running down the hall with a rustle of skirts—how had his sister got dressed so quickly?—and pulling open the door. There was no sound of it being slammed shut behind them; probably they had left it open, as so often happens in homes visited by a major calamity.

Gregory, however, felt much calmer. So they could no longer understand what he said, although his words had seemed to him quite clear, clearer than before; perhaps his ear had made the necessary adjustment. Still, they were now convinced that all was not well with him, and they were prepared to help. The confidence and assurance with which the first instructions had been issued had done him good. He felt involved once more in the body of mankind and expected both men, the doctor and the locksmith, without in fact distinguishing in any precise way between them, to achieve great and surprising things. In order to make his voice as clear as possible for the coming decisive discussion he gave a little cough, though taking great care to muffle it lest this sound too should turn out different from human coughing, which was an issue he no longer felt competent to judge. Meanwhile silence had fallen in the adjoining room. Possibly his parents were sitting around the table with the chief clerk and whispering; possibly they were all leaning against the door, listening.

101

Using the chair, Gregory slowly pushed himself towards the door, let go of it when he got there, threw himself against the door, used this to support himself in an upright position—the balls of his feet had a small amount of adhesive on them—and there took a moment's rest from his labours. Then he set about trying to use his mouth to turn the key in the lock. Unfortunately it seemed he had no proper teeth—how was he to grip the key?—although admittedly his jaws were very strong; and indeed with their help he actually managed to move the key, ignoring the fact that in doing so he was clearly damaging himself in some way since a brown fluid began to pour from his mouth, run down over the key, and drip onto the floor. 'Listen,' the chief clerk said in the adjoining room, 'he's turning the key.' This was an enormous encouragement to Gregory; but they should all have called out to him, including his father and mother: 'Go to it, Gregory,' they should have called, 'go on—turn that key!' And in the belief that they were all following his efforts in great excitement he bit down blindly on the key with all the strength he could muster. As the key gradually rotated in the lock he shuffled round in an arc; he was now supporting himself with his mouth alone, either hanging from the key or, if pressing was in order, pressing down on it once more with the whole weight of his body. The sharper sound as the bolt finally snapped back was literally a tonic to Gregory. With a sigh of relief he said to himself, 'I didn't need the locksmith, then.' And he laid his head on the door handle to finish opening the door.

His having to open the door in this way meant that he himself could still not be seen when the door was already open quite wide. He first had to work himself slowly round his leaf of the door, and he had to do it very carefully if he did not want to fall flat on his back before entering the other room. He was engaged in this difficult manoeuvre, too busy to notice anything else, when he heard the chief clerk suddenly utter a loud 'Oh!'—it sounded like a gust of wind—and then he saw too, because the chief clerk had been nearest to the door, how he pressed a hand to his gaping mouth and started slowly giving ground as if an invisible force had been driving him steadily backwards. His mother, who despite the presence of the chief clerk was standing there with her hair all undone and still tousled from the night, looked first with clasped hands at his father, then took two steps towards Gregory and sank down, her skirts billowing in circles around her, her face lowered to her bosom and quite invisible. His father looked hostile and clenched a fist as if to force Gregory back into his room; then, with a diffident glance round the living-room, he shaded his eyes with his hands and wept until his great chest shook.

Gregory did not in fact enter the room now but leant against the inside of the other, still bolted leaf of the door in such a way that only half his body could be seen, and above it his head, tilted to one side, peering out at them. It had grown much lighter meanwhile; clearly visible across the street was a section of the endless, grey-black building opposite—it was a hospital—with its hard, regular windows punched in the façade; rain was still falling, but only in huge, individually visible drops that were also being hurled to earth literally one by one. A superabundance of breakfast things littered the table, because for Gregory's father breakfast was the main meal of the day, which he used to sit over for hours, reading a variety of newspapers. Hanging on the wall opposite was a photograph of Gregory taken when he was in the army, showing him as a lieutenant: one hand on his sword, a carefree smile on his lips, his whole bearing and uniform commanding respect. The door to the hall was open, and since the front door stood open too one could see out onto the landing and the top of the stairs.

'Right,' said Gregory, well aware that he was the only one to have retained his composure, 'I shall now get dressed, pack my samples, and be off. You will let me go, won't you? You see, sir, I am not a stubborn person and I like my work; it's a wearisome business, travelling, but I couldn't live without it. Where are you off to, sir? Back to the office? Are you? Will you make a faithful report of all this? One may find oneself temporarily incapacitated as far as work is concerned, but that is precisely the time to look back on one's previous achievements and bear in mind that afterwards, once the hindrance has been overcome, one will undoubtedly work all the harder and with even greater application. I'm so deeply beholden to the boss, as you well know. On the other hand I have my responsibility towards my parents and my sister. I'm in a tight spot, but I shall work my way out of it. Only don't make it more difficult for me than it is already. Stick up for me in the office! We travellers are not liked, I know. People think we earn a mint of money and have a great life into the bargain. That is their preconception, and they have no particular occasion to review it. But you, sir, have a better grasp of the circumstances than the rest of the staff—indeed, between you and me, a better grasp than the boss himself, who in his capacity as employer readily allows his judgement to err to an employee's disadvantage. You also appreciate how easily the traveller, who spends almost the entire year away from the office, can fall victim to gossip, ill luck, and unjustified complaints—with not the slightest chance of defending himself, since he usually hears nothing whatever about them and it is only when he returns exhausted from a trip that he reaps the appalling consequences, the root causes of which can by then no longer be unravelled. Sir, before you go, just give me some indication that you agree with at least a small part of what I have said!'

But the chief clerk had turned away with a shrug at Gregory's first words, although he continued to look back at Gregory over his shoulder with pursed lips. And during the whole of Gregory's speech he was not still for a moment but kept moving, without taking his eyes off Gregory, towards the door—very slowly, though, inch by inch, as if there existed some secret injunction against leaving the room. He had reached the hall already, and from the sharp movement with which he withdrew his foot from the living-room for the last time one might have thought he had just scorched his sole. Once in the hall, he stretched his right hand out in front of him towards the stairs as if some almost supernatural deliverance awaited him there.

Gregory realized that he could under no circumstances allow the chief clerk to leave in this frame of mind if he did not want his position with the firm to be very seriously jeopardized. His parents did not understand these things too well; they had formed the conviction over the years that with this job Gregory was taken care of for life; moreover they were now so preoccupied with their immediate worries as to have quite lost the faculty of foresight. Gregory, however, had not. The chief clerk must be detained, mollified, persuaded, and ultimately won over; Gregory's future and that of his family depended on it! If only his sister had been there! She was clever; she had already been in tears when Gregory was still lying quietly on his back. Undoubtedly the chief clerk, who was quite a lady's man, would have allowed himself to be swayed by her; she would have closed the front door and talked him out of his panic in the hall. But his sister was not there, and Gregory must do something himself. So, forgetting that he was still quite unfamiliar with his present capabilities as far as moving about was concerned, forgetting too that his last speech had possibly if not probably been understood as little as the previous one, he let go of the door; thrust himself through the doorway; tried to go to the chief clerk, who was already—absurdly—clutching the landing banister with both hands; but promptly fell, giving a little cry as he groped for a hold, onto his many legs. No sooner had this happened than, for the first time that morning, he experienced a feeling of physical well-being; his legs, with firm ground under them, responded perfectly, as he discovered to his delight; indeed they strove impatiently to carry him where he wanted to go; and he was immediately convinced that an end to all the agony was at hand. But even as he lay there, swaying with pent-up movement, on the floor not far from his mother, just opposite where she knelt in a state of seemingly total self-absorption, she suddenly sprang up, arms outstretched, fingers splayed, cried, 'Help, for the love of God, help!'; craned her head forward as if trying to see Gregory better while on the contrary she was taking frenzied steps backwards; forgot the breakfast table behind her and, when she reached it, hopped distractedly up on it and sat on the edge; and seemed quite unaware of the fact that the overturned coffee pot beside her was emptying itself copiously onto the carpet.

'Mother, mother,' said Gregory softly, looking up at her. He had forgotten all about the chief clerk for the moment, though at the sight of the coffee pouring out he could not stop himself snapping at the air several times with his jaws. At this his mother let out another yell, fell off the table, and fled into the arms of his father as he hurried towards her. But Gregory had no time for his parents now; the chief clerk, already on the stairs, had laid his chin on the banister for one last look back. Gregory took a run to make doubly sure of catching him; the chief clerk must have suspected something then because he leapt down several steps at once and disappeared, his parting cry of 'Shoo!' echoing back up the stairwell. Unfortunately Gregory's father, who until now had been relatively composed, appeared to find the chief clerk's flight thoroughly unsettling, because instead of going after the man himself or at least not obstructing Gregory in his pursuit he seized the chief clerk's stick, which the latter had left behind on a chair together with his hat and coat, took a large newspaper from the table in his other hand, and with much stamping of his feet and brandishing of the stick and newspaper started to drive Gregory back into his room. None of Gregory's pleas availed, none were even understood; bend his head as meekly as he might, his father only stamped the louder. Across the room his mother, despite the cold weather, had thrown open a window and was leaning out, a long way out, pressing her face into her hands. This caused a powerful draught between street and stairwell that made the curtains billow, the newspapers rustle on the table, and one or two sheets even go floating across the floor. His father kept up the relentless pressure, hissing like a madman. Gregory, however, had had no practice at walking backwards and really could not go very fast. If only he could have turned round he would have been back in his room in an instant, but he was afraid of taxing his father's patience by so time-consuming a manoeuvre, with the stick in his father's hand threatening at any moment to deliver a mortal blow to his back or head. In the end, though, Gregory had no alternative, for he found to his dismay that he could not even control his direction in reverse; so with repeated anxious glances at his father he began to turn himself round as quickly as possible, which in the event was very slowly indeed. His father, perhaps realizing that he meant well, did not hinder him in this but even, from a distance, directed the rotation process intermittently with the end of his stick. If only it had not been for that unbearable hissing from his father! It threw Gregory into utter confusion. He was already nearly half-way round when, through continually listening for the hiss, he made a mistake and started turning the other way. But when, happily, he was facing the doorway at last, it became clear that his body was too wide to pass through just like that. His father, of course, given his state of mind at that moment, did not even begin to think of, for example, opening the other leaf of the door to provide Gregory with sufficient width of passage. His one and only idea was that Gregory must be got back into his room as quickly as possible. Nor would he ever have permitted the elaborate preparations Gregory would have had to make in order to assume an upright position and possibly get through the door that way. Instead he acted as if there had been no obstacle, urging Gregory on even more noisily than before; it no longer sounded like the voice of just one father behind him; things were really in earnest now, and Gregory thrust himself at the opening, come what might. One side of his body lifted up, he lay at an angle in the doorway, his flank was rubbed quite raw, some nasty-looking stains appeared on the white door, soon he was stuck fast and couldn't have moved another

107

inch unaided, his legs on one side hanging quivering in mid air while those on the other were squashed painfully against the floor—at which point his father gave him a truly liberating shove from behind and he went flying right into his room, bleeding profusely. The door was banged to with the stick, and at last there was silence.

II

Not until dusk did Gregory wake from a sleep so deep it had been like a coma. He would undoubtedly have woken before long even without being disturbed, because he felt quite rested and no longer sleepy, but his impression was that he had been roused by a quick footstep and by the door to the hall being carefully shut. The light of the electric street lamps shone wanly on the ceiling in places and on the upper parts of the various pieces of furniture, but down below, where Gregory lay, it was dark. Probing still rather awkwardly with his feelers, which he was only now beginning to appreciate, he pushed himself slowly over to the door to see what had happened there. His left side seemed to be one long scar; it pulled unpleasantly, and he was reduced to limping on his twin rows of legs. Moreover one leg had suffered severe damage during the course of the morning's events—it was almost a miracle that only the one had been damaged—and trailed lifelessly behind.

Not until he had reached the door did he notice what had in fact drawn him in that direction, namely the smell of something to eat. For there stood a bowl of sweetened milk with little slices of white bread floating in it. He could have laughed for joy, because he felt even hungrier than he had in the morning, and he promptly plunged almost his whole head into the milk. But he soon drew it out again in disappointment; it was not only that eating was difficult for him on account of his tender left side—and he could only eat if his whole body panted systematically—but also that he did not at all like the taste, although ordinarily milk was his favourite drink, which would have been why his sister had brought it for him; indeed it was with a feeling almost of disgust that he turned aside from the bowl and crawled back into the middle of the room.

In the living-room the gas had been lit, as Gregory could see through the gap between the doors, but whereas usually at this time Gregory's father liked to read the afternoon paper aloud to his mother and sometimes to his sister, too, now there was not a sound to be heard. Well, perhaps the reading aloud, which his sister was always telling him about in her letters, had dropped out of use in recent weeks. But the whole flat was so quiet, though it was surely not empty. 'What a peaceful life the family was leading!' Gregory said to himself, and as he stared fixedly into the darkness he felt enormously proud of having been able to provide his parents and his sister with such a life in so pleasant a flat. But what if all this peace, all this prosperity, all this satisfied contentment were to end in terror? Rather than risk losing himself in such thoughts Gregory preferred to move about, and he began crawling back and forth across the room.

Once during the long evening the door on one side and once the door on the other were opened a crack and then quickly closed again; someone had presumably felt the urge to come in but had had too many misgivings. Gregory stationed himself right by the door to the living-room, determined to get his diffident visitor into the room somehow or other or at least find out who it was; but from then on the door was not opened again, and Gregory waited in vain. In the morning, with the doors locked, everyone had wanted to come in; now that he had opened one door and the others had clearly been opened during the day no one came any more, and the keys had even been taken and put back in the locks from outside.

It was late into the night before the living-room light went out, and then it quickly became clear that his parents and his sister had in fact stayed up all that time, because the three of them could quite distinctly be heard tiptoeing

away. Now no one would be coming into Gregory's room
until morning, surely, so he had a long while in which to
consider in peace and quiet how best to reorganize his life.
But the tall, spacious room, in which he was obliged to lie
flat on the floor, frightened him without his being able to
discover why, because after all it was his room and he had
been living in it for five years—and with a half-
unconscious change of direction, and not without a slight
feeling of shame, he went scuttling under the couch,
where despite the fact that his back was a little squeezed
and he could no longer lift his head he immediately felt
very much at home, his only regret being that his body was
too wide to be accommodated under the couch in its
entirety.

There he spent the whole night, some of it in a doze
from which his stomach kept waking him with a start, but
some of it a prey to worries and obscure hopes, all of
which, however, led him to the conclusion that for the time
being he must keep calm and try, by being patient and
exercising great consideration, to make it easier for his
family to bear the inconvenience to which he was in his
present state quite frankly obliged to put them.

Early the next morning, almost before it was light,
Gregory had an opportunity to test the firmness of his new
resolutions when his sister, almost fully dressed, opened
the door from the living-room and nervously peered in.
She did not spot Gregory straight away, but when she
noticed him under the couch—God, he must be somewhere, he couldn't just have flown away—she got such a
fright that she involuntarily slammed the door shut again.
But as if thinking better of her action she opened it again
immediately and tiptoed into the room, rather as if she
were in the presence of a chronic invalid or even a
stranger. Gregory, his head pushed forward to the edge of
the couch, watched her. Would she notice that he had left
the milk—though not because he had no appetite, far
from it—and would she bring some other food that suited
him better? If she did not do so of her own accord he
would rather starve than tell her, despite what was really a

terrible urge to dart out from under the couch, hurl himself at his sister's feet, and beg her to bring him something good to eat. His sister, however, noticing immediately and with some surprise that the bowl was still full, with only a little milk spilt around it, picked it up—not, admittedly, with her bare hands but with a rag—and carried it out. Gregory was extremely curious to know what she would bring in its stead, and he devoted a great deal of thought to it. But never could he have guessed what his sister, in the goodness of her heart, actually did. She brought him a whole selection of things, all laid out on an old newspaper, to see what he liked. There were some old, half-rotten vegetables; the bones from supper, covered with congealed white sauce; some raisins and almonds; a piece of cheese that Gregory had pronounced inedible two days previously; a slice of dry bread, another spread with butter, and another spread with butter and salted. As well as all this she brought back the bowl, which it had probably been decided once and for all should be Gregory's, this time with water in it. Very tactfully, knowing that Gregory would not eat in her presence, she then withdrew and even turned the key in the lock to let Gregory know that he could set to as he pleased. Gregory's legs whirred as he crossed to where the food was. His wounds must incidentally have healed up completely by now, for he felt no further impediment; he was astonished at this and remembered how he had nicked his finger with a knife more than a month ago and how the wound had still been quite painful the day before yesterday. 'Have I perhaps become less sensitive?' he thought, sucking greedily at the piece of cheese, to which of all the things available he had been most immediately and emphatically drawn. With tears of contentment in his eyes, he demolished in quick succession the cheese, the vegetables, and the sauce. The fresh food did not appeal to him; in fact, finding even the smell of it intolerable, he went so far as to drag the things he wanted to eat a little way off. He had long finished all the food and was simply lazing about when, as a sign that he should withdraw, his sister began slowly turning the key. This roused him immediately, although he had been more than half asleep, and he hurried back beneath the couch. But it required enormous strength of mind for him to stay under the couch even for the short time his sister spent in the room, because as a result of his copious meal his body had swollen slightly and in that narrow space he could hardly breathe. Between bouts of near-suffocation he watched with somewhat protruding eyes as his unsuspecting sister swept together with a broom not only the scraps but even the food Gregory had left untouched, as if realizing that it too was no longer needed, and hurriedly threw everything into a pail that she covered with a wooden lid before carrying it out. Hardly was her back turned before Gregory emerged from beneath the couch to stretch and distend himself.

This was how Gregory now received his food each day, once in the morning when his parents and the maid were still asleep, and a second time after the family's lunch, because then his parents had another little sleep and the maid was sent off on some errand or other by his sister. Doubtless they no more wished Gregory to starve than she did, but perhaps it would have been too much for them to learn about his eating habits other than by hearsay, perhaps his sister was concerned to spare them even what might have been only a minor sorrow, for in all conscience they could be said to be suffering enough.

What excuses had been used on that first morning to get the doctor and the locksmith out of the flat again Gregory was never able to discover, because since there was no understanding him it did not occur to anyone, not even to his sister, that he might be able to understand other people, so that when his sister was in his room he had to content himself with her intermittent sighs and invocations of the saints. It was only later, when she had grown accustomed to things to a certain extent—there could never of course be any question of her becoming fully accustomed—Gregory occasionally caught a remark that was meant well enough or could be so interpreted. 'He enjoyed his food today,' she would comment if Gregory had scoffed the lot, whereas if the opposite was the case, and by degrees it came more and more often to be so, she would say almost sadly, 'Oh, he's left everything again.'

But while Gregory was unable to learn any news directly he did pick up a certain amount from the adjoining rooms, and as soon as he heard voices he would run to the door concerned and press his whole body up against it. Particularly in the early days there was no conversation that did not in some way, if only obliquely, have to do with him. For two days there were discussions at every meal as to how they should now conduct themselves, but between mealtimes, too, the same subject kept coming up, because there were always at least two members of the family at home; presumably no one wanted to stay at home on his or her own, and there could be no question of leaving the flat completely deserted. Also the maid had come to his mother on the very first day—it was not clear how much she knew of what had happened—and asked on bended knee to be discharged immediately, and when a quarter of an hour later she came back to say goodbye she expressed thanks for her discharge with tears in her eyes, as if it had been the greatest blessing ever bestowed on her in that house, and spontaneously delivered herself of a fearful oath to the effect that she would never breathe a word to anyone.

This meant that Gregory's sister, together with his mother, now had to do the cooking as well, although there was not much work involved as they were hardly eating anything. Again and again Gregory heard one of them vainly exhorting the others to eat, only to receive the inevitable reply, 'No, thank you, I've had enough,' or words to that effect. No drinking went on either. His sister was always asking his father if he wanted a beer, generously offering to go out for it herself, and when he said nothing she suggested, with a view to removing any misgivings he might have, that she could even send the janitor, but eventually Gregory's father told her firmly, 'No,' and the subject was not mentioned again.

113

In the course of the very first day his father gave both his mother and his sister a comprehensive account of the family's financial circumstances and prospects. Every now and then he got up from the table and went over to the small patent safe that he had retrieved from the collapse of his business five years before to fetch a receipt or a notebook or whatever it might be. He could be heard unlocking it—a complicated process—and, having removed what he wanted, locking it again. In part these elucidations of his father's were the first gratifying communications to have reached Gregory's ears since his captivity began. He had always assumed that his father had been left with nothing whatsoever from that business; at least, his father had never said anything to him to the contrary, nor as a matter of fact had Gregory ever asked him about it. The catastrophe had plunged them all into utter despair, and Gregory's sole concern at that time had been to do everything to erase it from the family's memory as swiftly as possible. That was when he had begun to work with quite exceptional enthusiasm and from being a minor clerk had become a traveller virtually overnight, as such of course enjoying an entirely different earning potential since his results, if he was successful, were immediately convertible, in terms of commission, into cash that could be taken home and laid on the table before the astonished and delighted eyes of the family. Those had been marvellous times, and they had never recurred since, at least not with the same splendour, although subsequently Gregory was earning so much money that he was in a position to meet the expenses of the entire family and indeed did so. They had simply started taking it for granted, not just the family but Gregory himself; they accepted the money gratefully, Gregory provided it willingly, but no special warmth seemed to be engendered any more. Only his sister had remained close to Gregory in spite of everything, and since unlike himself she was very fond of music and could play the violin most movingly it was his secret ambition, regardless of the expense that would inevitably be involved—he'd manage to cover that in some other

114

way—to send her to the Conservatory in the following year. During his brief stays in the city the Conservatory often cropped up in conversation with his sister, but never as anything more than a beautiful dream that could not possibly come true, and even those innocent references were unwelcome to their parents' ears; Gregory, however, had quite definite ideas on the subject and meant to make his announcement with some solemnity on Christmas Eve.

Such were the thoughts—quite futile in his present condition—that passed through his head as he stood glued to the door, listening. Once or twice, too tired to take in any more, he inadvertently let his head droop and knock against the door, but he lifted it again immediately because even the tiny sound it made had been heard in the next room, and they had all stopped talking. 'What's he up to now?' his father said after a while, obviously looking towards the door, and only then was the interrupted conversation gradually resumed.

Gregory now became thoroughly acquainted—for his father tended to be very repetitive, partly because he had not concerned himself with these matters for some time, partly too because Gregory's mother did not always grasp everything on first hearing—with the fact that, the catastrophe notwithstanding, an admittedly very small amount of capital still survived from the old days, now of course slightly swollen by the interest that had been allowed to accumulate in the mean time. Furthermore the money that Gregory had brought home each month—he had kept only the loose change for himself—had not all been used up and had itself accumulated to form a modest capital. Behind his door Gregory nodded enthusiastically, delighted to hear of this unexpected prudence and thrift. He could in fact have used the money to clear some more of his father's debt to the boss, and the day when he could write that item off completely would have been very much nearer, but as things were his father's arrangement was undoubtedly the better one.

The fact remained that the sum was nowhere near enough for the family to be able, for example, to live off the interest; it might be enough to support them for one or at most two years, but that was all. In other words it was money that ought not in fact to be touched at all but ought to be put aside for an emergency; the money for day-to-day expenses had to be earned. Now Gregory's father, though in good health, was an old man who had not worked for the past five years and in any case could not take on very much; during those five years, which had been the first holiday of his arduous yet unsuccessful life, he had put on a great deal of weight and become very clumsy in his movements as a result. And was Gregory's old mother to start going out to work when, crippled as she was by asthma, she found it an effort to walk round the flat and spent every other day lying on the sofa with the window open, gasping for breath? And was his sister to go out to work, a child of only seventeen whose life until then surely no one would have begrudged her, consisting as it had of dressing prettily, sleeping long hours, lending a hand with the housework, indulging in a few modest pleasures, and above all playing the violin? Whenever the talk turned to this necessity for earning money Gregory let go of the door and threw himself down on the cool leather sofa beside it, burning with shame and grief.

Often he lay there right through the night, not sleeping a wink but simply scratching at the leather for hours on end. Or he embarked on the laborious task of pushing a chair over to the window and crawling up the wall to the sill in order to brace himself in the chair and lean against the glass, obviously in response to some memory of the feeling of freedom it had once given him to look out of the window. Because the fact of the matter was that, as the days went by, even things that were quite close he saw less and less clearly; the hospital opposite, the all-too-frequent sight of which he had formerly cursed, he could not see at all now, and had he not known full well that he lived in the quiet but entirely urban Charlotte Street he might have thought his window overlooked a wilderness in which the grey sky and the grey earth merged indistinguishably. His thoughtful sister needed to see the chair standing there on only two occasions before she began, each time she had tidied up his room, pushing it carefully back beneath the window and even, from then on, leaving the inner casement open.

If only Gregory had been able to speak to his sister and thank her for everything she was having to do for him he could have borne her attentions more easily; as it was they pained him. Admittedly she tried to cover up the awkwardness of the situation as much as possible, and of course as time went by she became better and better at doing so, but in time, too, Gregory acquired a keener perception of things. Even her entrance was terrible for him. As soon as she had stepped over the threshold, and without even pausing to shut the door, for all her usual concern to spare everyone the sight of Gregory's room, she ran straight to the window, tore it open with fumbling hands as if she were on the point of suffocating, and stood by it for a while, no matter how cold the weather, taking deep breaths. She terrified Gregory twice daily with this running and banging; he spent the whole time trembling under the couch, yet he was perfectly sure she would have spared him the experience had she anyhow found it in her power to remain in a room occupied by Gregory with the window closed.

Once—this must have been a month after Gregory's metamorphosis, by which time his sister no longer had any particular reason to be astonished at his appearance—she came a little earlier than usual and found Gregory, motionless and at his most terrifying, still looking out of the window. Gregory would not have been surprised had she not come in, because his position made it impossible for her to open the window immediately, but not only did she not come in, she even withdrew smartly and shut the door; a stranger might almost have thought Gregory had been lying in wait for her with the intention of biting her. Gregory, of course, hid under the couch immediately, but he had to wait until noon before his sister returned, and when she did she seemed much more agitated than usual. He realized from this that she still found the sight of him

117

unbearable and would inevitably go on finding it unbearable, and that it probably cost her a great effort of self-control not to run at the sight of even the small portion of his body that stuck out from beneath the couch. To spare her even this sight he one day took his sheet, carried it over to the couch on his back—the job took him four hours—and there arranged it in such a way as to cover him completely, so that his sister could not see him even when she bent down. Had she considered the sheet unnecessary she could after all have removed it, because surely it was obvious that it could not be Gregory's idea of fun to cut himself off so utterly and completely, yet she left the sheet as it was, and Gregory even thought he detected a look of gratitude when at one point, to see how his sister was taking the new arrangement, he carefully lifted the sheet a little with his head.

For the first fortnight his parents could not bring themselves to enter his room, and he often heard them expressing unqualified approval of his sister's present efforts, whereas before they had thought her a fairly ineffectual sort of girl and had frequently lost patience with her. Now, however, both his father and his mother often waited outside Gregory's room while his sister cleaned it out, and no sooner had she emerged than she had to give them a detailed account of the state of the room, what Gregory had eaten, how he had behaved this time, and whether perhaps some slight improvement were noticeable. His mother in fact wanted to visit Gregory relatively early on, but his father and sister restrained her, initially using arguments based on common sense to which Gregory listened attentively and in full agreement. Subsequently they had to restrain her by force, and when she then cried out, 'Let me go to Gregory, my poor, unfortunate son! Don't you see that I must go to him?' Gregory thought it might not be a bad idea if his mother did come in, not every day of course but perhaps once a week; she understood things so much better than his sister, who for all her pluck was still a mere child and, when all was said and done, had perhaps only taken on so hard a task in a fit of childish exuberance.

Gregory's wish to see his mother was soon fulfilled. He did not like to show himself at the window during the day, if only for his parents' sake; he could not move about much in the few square metres of floor space; lying still he found difficult enough at night; eating no longer gave him the slightest pleasure; so to amuse himself he adopted the habit of crawling all over the walls and ceiling. He was particularly partial to hanging from the ceiling; this was quite different from lying on the floor; one could breathe more freely; gentle vibrations went coursing through the body; and in the almost blissful state of abstraction that Gregory found himself in up there it sometimes happened that, much to his own astonishment, he let go and went crashing to the floor. But of course he now had his body under much better control than before, and even a fall like that did not harm him. Gregory's sister noticed his new pastime straight away—he left traces of adhesive behind when he crawled—and took it into her head to give Gregory as much crawling-space as possible by removing such items of furniture, chiefly the wardrobe and the desk, as precluded it. She could not, however, do this on her own; she dared not ask her father to help; the maid would certainly not have lent a hand because, although for her sixteen or so years of age she had stuck it out bravely since the departure of the previous cook, she had asked as a special dispensation to be allowed to keep the kitchen permanently locked and to be obliged to open it only on receipt of a specific signal; so his sister had no alternative but to take advantage of one of the father's absences to fetch Gregory's mother. And along his mother promptly came, uttering cries of pleasure and excitement, though she fell silent at the door of Gregory's room. First, of course, his sister checked whether everything was all right in the room, only then letting the mother enter. Gregory had very hastily pulled the sheet down even lower and made more folds, and the whole arrangement really did look as if a sheet had simply been thrown over the couch at random. Gregory also refrained from stealing a glance

119

under the sheet this time; he was prepared to forgo seeing his mother on this occasion, content with the fact that she had come at last. 'Come on, you can't see him,' said his sister, obviously leading his mother by the hand. Gregory listened as the two frail women started to shift the old, rather heavy wardrobe; he could tell that his sister was deliberately doing most of the work herself the whole time, ignoring the anxious warnings of the mother, who was afraid she was going to strain herself. It took a very long time. After they had been at it for perhaps a quarter of an hour his mother said they should leave the wardrobe where it was: for one thing it was too heavy, they would not be finished before father came back, and with the wardrobe in the middle of the room they would be blocking Gregory's every move; for another thing it was by no means certain that in removing his furniture they were doing Gregory a favour. It seemed to her that the opposite was the case; she found the sight of the bare walls downright depressing; and who was to say that Gregory's reaction would not be the same, since he had had the furniture for ages, was used to it, and would feel lonely in the empty room. 'And isn't it,' his mother concluded in a low voice—in fact she had been virtually whispering the whole time as if to make sure that Gregory, of whose exact whereabouts she was unaware, should not even hear the sound of her voice, since she was already convinced he would not understand the words—'isn't it as if by removing the furniture we were showing that we had given up all hope of improvement and were callously leaving him to his own devices? I believe the best thing would be to try to keep the room exactly as it was, then when Gregory returns to us he will find everything the same and it will be that much easier for him to forget the time between.'

Hearing his mother's words, Gregory realized that the fact that no one had addressed him directly in the past two months, coupled with the monotony of life in the bosom of the family, must have considerably muddled his wits; this was the only explanation he could find of his seriously having wanted his room cleared. Did he really wish to have his warm, friendly room, cosily furnished as it was with family heirlooms, transformed into a cave in which he would admittedly be able to crawl all over the place unimpeded but at the price of rapidly and completely forgetting his human past? Why, he was on the verge of forgetting already, and he had been rallied only by hearing his mother's voice again after all this time. Nothing was to be removed; it must all stay; the positive influence that the furniture had on his condition was something he could not do without; and if the furniture prevented him from indulging in his stupid crawling, that was no disadvantage but a very good thing.

Unfortunately his sister thought otherwise; in discussions of Gregory's affairs she had taken to presenting herself, not without some justification, as something of an expert compared with her parents, so that on this occasion too the mother's advice was sufficient reason as far as the daughter was concerned for insisting on the removal not only of the wardrobe and the desk, which was all she had had in mind originally, but of every piece of furniture in the room, the indispensable couch excepted. It was of course more than mere childish defiance and the self-confidence she had so unexpectedly and laboriously acquired in recent weeks that impelled her to make this demand; she had also observed with her own eyes how Gregory required a great deal of space for crawling, whereas he did not, so far as one could see, have the slightest use for the furniture. But perhaps another contributory factor was the highly romantic nature of girls of that age, which, seeking gratification at every turn, had in the present instance led Meg into the temptation of trying to make Gregory's plight even more horrific, thereby putting herself in a position to render him even greater services. Because in a room in which Gregory patrolled empty walls probably no one but Meg would ever dare to set foot.

And so it was that she would not allow her resolve to be shaken by her mother, who even with the room as it was appeared to be nervous and unsure of herself, soon falling silent and giving the sister what help she could to move the wardrobe out. Well, Gregory could manage without the wardrobe at a pinch, but the desk must stay. And no sooner had the women left the room with the wardrobe, groaning as they flattened themselves against it, than Gregory poked his head out from under the couch to see how he might prudently and as far as possible tactfully intervene. As luck would have it, however, his mother came back first, leaving Meg in the other room with her arms around the wardrobe, rocking it to and fro without of course moving it an inch. Now his mother was not used to the sight of him; it might make her ill; so Gregory scurried backwards in some alarm until he was right at the far end of the couch, though he was too late to prevent the sheet at the front from swaying slightly, just enough to catch his mother's eye. She stopped short, stood quite still for a moment, then went back to Meg.

Although Gregory kept telling himself that nothing out of the ordinary was happening, it was only a few bits of furniture being moved about, he was soon forced to admit that the women's to-ing and fro-ing, their muttered cries, and the scraping of the furniture on the floor were affecting him like a great turmoil that was being fuelled from all sides, and however firmly he drew in his head and legs and pressed his body to the floor the conclusion was inescapable that he was not going to be able to put up with it for long. They were clearing his room out, taking away everything that was dear to him; the wardrobe, which contained his fret-saw and the other tools, was already gone; now they were freeing his desk from the holes it had dug in the floor, the desk at which as a student of commerce and before that as a schoolboy, in fact ever since his junior-school days, he had sat and laboured over his essays—no, he simply hadn't time to scrutinize the good intentions of the two women, whose existence he had in any case almost forgotten since they were now toiling in exhausted silence, and all that could be heard was the heavy tramp of their feet.

The upshot was that he darted from his hiding-place—

the women happened to be leaning against the desk in the next room, getting their breath back—changed direction four times, quite unable to decide what to salvage first, then, spotting the picture of the lady all in furs where it hung conspicuously on the otherwise bare wall, quickly crawled up to it and pressed himself against the glass, which offered a firm purchase and did his hot belly good. This picture at least, which Gregory was now completely covering, surely no one would take away from him. He twisted his head round towards the living-room door to observe the women's return.

They had not given themselves much of a rest and were already coming back; Meg had her arm around her mother and was virtually carrying her. 'All right, what shall we take next?' she said, looking about her. Then her eyes met Gregory's up on the wall. Probably only because her mother was there she retained her composure, bent her head closer to her mother to prevent her from looking about her, and said, if with somewhat tremulous haste, 'Come, let's go back in the living-room for a moment, shall we?' It was clear to Gregory what Meg was up to: she meant to get her mother out of harm's way and then chase him down from the wall. Well, just let her try! He was sitting on his picture and was not going to part with it. He'd leap off in Meg's face first.

But Meg's words had served only to increase the mother's agitation; she now stepped to one side, saw the huge brown blotch on the flowered wallpaper, cried out, before she had really registered the fact that it was Gregory she was looking at, in a shrill, strident voice, 'Oh God, oh God!' and with arms outstretched as if giving up altogether fell back on the couch and lay still. 'Gregory!' cried his sister, shaking her fist and glaring at him. It was the first time she had addressed him directly since the metamorphosis. She ran into the next room for some sort of essence that might revive her unconscious mother; Gregory wanted to help—time enough later to save the picture—but he was stuck fast to the glass and had to tear himself free; then he too ran into the next room as if there

123

were some advice he could give his sister, like in the old
days, but had to stand behind her doing nothing while she
rummaged among various bottles, and gave her a fright
when she turned round; one bottle fell to the floor and
broke; a sliver of glass flew in Gregory's face, wounding
him, and some pungent medicament swirled round him;
Meg wasted no more time but gathered up as many bottles
as she could and ran with them back to her mother,
slamming the door behind her with her foot. Gregory was
now cut off from his mother, who—and it was his fault—
might be on the point of death; he could not open the
door without frightening away his sister, and she must stay
with their mother; there was nothing he could do except
wait; and in an agony of anxiety and self-reproach he
began to crawl about, all over everything, walls, furniture,
ceiling, until eventually, in his despair, with the whole
room starting to spin round him, he fell right in the
middle of the big table.

For a while Gregory lay there weakly; around him all
was silence; possibly that was a good sign. Then there
came a ring at the door. The maid was of course locked in
her kitchen, so Meg had to go. It was Gregory's father.
'What's happened?' was the first thing he said; presumably
Meg's appearance had given the game away. Meg answered in a muffled voice, obviously with her face buried
against her father's chest, 'Mother fainted but she's all
right now. Gregory's got out.' 'I knew it,' said the father, 'I
kept telling you it would happen, but you women never
listen.' It was clear to Gregory that his father had misinter-
preted Meg's all-too-brief report and assumed that he had
been responsible for some act of violence. He must now
attempt to placate his father, having neither the time nor
the means to put him right. Accordingly he made a run for
the door of his room and pressed himself against it in
order that his father should see as soon as he entered the
living-room that his intentions were of the best, that he was
prepared to go back into his room immediately, and that it
was not necessary to drive him there but only to open the
door, when he would promptly disappear.

His father, however, was in no mood to spot such niceties; 'Ah!' he cried on entering, and his tone of voice suggested simultaneous rage and delight. Gregory pulled his head back from the door and swung it round towards his father. The man who stood there bore no resemblance to the mental image Gregory had had of him; admittedly he had neglected of late, through his new-found interest in crawling, to concern himself to the same extent as previously with events in the rest of the flat, and he ought in fact to have been quite prepared to find that things had changed. Yes, but, even so, could this really be his father? The same man as had lain wearily in bed, buried in his pillows, when Gregory left on a business trip; had greeted him from an armchair in his dressing-gown when Gregory returned home in the evening; had even found it beyond him to rise to his feet, merely raising his arms to indicate that he was pleased; and had, on the rare occasions when they went for a walk together, on a couple of Sundays a year and on the principal public holidays, shuffled along between Gregory and his mother, managing, though they were pretty slow walkers themselves, to go a little more slowly still, wrapped in his old overcoat, always placing his walking-stick with great care, and when he wanted to say something had almost invariably come to a complete halt and gathered his escort about him? Now, however, he was drawn up to his full height; dressed in a severe blue uniform with gilt buttons of the kind worn by bank commissionaires; the high, stiff collar of his jacket was topped by a powerful double chin; beneath the bushy eyebrows his piercing dark eyes had a fresh, alert look; the usually dishevelled white hair had been meticulously combed down, parted, and brilliantined. Tossing his cap, which bore a gold monogram, probably that of a bank, in an arc that took it right across the room onto the couch and pushing back the long flaps of his uniform jacket to thrust his hands into his trouser pockets, he bore down on Gregory with a look of grim determination on his face. Probably he did not know himself what he meant to do; nevertheless he raised his feet to an unusual height, and

125

Gregory was amazed at the enormous size of the soles of his boots. Not that he dwelt on his amazement, remembering as he did from the very first day of his new life that his father believed the only way to treat him was with the utmost severity; no, he fled from his father's advance, stopping whenever his father came to a halt and hurrying on again the moment his father moved. They made several circuits of the room like this without anything decisive happening, indeed without the whole performance, so slowly was it enacted, even having the appearance of a chase. For this reason Gregory also kept to the floor for the time being, especially since he was afraid his father might look upon a retreat to the walls or ceiling as evidence of conspicuous ill will. But he had to admit to himself that he would not be able to keep up even this kind of running for long, because where his father took one step he had to make a whole host of movements. He was beginning to experience difficulty in breathing, and it was a fact that even in his previous life his lungs had never been wholly reliable. As he staggered on, barely keeping his eyes open in order to save all his strength for his legs, not even, in his lethargy, considering any other escape than by running, having already almost forgotten that the walls were at his disposal, though in this room they were cluttered with elaborately carved furniture, all notches and protruberances—something was lobbed gently over his shoulder, struck the floor just in front of him, and rolled away. It was an apple; another went flying after it; Gregory came to a terrified halt, further running being pointless now that his father had decided to bombard him. He had filled his pockets from the fruit bowl on the sideboard and was throwing one apple after another without even taking aim first. The small, red apples rolled around the floor as if electrified, bumping into one another. One feebly tossed apple struck Gregory a glancing blow on the back, doing no damage. But another that came flying after it hit him on the back and sank right in; Gregory tried to drag himself forward as though the shocking, unbelievable pain might go away if he moved;

but it was like being pinned to the ground, and he stretched himself out, all his senses a complete blur. The last thing he saw was the door of his room being wrenched open and his mother rushing out past his shrieking sister, in her chemise because his sister had started undressing her to ease her breathing while she was unconscious, rushing up to his father with her tucked-up skirts spilling to the floor one by one as she ran, stumbling over the skirts as she fell upon his father and, with her arms around him, in absolute union with him—but Gregory's sight was already failing at this point—her hands cupping the back of his father's head, begged him to spare Gregory's life.

III

The severity of Gregory's wound, from which he suffered for more than a month—no one daring to remove the apple, it remained lodged in his flesh as a visible reminder—seemed to have brought home even to his father that, for all his present deplorable and repugnant appearance, Gregory was a member of the family and was therefore not to be treated as an enemy; on the contrary, family duty required them to swallow their loathing and simply grin and bear it.

And if in all likelihood Gregory had now, as a result of his injury, permanently lost some of his mobility and for the present resembled an elderly invalid in that it took him endless minutes to cross from one side of his room to the other—crawling on the walls and ceiling being out of the question—he felt fully compensated for this deterioration in his condition by the fact that every evening the door to the living-room, which he was in the habit of keeping a sharp eye on for as much as an hour or two beforehand, was thrown open and he was allowed to lie in the darkness of his room, invisible from next door, and observe the whole family around the brightly-lit table and listen to their conversation—all this as it were by general consent, in other words under very different circumstances from before.

Gone, of course, were the lively exchanges of earlier days, which Gregory had always recalled with a certain nostalgia in those tiny hotel rooms as he threw his weary body down on yet another damp bed. Now it was mostly a very peaceful time. His father fell asleep in his chair soon after supper; his mother and sister kept reminding each other to be quiet; his mother, leaning forward into the light, sewed lingerie for a fashion shop; his sister, who had taken a job as a shop assistant, spent her evenings learning shorthand and French with a view, possibly, to securing a better position later on. Occasionally his father would wake up, and as if unaware that he had been asleep he would say to the mother, 'You're doing a lot of sewing again today!' and go straight back to sleep, while mother and sister exchanged tired smiles.

With an almost mulish obstinacy Gregory's father refused to take off his commissionaire's uniform even in the house; and while his dressing-gown hung idle on the peg he slept fully dressed in his place at table as if permanently ready for duty, all ears, even here, for the dictates of his superior. As a result the uniform, which had not been new to start with, defied all Gregory's mother's and sister's efforts to keep it clean, and Gregory often spent whole evenings gazing at the appallingly stained garment, bright with its ever-polished buttons, in which the old man slept in great discomfort and yet at his ease.

As soon as the clock struck ten Gregory's mother tried by quietly talking to his father to wake him up and coax him into going to bed, because it was not proper sleep that he was getting where he was and sleep was something that, having to report for duty at six o'clock, he needed very badly. But with the wilfulness that had characterized him since he had taken this humble job he invariably insisted on staying up longer, although he regularly dozed off and afterwards it was only with the greatest difficulty that he could be persuaded to exchange chair for bed. No matter how much Gregory's mother and sister urged him with mild reproaches, for a quarter of an hour he went on slowly shaking his head with his eyes firmly closed, refusing to stand up. Gregory's mother plucked at his sleeve, whispering blandishments in his ear, and his sister left her work to go to her mother's aid, but the effect on Gregory's father was nil. He only slumped deeper into his chair. Not until the women grasped him under the armpits did he open his eyes, look from mother to sister, and say, 'What a life! So much for a quiet old age!' Then, leaning on the two women, he would rise awkwardly to his feet as if he were an enormous burden even to himself, allow the women to escort him to the door, and there wave them away to continue on his own, while Gregory's mother quickly put down her sewing and his sister her pen in order to run after him and offer further assistance.

Who in this overworked and exhausted family had time to give Gregory any more attention than was absolutely necessary? The housekeeping budget was progressively curtailed; the maid was dismissed after all; a big, raw-boned cleaning-woman with wispy white hair came in mornings and evenings to do the heaviest work; every-thing else Gregory's mother took care of, on top of all her sewing. It even reached the point where various pieces of family jewellery, formerly worn with great delight by Gregory's mother and sister on evenings out and other festive occasions, were sold, as Gregory learnt the same evening when the family discussed the prices fetched. But the main complaint was always that, while the flat was far too big for their present circumstances, they could not leave it because of the insoluble problem of how to move Gregory. Gregory, however, fully appreciated that he was not the only consideration in the way of a move, since it would have been a simple matter to transport him in a suitable crate fitted with a few air-holes; no, what chiefly held the family back from finding a new flat was their feeling of utter despair and the idea that they had been struck by a misfortune exceeding anything ever experi-enced within their entire circle of friends and relations. What the world requires of poor people they were

fulfilling to the last degree; the father fetched breakfast
for minor bank officials; the mother sacrificed herself for
the underwear of total strangers; the sister ran back and
forth behind the counter at her customers' beck and call;
to do any more was beyond the family's power. And the
wound in Gregory's back began to hurt all over again
when his mother and sister, having put his father to bed,
came back, left their work where they had dropped it,
moved their chairs closer together until they were sitting
cheek to cheek; and when his mother, indicating Gregory's
room, said, 'Shut the door now, Meg,' and he was in
darkness again, while in the other room the women wept
together or possibly sat dry-eyed, staring at the table-top.

Gregory's nights and days passed almost entirely without sleep. He thought intermittently of taking the affairs
of the family in hand again just as before, the very next
time the door opened; after a long interval the boss and
the chief clerk reappeared in his thoughts together with
the other clerks and the apprentices, the dim-witted
errand boy, two or three friends from other firms, a
provincial hotel chamber-maid of brief, fond memory, a
cashier in a hat shop whom he had courted in earnest but
rather too slowly—they all appeared, interspersed with
strangers or people he had forgotten, but instead of
helping him and his family they were without exception
unapproachable and he was glad to see them go. Afterwards, however, he was again in no mood to bother about
his family; he was merely angry at the appalling service,
and although he could think of nothing he might have felt
like eating he began to plan ways of gaining access to the
larder, there to help himself to what, even if he was not
hungry, was after all no more than his due. With no
thought any longer of how she might particularly please
Gregory, his sister now hurriedly shoved any old thing
into his room with her foot before leaving for work in the
morning and again after lunch, and in the evening,
regardless of whether the food had perhaps merely been
picked at or—as was usually the case—left completely
untouched, she swept it out again with a whisk of her

broom. The cleaning, which she now always did in the evenings, could not have taken less time. The walls of Gregory's room were streaked with dirt, and balls of dust and little heaps of excrement dotted the floor. At the beginning Gregory used to position himself, when his sister arrived, in corners that were particularly bad in this respect, intending his action as a sort of reproach to her. But he could have stayed there for weeks without his sister mending her ways; the fact was, she could see the dirt as clearly as he could, only she had made up her mind to leave it. At the same time she watched with, for her, a quite novel sensitivity—it had come over the whole family, in fact—that the cleaning of Gregory's room should remain her prerogative. On one occasion Gregory's mother had subjected his room to a major spring-clean, which had taken several buckets of water to complete successfully —all the humidity upsetting Gregory too, of course, so that he flopped down on the couch in a sulk and lay still —but she did not go unpunished. As soon as Gregory's sister saw the change in his room that evening she ran into the living-room, deeply hurt, and despite her mother's imploringly upraised hands burst into a paroxysm of tears of which her parents—the father had of course started up out of his chair in alarm—were at first astonished and helpless witnesses; until they too began to get excited; father upbraiding mother to his right for not leaving the cleaning of the room to Gregory's sister; and to his left yelling at the sister that she would never be allowed to clean Gregory's room again; while Gregory's mother tried to drag his father, who was beside himself with rage, into the bedroom; his sister, shaking with sobs, pounded the table with her little fists; and Gregory himself hissed aloud in his fury at the fact that no one thought of shutting the door and sparing him this noisy scene.

But even if his sister, exhausted from her day's work, had had enough of looking after Gregory as she had once done, there was still no need for Gregory's mother to have taken her place and still no reason why Gregory should be neglected. For now the cleaning-woman was there. This

elderly widow, whose powerful build had presumably
helped her to weather the worst in the course of her long
life, had no particular horror of Gregory. Without as it
were being nosy she had once inadvertently opened the
door of Gregory's room, and at the sight of Gregory, who
was taken completely by surprise and began running to
and fro although no one was chasing him, she had stood
there in amazement with her hands clasped before her.
Since then she had not let a day go by without, morning
and evening, opening the door a crack and peeping in at
Gregory. The first few times she had also called him to
her, using words she probably regarded as affable, such as
'Come on, you old dung beetle, come over here!' or 'Look
at the old dung beetle!' Addressed in this fashion, Gregory
had made no reply but stayed where he was without
moving as though the door had never been opened. If
only, instead of letting the woman plague him to no
purpose as the mood took her, they had told her to clean
his room out every day! One early morning—heavy rain,
possibly in token of the coming of spring, was beating at
the window-panes—Gregory felt so bitter when the
cleaning-woman started using those words again that he
turned, though very slowly and rather decrepitly, as if to
attack her. Instead of taking fright, however, the cleaning-
woman merely picked up a nearby chair and raised it high
in the air, and from the way in which she stood there with
her mouth wide open it was clear that she would shut her
mouth only when the chair in her hand had come crashing
down on Gregory's back. 'You keep your distance, all
right?' she asked as Gregory turned away again; then she
calmly put the chair back in the corner.

Gregory was now eating almost nothing. Only when he
happened to walk past the food put down for him did he
aimlessly take a bite, which he kept in his mouth for hours
and then usually spat out again. At first he thought it was
sadness at the state of his room that had spoilt his appetite,
but in fact the changes in his room were something to
which he became reconciled very quickly. They had got
into the habit of putting in with him things that could not

be accommodated elsewhere, and there were now a great many such things because they had let one room of the flat to three lodgers. These earnest gentlemen—all three wore full beards, as Gregory discovered on one occasion through a crack in the door—were sticklers for order, not only in their room but also, now that they were installed as lodgers, as far as the whole household was concerned, which meant particularly the kitchen. They had no time for useless junk and even less if it was dirty. Moreover they had brought most of their furniture with them. As a result, many things had become superfluous for which there was no market but which on the other hand no one wanted to throw away. All of them found their way into Gregory's room, as did the ash bucket and the rubbish bin from the kitchen. Everything that was temporarily out of use the cleaning-woman, who was always in a great hurry, simply flung into Gregory's room; Gregory was usually lucky enough to see only the object in question and the hand holding it. The cleaning-woman may have meant to fetch the things again when she had a moment or throw them all out at one go; in fact they stayed where they had landed, except when Gregory forced a path through the stuff and shifted it, at first because he had to, there being no other space for crawling, but subsequently with ever-increasing pleasure, although the aftermath of such expeditions was that he relapsed, dead-tired and in a mood of deep gloom, into hours of lying without moving.

As the lodgers sometimes had supper at home as well, eating in the communal living-room, there were evenings when the living-room door stayed shut, but Gregory found it quite easy to forgo the opening of the door; there had already been evenings when, with the door open, he had not taken advantage of the fact but had lain motionless in the darkest corner of his room, unnoticed by the family. On one occasion, however, the cleaning-woman having left the door to the living-room ajar, it stayed that way and was still ajar when the lodgers came home in the evening and the lamp was lit. They sat down at the head of the table, where Gregory's father and mother and Gregory

himself had formerly eaten, unfolded their napkins, and
picked up their knives and forks. Promptly Gregory's
mother appeared in the doorway with a dish of meat and
right behind her his sister with another dish piled high
with potatoes. Steam rose thickly from both. The lodgers
bent over the dishes as they were placed in front of them;
it was as if they wanted to inspect the food before eating it,
and indeed the one in the middle, evidently an authority
in the eyes of the other two, actually cut through a piece of
meat while it was still on the dish, clearly in order to
establish whether it was done or whether it should perhaps
be sent back to the kitchen. He was satisfied, and Gregory's
mother and sister, who had been watching apprehensively,
broke into relieved smiles.

The family ate in the kitchen. Gregory's father, however, before going to the kitchen, came into the living-
room and with a bow, cap in hand, made a tour of the
table. The lodgers rose as one man and mumbled something into their beards. Afterwards, when they were alone,
they ate in almost complete silence. It struck Gregory as
odd that, of all the multifarious sounds of eating, the one
that stood out most persistently was the champing of their
teeth; it was as if they meant to show him that one needed
teeth to eat and that even the finest of toothless jaws were
good for nothing. 'I do feel like eating,' Gregory said
worriedly to himself, 'but not these things. The way these
lodgers stuff themselves—and I'm starving!'

That same evening—and Gregory could not remember
hearing it once during the whole time—the sound of the
violin came from the kitchen. The lodgers had finished
their supper, the middle one had produced a newspaper
and given the other two a page each, and they were now
leaning back in their chairs, reading and smoking. When
the violin began to play they looked up, got to their feet,
and tiptoed to the hall doorway, where they stood huddled
together. Their movements must have been audible in the
kitchen because Gregory's father called out, 'Would the
gentlemen perhaps rather not have the violin played? It
can be stopped immediately.' 'On the contrary,' said the

middle lodger, 'would the young lady not like to come in here and play in the living-room where it's much cosier and more relaxed?' 'Why, certainly!' cried Gregory's father as if he had been the violinist. The lodgers came back into the room and waited. Soon Gregory's father entered with the music stand, his mother with the music, and his sister with the violin. His sister calmly got everything ready to play; his parents, who had never let rooms before and consequently overdid the politeness towards their lodgers, dared not even sit in their own chairs; Gregory's father leant against the door, his right hand inserted between two buttons of his livery jacket; his mother, however, offered a chair by one of the lodgers, sat down where the gentleman had happened to put it, which was tucked away in a corner.

Gregory's sister began to play, while his father and mother, one on each side of her, followed the movements of her hands with close attention. Drawn by her playing, Gregory ventured forward a little way until his head was inside the living-room. He gave scarcely a thought to the fact that he had been showing so little regard for others recently, whereas before he had prided himself on his altruism. And now there was even more reason for his staying out of sight because, as a result of the dust that lay everywhere in his room and blew about at the slightest disturbance, he too was covered in dust; he dragged lengths of thread, hairs, and scraps of left-over food around with him on his back and flanks; he was far too apathetic altogether to do as he had previously done several times a day, which was to lie on his back and rub himself on the carpet. Yet in spite of it all he had no inhibitions about edging forward onto the spotless floor of the living-room.

Not that anyone paid any attention to him. The family was completely absorbed in the violin-playing; the lodgers, however, having begun by stationing themselves, hands in pockets, much too close behind his sister's music stand where they could all see the score, which must surely have bothered his sister, soon retired muttering to the window and stood there with heads lowered, watched anxiously by Gregory's father. It now looked very much as if, disappointed in their expectation of hearing some beautiful or entertaining violin-playing, they were fed up with the whole performance and were allowing their peace to be disturbed further only out of politeness. Particularly the way in which they all blew their cigar smoke into the air out of nose and mouth together suggested a high degree of irritation. Yet his sister was playing so beautifully. Her face was tilted to one side; her eyes had a sad, searching look as they followed the lines of the score. Gregory crawled a little farther into the room and pressed his head to the floor in the hope of perhaps meeting her gaze. Could he really be an animal, if music affected him so deeply? He felt as if he were being shown the way to that food he so longed for without knowing what it was. He was determined to reach his sister and suggest by tugging at her skirt that she should bring her violin and come into his room, because no one here was rewarding her playing as he wished to reward it. He wanted to keep her in his room and not let her go, at least not while he lived; for the first time his nightmarish appearance would serve some useful purpose; he meant to be at all the doors of his room simultaneously and spit in his attackers' faces; his sister, though, must not be coerced but must stay with him of her own free will; she should sit beside him on the couch and lower her ear to his mouth, and he would then confide to her that it had been his firm intention to send her to the Conservatory and that if this mishap had not intervened he would have told everyone so at Christmas—presumably Christmas had already passed—and would have turned a deaf ear to any objections. Following this declaration his sister would burst into tears of emotion and Gregory would lift himself up to the level of her shoulder and kiss her bare neck, for since she had been going out to work she had worn neither neckband nor collars.

'Mr Samsa!' the middle lodger cried, addressing Gregory's father and pointing, without another word, at the slowly advancing Gregory. The music stopped; the middle lodger looked at his friends with a smile and a shake of the head before turning back to Gregory. Gregory's father seemed to feel that getting rid of Gregory was less urgent for the moment than reassuring the lodgers, although the lodgers, far from being upset, appeared to be deriving more amusement from Gregory than they had from the violin-playing. He hurried over to them and tried by spreading his arms to drive them into their room, at the same time using his body in an attempt to block their view of Gregory. At this they did in fact turn a little nasty, though there was no knowing whether it was because of the father's behaviour or because of the realization now dawning on them that they had unwittingly had such a creature as Gregory for a next-door neighbour. They demanded explanations of Gregory's father, their own arms flew up, they plucked nervously at their beards and only slowly gave ground in the retreat to their room. Meanwhile his sister had recovered from the forlorn mood into which she had lapsed following the abrupt interruption of her playing; after dangling violin and bow loosely in her hands for a while and continuing to gaze at the score as if she were still playing, she had suddenly pulled herself together, laid the instrument in her mother's lap where she sat fighting for breath with labouring lungs, and run into the next room, which the lodgers, driven on by Gregory's father, were now approaching more rapidly. Quilts and pillows could be seen flying into the air and falling back into place, guided by his sister's practised hands. Before the lodgers even reached the room she had finished making the beds and slipped out again. Gregory's father appeared to have fallen a prey to his own obstinacy once more, this time to the point of forgetting completely the respect that, after all, he owed his paying guests. He kept driving them on and driving them on until, right in the doorway of the room, the middle lodger stamped his foot with a sound like thunder and stopped Gregory's father in his tracks. 'I hereby give notice,' he said with upraised hand, looking round to include Gregory's mother and sister as well, 'that in view of the disgusting

circumstances obtaining in this flat and in this family'—
here he suddenly decided to spit on the floor—'I intend to
quit my room immediately. I shall not of course pay a
thing for the days I have already spent in residence here;
on the contrary, I shall be considering whether to lodge
a—believe me—very easily justifiable claim against you for
damages.' He stopped talking and looked straight ahead
of him as if waiting for something. And indeed his two
friends chimed in promptly with the words, 'We too give
notice as of now.' At that he seized the door handle and
slammed the door.

Gregory's father groped his way to his chair and
slumped into it; he might have been stretching out for his
customary evening nap, except that the violent nodding of
his head, almost as though it had come loose, showed that
he was anything but asleep. All this time Gregory had been
lying motionless where the lodgers had first spotted him.
Disappointment at the failure of his plan but perhaps also
the weakness brought on by prolonged starvation had
robbed him of all possibility of movement. Dreading with a
kind of certainty that a general state of collapse was about
to break over him at any moment, he waited. Not even the
violin alarmed him when, having slipped from his
mother's trembling fingers, it fell from her lap and hit the
floor with a loud, ringing sound.

'My dear parents,' said Gregory's sister, banging her
hand down on the table by way of an introduction, 'we
can't go on like this. I see that even if you perhaps don't. I
refuse to utter my brother's name in front of this creature,
so all I say is: we must try to get rid of it. We've tried our
level best to look after it and put up with it, and I believe
no one can reproach us in the slightest.'

'She's right, by God,' Gregory's father said to himself.
His mother, who had still not managed to get her breath
back, now put a hand to her mouth and with a crazed look
in her eyes began coughing hollowly.

His sister hurried over to her and put a hand on her
forehead. His father appeared to have been set thinking
along more specific lines by the girl's words; he had sat up

in his chair and was playing with his cap among the plates that still lay on the table from the lodgers' supper, casting occasional glances at the motionless Gregory.

'We must somehow get rid of it,' said Gregory's sister, now addressing only his father because the mother could hear nothing above her coughing, 'or it will be the death of you both, I can see it coming. When people have to work as hard as we do they cannot take this everlasting worry at home as well. I can't either.' And she burst into such floods of tears that they splahed down onto her mother's face, from which she wiped them with perfunctory movements of her hands.

'But, my child,' said her father pityingly and with evident understanding, 'what are we to do?'

Gregory's sister merely shrugged her shoulders in token of the perplexity that had come over her with her tears, contrasting with her earlier assurance.

'If he understood what we said,' Gregory's father began half wonderingly, but his sister, still weeping, waved a hand violently to show that it was out of the question.

'If he understood what we said,' Gregory's father repeated as, by closing his eyes, he took in the girl's conviction that this was impossible, 'we might perhaps be able to come to an arrangement with him. But as things are . . .'

'It has to go,' his sister cried. 'It's the only way, Father. You must just try to get out of the habit of thinking it's Gregory. That's been our undoing, in fact, that we've believed it for so long. But how can it be Gregory? If it were he would long ago have seen the impossibility of people living in the same house as such an animal and would have gone away of his own accord. In which case we would have no brother but could at least go on living and could honour his memory. As it is, the brute persecutes us, drives away the lodgers, and clearly means to take over the whole flat and have us sleeping out on the street. Look, Father,' she screamed suddenly, 'there he goes again!' And in a state of panic that Gregory found quite incomprehensible she even left her mother's side, actually using the back of the chair to push herself off as though she would rather sacrifice her mother than remain in Gregory's vicinity, and dashed behind her father, who then, prompted purely by her reaction, also stood up and half raised his arms in front of the girl as though to protect her.

But of course nothing was further from Gregory's mind than to try to inspire fear in anyone, let alone his sister. He had simply begun to turn himself round in order to make his way back to his room, only it looked rather spectacular because in his ailing condition he had to help this difficult process along with his head by repeatedly lifting it in the air and bringing it down on the floor with a bang. He stopped and looked round. Apparently they had recognized that he meant well; the alarm had been only a momentary one. Now they were looking at him in sad-eyed silence. His mother was lying in her chair with her legs outstretched and pressed together, so exhausted that she could barely keep her eyes open; his father and sister were sitting together, she with one arm draped round his father's neck.

'I suppose it's all right to turn round now,' thought Gregory, and he went back to work. He could not help panting with the effort, and every now and then he had to pause for a rest. Not that anyone put him under pressure: it was all left to him. As soon as he had completed his turn he set off in a straight line. He was amazed at the enormous distance separating him from his room and could not understand how in his enfeebled state he had made the same journey almost without realizing it a short while before. Concentrating entirely on crawling fast, he hardly noticed the fact that not a word, not a cry from any member of his family disturbed his progress. Not until he had reached the doorway did he turn his head, and then not completely because he could feel his neck becoming stiff; nevertheless he saw that behind him nothing had changed except that his sister had risen to her feet. His last glimpse was of his mother, now fast asleep.

Almost before he was inside his room the door was hurriedly pushed to, bolted, and locked. The sudden noise behind him frightened Gregory so much that his legs gave way. It was his sister who had been in such a hurry. She had been on her feet already, waiting; she had then sprung forward nimbly—Gregory had not even heard her coming—and, with a cry of 'At last!' for her parents' benefit, she had turned the key in the lock.

'Now what?' Gregory asked himself as he looked about him in the darkness. He quie soon discovered that he could no longer move at all. He was not surprised; in fact what struck him as unnatural was that he had actually been able to get about until then on such thin legs. Otherwise he felt comparatively comfortable. Admittedly he hurt all over, but he had the impression that the pains were gradually becoming fainter and fainter and would eventually go away together. The rotten apple in his back and the inflamed area around it, now completely covered with a soft dust, were almost forgotten. He recalled his family with sympathy and love. His own belief that he must go was if possible even firmer than his sister's. He remained in this state of vacant and peaceable reflection until the church clock struck three in the morning. He lived to see the first signs of the general brightening outside the window. Then, independently of his will, his head sank to the floor and his last breath streamed feebly from his nostrils.

When the cleaning-woman arrived in the early morning—out of sheer, bustling energy she slammed all the doors, no matter how often she had been asked not to, so hard that throughout the flat, from the moment of her arrival onwards, peaceful sleep was an impossibility—she noticed nothing out of the ordinary about Gregory at first on her customary brief visit. She thought he was deliberately lying so still, playing the injured party; she credited him with boundless intelligence. Happening to have the long-handled broom in her hand, she tried to tickle Gregory with it from the door. When even this was unsuccessful she lost patience and gave Gregory a little prod, and it was only when she had shifted him from his place without encountering any resistance that her attention was aroused. She was quick to grasp the true state of affairs, reacting with a look of surprise and a low whistle; then, without wasting any more time, she tore open the bedroom door and bellowed into the darkness within, 'Take a look at this—the thing's snuffed it! It's lying here dead as a doornail!'

The Samsas were sitting up in the matrimonial bed and had first to overcome their alarm at the cleaning-woman's irruption before there was any question of registering her announcement. Then, however, Mr and Mrs Samsa got quickly out of bed, one on each side, Mr Samsa throwing the quilt round his shoulders, Mrs Samsa wearing only her nightdress; thus attired, they entered Gregory's room. Meanwhile the door to the living-room, where Meg had been sleeping since the lodgers moved in, had also opened; Meg was fully dressed as though she had not even been to bed, an impression her pale face seemed to confirm. 'Dead?' said Mrs Samsa, looking inquiringly up at the cleaning-woman although she could verify everything herself and even see for herself without verification. 'I reckon so,' said the cleaning-woman, and to prove it she gave Gregory's corpse another great sideways shove with the broom. Mrs Samsa made as if to put a restraining hand on the broom but did not do so. 'Well,' said Mr Samsa, 'thanks be to God.' He crossed himself, and the three women followed his example. Meg, her eyes fixed on the corpse, said, 'See how thin he was. Well, he hadn't eaten anything for ages, had he? The food used to come out exactly as it had gone in.' Gregory's body was indeed completely flat and dried out, as could be seen only now that it was no longer raised on its legs and there was nothing else about it to distract the eye.

'Meg, come into our room for a moment,' said Mrs Samsa, smiling wistfully, and Meg, not without a backward glance at the corpse, followed her parents into their bedroom. The cleaning-woman closed the door and opened the window wide. Despite the earliness of the hour the fresh air already held a trace of mildness, for by this time it was the end of March.

The three lodgers emerged from their room and stared about them in astonishment, looking for their breakfast; they had been forgotten. 'Where's our breakfast?' the middle lodger gruffly demanded of the cleaning-woman. But she put a finger to her lips and in silence gestured quickly to the lodgers to come into Gregory's room. They came, and in the already quite bright room, with their hands in the pockets of their somewhat threadbare jackets, they stood around Gregory's corpse.

Then the bedroom door opened and Mr Samsa appeared in his livery, his wife on one arm and his daughter on the other. They were all slightly red-eyed from crying, Meg occasionally pressing her face against her father's arm.

'Get out of my flat this instant,' said Mr Samsa, pointing to the door without letting go of the women. 'How do you mean?' said the middle lodger, stunned but managing a honeyed smile. The other two had their hands behind their backs and were rubbing them together as if in delighted anticipation of a major row that, moreover, promised to turn out in their favour. 'I mean precisely what I say,' replied Mr Samsa, and with his two escorts he began to walk straight towards the middle lodger. The latter made no move at first but stood looking at the floor as if things were falling into a fresh pattern in his mind. 'All right, we'll go,' he concluded, looking up at Mr Samsa as though, in a sudden access of humility, he were even seeking fresh approval for this decision. Mr Samsa merely nodded curtly several times, glaring at him. Sure enough, the lodger promptly turned and strode out into the hall. His two friends, who had stopped rubbing their hands and started listening intently some time ago, now went literally scurrying after him as if afraid that Mr Samsa might reach the hall before them and cut them off from their leader. Out in the hall all three of them took their hats from the hat stand, drew their sticks from the stick rack, bowed silently, and left the flat. Prompted by what turned out to be a quite unfounded distrust, Mr Samsa stepped out onto the landing with the two women; there they leant on the banister and watched the three gentlemen slowly but surely descending the long stairwell, disappearing at a particular turn of the staircase between each floor and re-emerging a moment or two later; the lower they went, the more the Samsa family lost interest in them, and as a butcher's man passed them coming up and then climbed high above them, proudly bearing his tray on his head, Mr Samsa soon left the landing with the women, and they went back into their flat as though relieved.

They decided to spend the day resting and going for a walk. They had not only earned this break from work; they needed it, and needed it badly. So they sat down at the table and wrote three letters of apology, Mr Samsa to his superiors, Mrs Samsa to the man who sent her needlework, and Meg to the proprietor of the shop she served in. While they were writing, the cleaning-woman came in to say that she was going since her morning work was done. The three letter-writers merely nodded at first without looking up; only when the cleaning-woman continued to show no sign of leaving did they look up in some irritation. 'Well?' Mr Samsa asked. The cleaning-woman stood smiling in the doorway as though she had some excellent news to announce to the family but would surrender it only on being quizzed at length. The little ostrich feather that stood up almost vertically from her hat and had been a source of irritation to Mr Samsa throughout her period of service bobbed and dipped in all directions. 'What was it you wanted?' asked Mrs Samsa, who was the person for whom the cleaning-woman still had most respect. 'Yes, well,' the cleaning-woman replied before a peal of amiable laughter prevented her from continuing for a moment, 'if you were worrying about how to get rid of that rubbish next door, you needn't. It's already dealt with.' Mrs Samsa and Meg bent over their letters as if to go on writing; Mr Samsa, realizing that the cleaning-woman now intended to launch into a full description, countered with a resolutely outstretched hand. Prevented from telling her story, she recalled the great hurry she was in, and with a clearly offended "Bye,

144

all,' she whirled round and left the flat amid a fearful banging of doors.

'She'll be getting her notice this evening,' said Mr Samsa, but neither his wife nor his daughter offered any response, the cleaning-woman having apparently shattered their so recently acquired peace of mind once more. They got up, crossed to the window, and stood with their arms around each other. Mr Samsa turned in his chair to face them and watched them in silence for a while. Then he called out, 'Look, come over here. Forget about the past, can't you? And have a bit of consideration for me.' The women obeyed him immediately, hurrying over to him, caressing him, and quickly finishing their letters.

Afterwards the three of them left the flat together, which was something they had not done for months, and took the tram out into the country. They had the carriage to themselves, and it was full of warmth and sunlight. Leaning back comfortably in their seats, they discussed their prospects, which closer examination revealed to be not at all bad, because all three employments—and they had never really questioned one another about this before —were most advantageous and, particularly as far as the future was concerned, very promising indeed. The chief immediate improvement in their situation could of course be expected from a simple change of accommodation; they now wanted to take a smaller, less expensive flat that was at the same time better located and altogether more practical than their present one, which Gregory had found. As they discussed these things Mr and Mrs Samsa, watching their daughter become increasingly animated, were struck almost simultaneously by the realization that in recent months, despite all the troubles that had drained the colour from her cheeks, she had blossomed into a beautiful, full-bosomed girl. Speaking more quietly now, and communicating almost unconsciously through glances, they thought about how the time was also coming when they must start looking round for a nice husband for her. And they saw it as a sort of confirmation of their new-found dreams and good intentions when, at the end of the

journey, their daughter was the first to stand up, stretching her young body.

In the Penal Colony

(*In der Strafkolonie*, written in October 1914; volume publication by Kurt Wolff in May 1919.)

'It's a curious device,' said the officer to the traveller, surveying with a look almost of admiration the device with which he was of course so familiar. The traveller appeared to have acted purely out of politeness in complying with the commandant's request that he attend the execution of a soldier condemned for insubordination and insulting a superior. Interest in the execution was clearly not very great even within the penal colony itself. At least, the only persons present in that deep sandy valley with its barren slopes all around were, apart from the officer and the traveller, the condemned man, a stolid, broad-mouthed individual with a look of neglect about his hair and face, and a soldier who held the heavy chain gathering up the little chains that were fixed to the condemned man's ankles, wrists, and neck as well as being fastened to each other by interconnecting chains. In fact the condemned man had an air of such doglike subservience as to suggest that one could have given him the run of the surrounding slopes and a mere whistle would have fetched him back when the execution was due to begin.

The traveller was not greatly interested in the device, and his uninvolvement was little short of obvious as he paced up and down behind the condemned man while the officer attended to the final preparations, now crawling underneath the device, which was sunk some way into the earth, now climbing a ladder to inspect its upper parts. These were tasks that could really have been left to a mechanic, yet the officer performed them with enormous enthusiasm, either because he was a particular devotee of this device or because there were other reasons why the work could be entrusted to no one else. 'All ready now!' he called out at last, stepping down from the ladder. He was dreadfully tired, his mouth hung wide open as he breathed, and he had wedged two delicate lady's handkerchiefs inside the collar of his uniform. 'They're too heavy for the tropics, those uniforms,' said the traveller instead of, as the officer had expected him to, asking questions about the device. 'That's right,' said the officer as he washed the oil and grease from his hands in the bucket of water that stood there for the purpose, 'but they mean home; we don't want to lose touch with home. Now, take a look at this device,' he went on briskly, drying his hands on a towel and at the same time pointing at the device. 'Up to now I've still had to do some things by hand, but from here onwards the device is entirely automatic.' The traveller nodded and followed the officer. To cover himself against all eventualities, the latter added, 'We get the odd breakdown, of course. I hope nothing will happen today, but one has to be prepared for it; after all, the device is required to run for twelve hours without interruption. But even if breakdowns do occur they're only very minor and we repair them straight away. Won't you take a seat?' he asked in conclusion, pulling a cane chair out of a pile of such chairs and offering it to the traveller, who could not refuse.

He found himself sitting at the edge of a pit, into which he cast a quick glance. It was not very deep. On one side of the pit the excavated earth had been piled up to form an embankment; on the other side stood the device. 'I don't know,' the officer said, 'whether the commandant has already explained the device to you.' The traveller gestured vaguely, which was all the officer wanted because now he could go ahead and explain the device himself. 'This device,' he said, grasping a connecting-rod and leaning his weight on it, 'is an invention of the late commandant's. I worked on the very first experiments, and I was involved at every stage of the job up to its completion, but the credit for the invention is his and his alone. Have you heard of our late commandant? No? Well, I'm not exaggerating when I say that the entire set-up here is his work. We, his friends, knew when he died that the whole way the penal colony had been constituted was so complete, so self-contained, that his successor, no matter how many new projects he had in mind, would be able to alter nothing of the original concept for many years at least. And we were right; the new commandant has had to admit as much. What a shame you never knew our late commandant! But,' the officer interrupted himself, 'here am I, blathering on, and we have his device before us. It consists, as you see, of three parts. Over the years each of those parts has acquired a popular name, as it were. The bottom part is called the bed, the top part the scriber, and this middle part, suspended between them, is known as the harrow.' 'The harrow?' inquired the traveller. He had not been paying full attention; the valley was without shade and trapped too much sun, which made it difficult to collect one's thoughts. All the greater was his admiration for the officer, who in his tight parade-ground tunic with its heavy epaulettes and loops of braid was explaining his job with such enthusiasm while at the same time, screwdriver in hand, also busying himself with the odd screw here and there. The soldier appeared to be in much the same state as the traveller. He had wound the condemned man's chain round both his wrists and was leaning with one hand on his rifle, head flung back, paying no attention to anything. The traveller was not surprised at this, because the language the officer was speaking was French, which surely neither the soldier nor the condemned man understood. It did, however, make all the more remarkable the fact that the condemned man was nevertheless doing his utmost to follow the officer's explanations. With a kind of drowsy obstinacy he would direct his gaze wherever the officer happened to be pointing, and when the latter was interrupted by a question from the traveller he too, like the officer, turned to look in the traveller's direction.

'The harrow, yes,' said the officer. 'It's a good name. The needles are set in the same pattern as on a harrow, and the whole thing is driven in much the same way except that it stays in one place and works much more neatly and efficiently. You'll get the picture in a moment. The condemned man is laid on the bed here. You see, I want to describe the device first and then afterwards have it go through the actual process. You'll be able to follow it better then. Also one of the cogwheels in the scriber is rather worn; it grates badly as it turns, and one can hardly hear oneself speak; spares are difficult to get hold of here, unfortunately. Right, here's the bed, as I was saying. It is completely covered with a layer of cotton wool, you'll discover why later. The condemned man is laid on the cotton wool on his stomach—naked, naturally; these straps here are for his hands, his feet, and his neck, to fasten him down. Here at the head end of the bed, where as I've said the man starts off lying on his face, there's this little stub of felt that can be easily adjusted to push right into the man's mouth. The object of that is to prevent screaming and biting of the tongue. The man has to take the felt, of course, because otherwise the neck straps would break his neck.' 'That's cotton wool?' asked the traveller, leaning forward. 'Oh, yes,' said the officer with a smile. 'Feel.' And he took the traveller's hand and passed it over the surface of the bed. 'It's a specially treated type of cotton wool, which is why it looks so different; I'll come back to what it's for in a moment.' The device was beginning to capture the traveller's imagination; using his hand to keep the sun out of his eyes, he stared up at it. It was a sizable structure: The bed and the scriber were about equally large and resembled two dark-coloured chests. The scriber was mounted some two metres above the bed, and the two were joined at the corners by four brass rods that almost shone in the sun. Suspended between the two chests on a steel strap was the harrow.

The officer, who had hardly noticed the traveller's earlier indifference, evidently sensed these first stirrings of interest and paused in his elucidations to give the traveller time to view the device at his ease. The condemned man aped what the traveller was doing except that, being unable to put his hand over his eyes, he blinked upwards with his eyes unprotected.

'All right, the man's lying there,' said the traveller; he leant back in his chair and crossed his legs.

152

'Yes,' said the officer, tipping his cap back and passing a hand over his hot face, 'now, listen to this! Both the bed and the scriber have their own batteries, the bed for itself, the scriber for the harrow. As soon as the man is fastened down, the bed is set in motion. It quivers with tiny, very rapid jerks from side to side and at the same time up and down. You'll have seen similar devices in sanatoria; the only difference is, with our bed all the movements are painstakingly calculated; they have to be, to mesh in with the movements of the harrow. But it's this part, the harrow, that actually carries out the sentence.'

'What is the sentence, in fact?' asked the traveller. 'You don't even know that?' said the astonished officer, beginning to bite his lips. 'Forgive me—my explanations are perhaps a trifle muddled. I'm very sorry, I really am. The commentary always used to be given by the commandant, but the new commandant has been evading his duty in this respect. Still, that so eminent a visitor as yourself'—the traveller tried with both hands to parry this distinction, but the officer insisted—'that so eminent a visitor as yourself should not even have been told about the form our sentence takes is yet another innovation on his part that—' There was an oath on his lips, but he recovered himself and said merely, 'I wasn't informed; it's not my fault. In point of fact I am the person best qualified to explain our sentences because I have here'—he tapped his breast pocket—'the relevant drawings in the late commandant's own hand.'

'Drawings in his own hand?' the traveller asked. 'Did he do everything, then? Was he soldier, judge, mechanical engineer, chemist, draftsman?'

'He certainly was,' said the officer, nodding with a fixed, thoughtful look. Then he examined his hands; they did not seem to him clean enough to touch the drawings; so he went to the bucket and washed them a second time. Then he pulled out a small leather wallet and said, 'Our sentence doesn't sound particularly severe. The condemned man has the law that he has broken inscribed on his body with the harrow. This man, for instance,'—the officer pointed

to him—'will have "Honour your superiors!" inscribed on
his body.'

The traveller cast a quick glance at the condemned man;
his head was bowed as the officer pointed at him, and he
appeared to be straining his ears in an attempt to learn
something, though it was evident from the movements of
his thick, pouting lips that he understood nothing. The
traveller had various questions in mind but at the sight of
the man asked only, 'Does he know his sentence?' 'No,' said
the officer. He was about to go on with his explanations,
but the traveller cut him short: 'He doesn't know his own
sentence?' 'No,' the officer said again; he was still for a
moment as if expecting the traveller to volunteer some
reason for his question, then he said, 'There would be no
sense in telling him. He experiences it on his own body.'
The traveller, who would have said no more, became
aware that the condemned man was looking at him,
apparently to ask whether he was able to sanction the
process being described. The traveller therefore bent
forward again, having leant back in his seat, and asked
another question: 'But he knows he has been sentenced?'
'He doesn't know that either,' said the officer, smiling at
the traveller as if in anticipation of further strange
disclosures on his part. 'You mean,' said the traveller,
passing a hand over his forehead, 'that even now the man
doesn't know how his defence was received?' 'He's had no
opportunity to defend himself,' said the officer, looking
away as if he were talking to himself and did not wish to
humiliate the traveller with an account of things that, to
him, were self-evident. 'But he must have had an opportunity to defend himself,' the traveller said, rising to his
feet.

The officer, recognizing the risk of a serious hold-up as
far as his explaining the device was concerned, went over
to the traveller, placed an arm in his, pointed to the
condemned man, who was standing stiffly erect, now that
he was so obviously the centre of attention—also the
soldier was pulling on the chain—and said, 'It's like this. I
hold the office of judge here in the penal colony. In spite

of my youth. The reason being that I used to help the late commandant with all the criminal cases, and I also know the device better than anyone else. The principle on which I base my decisions is: guilt is invariably beyond doubt. Other courts are unable to abide by this principle because they consist of several persons and also have higher courts above them. This is not the case here, or at least it wasn't under the late commandant; the new one has shown signs of wanting to meddle in my jurisdiction, but so far I have managed to ward him off, and I shall continue to do so. You wanted to know about this case; it's as straightforward as they all are. A captain laid a charge this morning to the effect that this man, who is assigned to him as a servant and sleeps outside his door, had been asleep on duty. Part of his duty, you see, is to get up every time the hour strikes and salute the captain's door. A simple enough duty, surely, but a very necessary one because for both watching over and waiting on his superior the man has to remain alert. Last night the captain wanted to check whether the servant was performing his duty. Opening the door on the stroke of two, he found him curled up asleep. He fetched the horsewhip and hit him in the face. Instead of then standing up and apologizing the man seized his master round the legs, shook him, and yelled, "Drop that whip or I'll make mincemeat of you!" Those are the facts. The captain came to me an hour ago; I wrote down his statement and immediately after it the sentence. Then I had the man put in chains. It was all very simple. Had I first called the man in and questioned him it would only have led to confusion. He would have lied; when I succeeded in refuting the lies he would have told fresh ones in their stead; and so on. Now, though, I've got him and I won't let him go. Does that explain everything? But time's getting on, we ought to be starting with the execution, and I haven't finished explaining the device.' Urging the traveller to resume his seat, he went back to the device and began, 'As you can see, the harrow is in the shape of a man; here is the harrow for the abdomen, here are the harrows for the legs. For the head there's just this one little cutter. Is that clear?' He leant amiably towards the traveller, ready to supply the fullest possible explanations.

The traveller was looking at the harrow with a frown. The information about the trial procedure had failed to satisfy him. He had to admit, of course, that this was a penal colony, that therefore special measures were called for, and that the procedure must be military throughout. On the other hand he placed a certain amount of hope in the new commandant, who clearly intended, however slowly, to introduce a new form of procedure, which was beyond this officer's limited understanding. Pursuing this train of thought, the traveller asked, 'Will the commandant be attending the execution?' 'It's not certain,' said the officer, embarrassed by the abrupt question, his friendly features twisting into a grimace. 'That's why we have to get a move on. I shall even, much against my will, have to cut short my remarks. But I could fill in the details tomorrow, when the device has been cleaned—that's the only trouble with it, that it gets in such a mess. All right, just the essentials now. When the man is lying on the bed and the bed has started vibrating, the harrow is lowered onto the body. It sets itself automatically with the tips of the needles just touching the body. Once it is set, this hawser tautens to form a rod. Now we're in business. Outwardly the layman sees no difference between the punishments. The harrow appears to operate quite uniformly, vibrating away and stabbing its needles into the body as the body, itself quivering, is offered up by the bed. Now, to enable everyone to study the execution of the sentence the harrow is made of glass. Mounting the needles presented one or two technical snags, but after a lot of experimenting we eventually managed it. No effort was spared, you understand. And now everyone can watch through the glass as the inscription is made on the body. Come over here, won't you, and have a closer look at the needles.'

The traveller got slowly to his feet, walked forward, and bent over the harrow. 'You have here,' the officer said, 'two sorts of needle in a multiple arrangement. Each long one has a short one beside it. The long one writes, you see, and the short one squirts out water to wash away the blood and keep the writing clear at all times. The blood water is then channelled through a system of little gutters into this main gutter here and down the drainpipe into the pit.' The officer's finger indicated the precise path the mixture of blood and water must take. When in the interests of maximum clarity he actually made as if to catch it in his cupped hands at the mouth of the pipe, the traveller raised his head and, feeling behind him with one hand, began to back towards his chair. He saw then to his horror that the condemned man had likewise accepted the officer's invitation to inspect the harrow at close quarters. He had pulled the sleepy soldier forward a little way on the chain and was leaning over the glass. One could see him searching with a puzzled look in his eyes for what the two gentlemen had just spotted and, without the accompanying explanation, failing to find it. He was leaning this way and that, running his gaze repeatedly over the glass. The traveller wanted to push him back because he was surely committing a punishable offence. The officer, however, restraining the traveller with one hand, used the other to pick up a clod from the embankment and hurl it at the soldier. The latter looked up with a start, saw what the condemned man had dared to do, dropped his rifle, dug his heels in, hauled the condemned man back so that he fell over, and stood looking down at him as he writhed about in his clinking chains. 'Stand him up!' the officer shouted, aware that the traveller was being very seriously distracted by the condemned man. Indeed he was even leaning out over the harrow again, taking no notice of it but merely trying to see what was happening to the condemned man. 'Careful with him!' the officer shouted again. He ran round the device, grasped the condemned man under the armpits, and with the soldier's help, and after much slipping and sliding on the condemned man's part, stood him on his feet.

'Now I know all about it,' said the traveller as the officer came back. 'All but the most important thing,' the latter replied, grasping the traveller's arm and pointing upwards. 'The scriber there houses the machinery that governs the movements of the harrow, and that machinery is geared up to match the drawing on which the sentence is set out. I still use the late commandant's drawings. Here they are,'—he pulled several sheets from the leather wallet—'only I'm afraid I can't let you handle them yourself; they're my most treasured possession. Sit down and I'll show you them from here; you'll see everything perfectly.' He held up the first sheet. The traveller would have liked to say something appreciative, but all he could see was a maze of criss-cross lines covering the paper so closely that it was difficult to make out the white spaces between. 'Read it,' said the officer. 'I can't,' said the traveller. 'But it's quite clear,' said the officer. 'It's most artistic,' the traveller said evasively, 'but I can't decipher it.' 'Right,' said the officer, putting the wallet away with a chuckle. 'This is no copybook calligraphy. It takes a lot of reading. Even you could make it out in the end, I'm sure. It can't be plain lettering, you see; it's not supposed to kill straight away but only after a twelve-hour period, on average, with the turning-point calculated to occur at the sixth hour. So the actual lettering has to be accompanied by a great deal of embellishment. The text itself forms only a narrow band running round the waist, the rest of the body being set aside for flourishes. Are you in a position now, do you think, to appreciate the work of the harrow and of the device as a whole? Well, watch!' He shinned up the ladder, spun a wheel, called down, 'Out of the way, please!' and the whole thing started working. Had the wheel not grated, it would have been magnificent. As if the offending wheel had come as a surprise to him, the officer threatened it with his fist, then spread his arms apologetically for the traveller's benefit and came hurrying down the ladder to observe the operation of the device from below. Something was still not right, though only he was aware of it; he climbed up again, reached inside the scriber with both hands, and then, to get down faster, instead of using the ladder, slid down one of the poles and started yelling in the traveller's ear as loudly as he could in order to make himself heard: 'Do you understand the process? The harrow starts to write; as soon as it has completed the first draft of the inscription on the man's back the cotton-wool layer rolls round and turns the body slowly onto its side, offering a fresh area for the harrow to work on. Meanwhile the parts already inscribed are presented to the cotton wool, which being specially treated immediately staunches the bleeding and prepares the way for a deepening of the inscription. These teeth here along the edge of the harrow then catch the cotton wool as the body rolls on round, hook it out of the wounds, toss it into the pit, and the harrow can get to work again. So it goes on, for the full twelve hours, writing deeper and deeper all the time. For the first six hours the condemned man lives almost as before; he merely suffers pain. After two hours the felt is removed because the man no longer has the strength to scream. Here in this electrically-heated bowl at the head end we put warm rice pudding, from which, if he wishes, the man can help himself to as much as he can reach with his tongue. Not one of them passes up the chance. I know of none, and my experience is considerable. Not until around the sixth hour does the man lose his pleasure in eating. I usually kneel down here at that point and observe the phenomenon. The man seldom swallows the last bite; he simply turns it round in his mouth and spits it into the pit. I have to duck then, otherwise I get it in the face. How quiet the man becomes, though, around that sixth hour! The dimmest begin to catch on. It starts around the eyes. From there it gradually spreads. A sight to make you feel like lying down beside him under the harrow. Nothing else happens; the man is simply beginning to decipher the text, pursing his lips as if listening. It's not easy, as you saw, to decipher the text when looking at it; our man, remember, is doing it with his wounds. There's a good deal of work involved, of course; he needs six hours to complete the job. But then the harrow runs him right through, hoists him up, and throws him into the pit, where he lands with a splash in the blood water and the cotton wool. Judgement is then complete, and we, the soldier and I, shovel a bit of earth on top of him.'

The traveller, one ear inclined towards the officer, stood with his hands in his pockets, watching the machine in operation. The condemned man was watching too, but uncomprehendingly. Bent forward slightly, he was trying to follow the swaying needles when the soldier, at a signal from the officer, took out a knife and slit the condemned man's shirt and trousers open from behind so that they fell from his body; he tried to grab them as they fell in order to cover his nakedness, but the soldier lifted him up and shook the remaining rags off him. The officer stopped the machine, and in the ensuing silence the condemned man was laid beneath the harrow. The chains were removed and the straps done up instead, which for the condemned man seemed at first almost to be a relief. The harrow now came down a little lower, because this was a thin man. As the points made contact a shudder ran over his skin; he stretched out his left hand—the soldier was busy with his right—not knowing in which direction; but it was towards where the traveller was standing. The officer was looking steadily at the traveller from the side as if trying to tell from his face what impression the execution, which he had now at least superficially explained, was having on him.

The strap that was meant to go round the wrist tore; probably the soldier had pulled it too tight. The soldier held up the broken piece of strap, appealing to the officer for help. The officer went over to him and said, looking at the traveller, 'The machine is extremely complex; something's bound to give here and there; one shouldn't let that cloud one's overall judgement. In any case, for the straps we can find a substitute straight away; I'll use a chain, though of course it will spoil the subtlety of the oscillations as far as the right arm is concerned.' And as he fixed the chain he added, 'The money available for upkeep is very limited now. Under the late commandant I had access to a special fund set aside for the purpose. There used to be a storage depot here that stocked all kinds of spares. I admit I made almost extravagant use of it—before, I mean; not now, as the new commandant claims, but then for him everything's an excuse to attack ancient institutions. Now he administers the machine fund himself, and if I send for a new strap I have to submit the old one as evidence, the new one takes ten days to arrive, and when it does it's of inferior quality and not much use to me. How I'm supposed to operate the machine without straps in the mean time doesn't appear to bother anyone.'

The traveller thought: it is always a serious matter, intervening decisively in other people's affairs. He was neither a citizen of the penal colony nor a citizen of the country to which it belonged. Were he to attempt to pass judgement on or, worse, prevent this execution, they could have told him: be quiet, you're a foreigner. He would have had no rejoinder; he could only have added that in this instance he found his own behaviour puzzling, travelling as he did purely for the purpose of seeing things and not at all, for example, in order to alter the way in which other countries constituted their legal systems. Here, though, the circumstances were extremely tempting. The injustice of the procedure and the inhumanity of the execution were beyond doubt. No one could presume self-interest of any kind on the traveller's part since the condemned man was a stranger to him, not even a fellow countryman, and by no means a person to inspire sympathy. The traveller himself carried letters of recommendation from people in high places, he had been most courteously received here, and the fact that he had been invited to attend the execution even seemed to indicate that his opinion of this trial was sought after. This was all the more likely in view of the commandant's being, as he had just heard in the clearest possible terms, no supporter of this procedure and maintaining an attitude almost of hostility towards the officer.

At this point the traveller heard the officer let out a yell of rage. He had just succeeded, not without difficulty, in shoving the stub of felt into the condemned man's mouth when the condemned man, nauseated beyond bearing, closed his eyes and vomited. Hastily the officer yanked him up off the stub and tried to turn his head towards the pit, but it was too late; vomit was already running down the machine. 'This is all the commandant's fault!' the officer yelled, shaking the front two brass rods in a blind fury. 'My machine's being fouled like a pigsty!' His hands trembled as he pointed out to the traveller what had happened. 'Have I not spent hours of my time trying to make the commandant see that for one day before the execution no further food is to be served? Oh, no: the new leniency begs to differ. The commandant's ladies stuff the man full of sweets before he is led away. His whole life he's lived on stinking fish and now he has to eat sweets. All right, I don't mind that, but why don't they get hold of a new felt as I've been asking them to do for the past three months? How can anyone take this piece in his mouth without feeling sick when upwards of a hundred men have sucked and chewed on it as they died?'

The condemned man had laid his head down again and was looking peaceful; the soldier was busy wiping the machine with the condemned man's shirt. The officer went over to the traveller, who in response to some premonition took a step backwards; the officer, however, grasped his hand and drew him aside. 'I want to tell you something in confidence,' he said. 'I may, I take it?' 'Certainly,' said the traveller, and he listened with lowered gaze.

'This procedure and this form of execution, which you now have the opportunity of admiring, currently have no open supporters left in our colony. I am their sole champion, just as I am the sole champion of the old commandant's legacy. Further improvement of the procedure is more than I can contemplate undertaking; it requires all my strength to maintain what we have. When the old commandant was alive the colony was full of his supporters. I have something of the old commandant's persuasiveness but none of his power; consequently the supporters have gone into hiding; there are still plenty of them but none will own up to the fact. If you go into the tea-house today—in other words, on an execution day —and listen to what people are saying you may well hear nothing but ambiguous remarks. They'll all be supporters, but under the present commandant and given his present views they're completely useless as far as I'm concerned. And now I ask you: Is the achievement of a lifetime'—he indicated the machine—'to be utterly ruined because of this commandant and the women who influence him? Is that something one can allow to happen? Even as a foreigner who is only visiting our island for a few days? But there's no time to be lost; they're planning something to curb my jurisdiction. Already discussions are being held in the commandant's office to which I am not invited to contribute; even your visit today strikes me as typical of the whole situation; the man's a coward and sends you, a foreigner, out to reconnoitre. How different it all used to be! A full day before the execution the entire valley would be crammed with people, all there just to watch; early in the morning the commandant appeared with his ladies; fanfares roused the entire camp; I reported that everything was ready; the top people—and every high-ranking official had to be there—took their places around the machine; the pile of cane chairs over there is a pathetic reminder of those days. The machine sparkled; it was always freshly cleaned, and I used to take new parts for nearly every execution. Hundreds of pairs of eyes—there were spectators standing on tiptoe all the way to the rising ground over there—watched as the condemned man was laid beneath the harrow by the commandant himself. What a common soldier is allowed to do today was then my job as presiding judge, and I counted it an honour. And then the execution began! No jarring note interfered with the work of the machine. Many people stopped watching altogether and lay down in the sand with their eyes closed; they all knew: Justice was being done. In the silence you could hear only the moaning of the condemned man, muffled by the felt. Nowadays the machine can no longer force a louder moan out of the condemned man than the felt is able to stifle, but then the scribing needles used to drip a caustic fluid that we're not allowed to use today. Ah, and then came the sixth hour! We couldn't possibly let

everyone watch from close up that wanted to. The
commandant in his wisdom gave orders that the children
should be considered first; I was of course always allowed
to be present by virtue of my job, and many were the times
I squatted there with a little child in either arm. The way
we all took in the look of enlightenment on the tortured
face, the way we held our cheeks up to the glow of a justice
accomplished at last and already beginning to fade! Those
were the days, my friend!' The officer had evidently
forgotten who was standing there; he had taken the
traveller in his arms and pressed his face to the man's
shoulder. The traveller, deeply embarrassed, was looking
impatiently over the officer's head. The soldier had
finished cleaning up and had just shaken some rice
pudding into the bowl from a tin. As soon as he saw this
the condemned man, now apparently quite recovered,
began reaching for the pudding with his tongue. The
soldier kept pushing him away, the pudding being probably intended for later, but surely it was also highly
irregular that the soldier should stick his dirty hands in it
and eat some before the eyes of his ravenous charge.

The officer quickly regained his composure. 'I didn't
mean to upset you,' he said. 'I know how impossible it is to
make anyone understand what times were like then.
Anyway, the machine still works and is its own justification, even standing by itself in this valley. And the end is
still that incredibly smooth flight of the corpse into the pit
even when, unlike then, people are not swarming round
the pit in their hundreds like flies. Then we had to have a
stout railing running round the pit; it was pulled up long
ago.'

The traveller wanted to conceal his face from the officer
and looked aimlessly about him. The officer, thinking he
was contemplating the desolation of the valley, seized his
hands, moved round him to look into his eyes, and
demanded, 'You see the shame of it?'

But the traveller said nothing. The officer left him alone
for a moment; legs apart, hands on hips, he stood still and
looked at the ground. Then he gave the traveller a cheery

smile and said, 'I was not far away from you yesterday
when the commandant invited you. I heard the invitation.
I know the commandant. I saw immediately what he was
trying to achieve by inviting you. Although he has the
power to take steps against me he still dare not do so, yet
he is quite prepared to expose me to the judgement of a
distinguished foreigner such as yourself. He's worked it all
out very carefully: this is your second day on the island,
you didn't know the old commandant and the way his
mind worked, you have your European preconceptions,
possibly you're opposed on principle to the death penalty
in general and this type of mechanical method of execution in particular, you're also seeing how the execution
takes place with no public participation, joylessly, and on a
somewhat damaged machine—might you not, in the light
of all these things (thinks the commandant), very possibly
be inclined to regard my procedure as wrong? And if you
do regard it as wrong you will not fail (I'm still speaking
from the commandant's point of view) to say so, because
you surely have confidence in your tried and tested
convictions. On the other hand you have seen and learnt
to respect many peculiarities of many peoples, so you will
probably not put your whole energy, as you might have
done back in your own country, into speaking out against
the procedures here. But the commandant doesn't even
need that. A single unguarded remark will be enough. It
need not even represent your conviction, as long as it
appears to be in line with what he wants. He will question
you with enormous cunning, I'm sure of that. And his
ladies will sit around in a circle and prick up their ears;
you'll say, for example, "Our trial procedure is different,"
or, "We examine the accused before passing sentence," or,
"In our system the condemned man is told the sentence,"
or, "We have other punishments besides the death penalty," or, "In our country people were tortured only in the
Middle Ages." All remarks that are as correct as they seem
to you self-evident; innocent remarks that in no way
impugn my procedure. But how will they be received by
the commandant? I can see him, our excellent comman-

dant, pushing his chair aside immediately and hurrying
out to the balcony; I see his ladies go streaming out after
him; I hear his voice—like thunder, as the ladies describe
it—and what he says is: "One of the West's great explorers,
appointed to investigate trial procedure in every country
in the world, has just said that our procedure, based on
ancient custom, is inhumane. Given this verdict by a
person of such standing, I naturally cannot tolerate this
procedure any longer. With effect from today I therefore
give orders that—and so on." You want to intervene, you
didn't say what he reported you as saying, you didn't call
my procedure inhumane, on the contrary it is your deeply
held conviction that it is the most humane and dignified
procedure possible, you also admire this piece of
machinery—but it's too late; you can't even get onto the
balcony, which by now is full of ladies; you want to draw
attention to yourself; you want to shout; but a lady's hand
holds your mouth closed—and I and the old commandant's work are done for.'

The traveller had to suppress a smile; so it was that easy,
the task he had thought would present such difficulty. He
said evasively, 'You overestimate my influence; the commandant has read my letters of recommendation and
knows I am no authority on legal procedures. Were I to
express an opinion it would be the opinion of a private
person, carrying no more weight than that of anyone else
and certainly a great deal less than the opinion of the
commandant, who has, I understand, very extensive rights
in this penal colony. If his opinion regarding this procedure is as definite as you believe, then I am afraid the
procedure is indeed doomed without my modest assistance being necessary.'

Did the officer understand now? No, he did not. He
shook his head vigorously, glanced back at the condemned
man and the soldier, both of whom flinched away from the
rice, he went right up to the traveller, looking not in his
face but at some point on his jacket, and said more quietly
than before, 'You don't know the commandant; as far as
he and all of us are concerned you're as it were—if you'll

pardon the expression—untouchable; believe me, your influence cannot be rated too highly. I was delighted to learn that you were to attend the execution on your own. The commandant's directive was in fact aimed at me, but I'm going to turn it to my advantage. Undeterred by false insinuations and scornful looks—which given a bigger attendence at the execution would have been inevitable—you have listened to my explanations, seen the machine, and are now viewing the execution. Your mind, surely, is already made up; any lingering doubts will be removed as you watch the execution. So I now appeal to you: please take my side against the commandant!'

The traveller let him go no further. 'How could I?' he exclaimed. 'It's out of the question. I can no more be of use to you than I can damage your interests.'

'You can,' said the officer. The traveller saw with some alarm that the officer's fists were clenched. 'You can,' the officer repeated with even greater urgency. 'I have a plan that's sure to succeed. You don't think you wield sufficient influence. I know you do. But even accepting that you are right, if we are to save this procedure we surely need to mobilize all our resources, don't we, even the possibly inadequate? Let me tell you my plan. If we're to bring it off it's very important that, today in the colony, you should keep as quiet as possible about your opinion of the procedure. Unless you're asked straight out, you should say nothing at all; what you do say must be brief and non-committal; let them see that you find it difficult to talk about it, that you feel bitter, that, were you to speak frankly, you would have almost to break out into cursing and swearing. I'm not asking you to tell lies; not at all; just to keep your answers brief, as, "Yes, I saw the execution," or, "Yes, I heard all the explanations." That's all, nothing more. There's reason enough, after all, for the bitterness we want them to hear in your voice, even if it's not quite what the commandant intended. He of course will get it completely wrong and interpret everything in his own way. That's the gist of my plan. Tomorrow there's to be a big meeting in the commandant's office, under the com-

mandant's chairmanship, of all the top administrative
officials. The commandant, of course, has managed to
turn such meetings into a public spectacle. A gallery has
been built and it's invariably packed. I am forced to take
part in the discussions, though I shudder with loathing.
Now, you are sure to be invited to the meeting, whatever
happens, and if today you act in accordance with my plan
the invitation will become an urgent request to attend. If,
however, for some mysterious reason you should not be
invited, you must certainly demand an invitation; that you
will then receive one is beyond any doubt. So tomorrow
there you are, sitting with the ladies in the commandant's
box. He looks up repeatedly to satisfy himself that you are
there. After various trifling, ridiculous items aimed solely
at the audience—usually to do with harbour works, they're
always talking about harbour works—the question of trial
procedure comes up. If this fails to happen or takes too
long to happen on the commandant's initiative, I shall
make sure that it happens. I shall stand up and report
today's execution. Very briefly, just saying it took place.
It's not the usual thing to make such reports there, but I
do so all the same. The commandant thanks me, as he
always does, with a pleasant smile and then, unable to
restrain himself, seizes his opportunity. "We have
just"—this is what he'll say, or something like it—"had the
report of the execution. I should merely like to add a note
to the effect that this particular execution was attended by
the great explorer of whose visit to our colony as well as
the quite exceptional honour it does us you are all aware.
Our meeting today is likewise lent greater significance by
his presence. Why don't we now turn to this great explorer
and ask him what he thinks of our traditional method of
execution and the procedure leading up to it?" Lots of
applause, of course; unanimous approval, with me making
more noise than anyone. The commandant bows to you
and says, "Then, sir, on behalf of us all I put that question
to you." And now you step up to the rail. Put your hands
where everyone can see them, otherwise the ladies will get
hold of them and play with your fingers. And at last you

speak. I don't know how I'm going to stand the tension of the intervening hours. In your speech you mustn't set yourself any limits; let the truth ring out, lean over the rail and shout at the commandant, really shout out your opinion, your unshakable opinion. But perhaps you'd rather not, it's not in your character, where you come from people may behave differently in such situations, that doesn't matter, that will do fine, don't even get up, merely say a few words, whisper them so that they just reach the ears of the officials sitting below you, that will be enough, you needn't even talk about the lack of attendance at the execution, the wheel that grates, the broken strap, the revolting felt, you needn't even mention those things yourself, I'll see to all the rest, and believe me, if my speech doesn't drive him from the room it'll force him to his knees: "Old commandant," it'll make him say, "I humble myself before you." That's my plan; will you help me carry it out? But of course you will—what am I saying?—you must.' And the officer seized the traveller by both arms and stared into his face, panting for breath. The last few phrases had been yelled at such a pitch that even the soldier and the condemned man had begun to take notice; though they understood nothing they had paused in their eating and were staring across at the traveller, chewing.

The answer he must give had, as far as the traveller was concerned, been beyond doubt from the very beginning; he had been through too much in his life for there to have been any question of his wavering here; he was fundamentally honest, and he was not afraid. Even so he did, at the sight of the soldier and the condemned man, hesitate for a moment. But eventually he said, as he had to, 'No.' The officer blinked several times but without taking his eyes off him. 'Do you want an explanation?' the traveller asked. The officer nodded wordlessly. 'I am opposed to this procedure,' the traveller went on. 'Even before you took me into your confidence—a confidence that I shall of course under no circumstances abuse—I was already wondering whether I had any right to intervene against this procedure and whether my intervention had even the remotest prospect of success. It was clear to me whom I must approach first: the commandant, of course. You have made that even clearer, though without doing anything in the way of strengthening my resolve; on the contrary, the sincerity of your conviction affects me deeply, even if it cannot distract me from my purpose.'

The officer, still without a word, turned to the machine, grasped one of the brass rods, and, leaning back slightly, looked up at the scriber as if checking whether everything was in order. The soldier and the condemned man appeared to have struck up a friendship; the condemned man was making signs to the soldier, difficult though this was with the straps pulled so tight; the soldier bent over him; the condemned man whispered something to him, and the soldier nodded.

The traveller went over to the officer and said, 'You don't know yet what I intend to do. I shall certainly be telling the commandant what I think of the procedure but not at a meeting; I shall do so in private; nor shall I be staying here long enough to be called into any meeting; I sail tomorrow morning or shall at least be rejoining my ship then.'

It did not look as if the officer had been listening. 'So the procedure didn't convince you,' he murmured, smiling as an old man smiles at the nonsense of a child and uses the smile to hide what he is really thinking. 'The time has come, then,' he concluded, and suddenly he looked at the traveller with eyes that were bright with a kind of challenge, almost a call to complicity.

'The time for what?' the traveller asked uneasily, but he received no answer.

'You're free,' the officer told the condemned man in his own language. The man did not believe it at first. 'I said you're free,' the officer repeated. For the first time genuine life came into the condemned man's face. Was this true? Was it just a whim of the officer's that might pass? Had the foreign visitor got him off? What was it? his face seemed to be asking. But not for long. Whatever it might be, he wanted, if he could, to be actually at liberty, and he began to shake himself about as much as the harrow allowed.

'You're tearing my straps!' the officer shouted. 'Keep still! We'll undo them for you!' He beckoned to the soldier, and the two of them set to work. The condemned man said nothing but chuckled quietly to himself, turning his face now to the left towards the officer, now to the right towards the soldier, and in between even towards the traveller.

'Pull him out,' the officer ordered the soldier. This had to be done with a certain amount of care because of the harrow. The condemned man already had a number of minor lacerations on his back as a result of his earlier impatience.

From this point on, however, the officer took very little notice of him. He went over to the traveller, pulled out the small leather wallet once more, leafed through it, eventually found the sheet he was looking for, and held it up for the traveller to look at. 'Read it,' he said. 'I can't,' said the traveller. 'I told you, I can't read those sheets.' 'Look carefully,' the officer said, moving round beside the traveller to read the sheet with him. When even this failed he stuck out his little finger and, holding it well away as if the sheet must not on any account be touched, ran it over the paper to make it easier for the traveller to read. The traveller really tried, hoping to be able to accommodate the officer at least in this respect, but he found it impossible. The officer then started spelling out what was written there and in the end read out the whole thing: '"Be just," it says. Now you can read it, surely?' The traveller bent so low over the paper that the officer, afraid he might touch it, moved it farther away; the traveller said nothing more, but it was obvious that he had still not been able to read it. '"Be just," it says,' the officer repeated. 'Possibly,' said the traveller. 'I believe you.' 'Right,' the officer said, partially satisfied at least, and he took the sheet with him and climbed the ladder; very carefully he bedded the sheet in the scriber and then appeared to rearrange the entire gear mechanism; this was an extremely laborious operation, some of the gear wheels evidently being very small, and from time to time the officer's head would disappear completely inside the scriber, so closely did he have to inspect the mechanism.

The traveller kept uninterrupted watch on the operation from below until his neck was stiff and his eyes ached from the sunlight flooding the sky. The soldier and the condemned man were concerned only with each other. The condemned man's shirt and trousers, which lay in the pit, were hauled out on the end of the soldier's bayonet. The shirt was horribly filthy, and the condemned man washed it in the bucket of water. When he then donned it and the trousers, neither the soldier nor he could refrain from laughing, because of course the garments had been slit up the back. Possibly in the belief that it was his duty to entertain the soldier, the condemned man pirouetted in front of him in his ruined clothing; the soldier, squatting on the ground, slapped his knees as he laughed. With the gentlemen present, however, they kept themselves under control.

When the officer had finally finished up on top, he smilingly surveyed the whole thing once more, part by part, slammed the scriber lid shut this time, it having been open until now, climbed down, looked into the pit and then at the condemned man, saw to his satisfaction that the latter had taken his clothes out, walked over to the bucket of water to wash his hands, noticed the revolting filth too late, was distressed that he could not now wash his hands, finally plunged them – it was an inadequate substitute but he had to bow to circumstances – into the sand, then stood up and began unbuttoning his tunic. As he did so the two lady's handkerchiefs that he had wedged inside the collar fell out into his hands. 'Here – your handkerchiefs,' he said, tossing them to the condemned man. And for the traveller's benefit he explained, 'Presents from the ladies.'

Despite the evident haste in which he removed his tunic and then all the rest of his clothes, he handled each garment with great care, even running his fingers deliberately over the silver braid of the tunic and shaking the odd tassel straight. It was then rather out of keeping with this carefulness that, as soon as he had finished with a garment, he tossed it into the pit with an impatient jerk. The last thing he was left with was his short sword on its sling. He unsheathed it, broke it into pieces, then, gathering everything together, the bits of sword, the scabbard, and the sling, hurled it all from him with such force that it hit the bottom of the pit with a clang.

He stood there, naked. The traveller bit his lips and said nothing. He knew what was going to happen, but he had no right to hinder the officer in any way. If the trial procedure to which the officer was so attached was really on the point of being abolished—possibly in consequence of actions to which the traveller, for his part, felt committed in advance—then he was acting quite properly; the traveller would have acted no differently in his place.

The soldier and the condemned man, understanding nothing, at first did not even watch. The condemned man was delighted to have his handkerchiefs back. His delight was short-lived, though, the soldier snatching them back with a swift, unforseeable movement. The condemned man then tried to pull the handkerchiefs out from behind the soldier's belt, where the latter had put them for safe keeping, but the soldier was on his guard. They went on struggling like this, half jokingly, and it was not until the officer was completely naked that they began to take notice. The condemned man in particular appeared to have sensed some kind of major reversal. What had been happening to him was now happening to the officer. Perhaps this time it would be taken to the last extreme. Probably the foreign traveller had given the order. Vengeance, then. Without himself having suffered all the way, he was going to be revenged all the way. A broad, soundless laugh materialised on his face and stayed there.

The officer, meanwhile, had turned to the machine. It had been clear enough all along how well he understood the machine, but now one might almost have been staggered by his handling of it and by its response. All he did was to hold a hand out towards the harrow and it

173

raised and lowered itself several times until it was in the
right position to receive him; he simply gripped the edge
of the bed and it began to vibrate; the stub of felt moved
towards him, you could see that the officer did not really
want to take it, but after only a moment's hesitation he
submitted and accepted it in his mouth. Everything was
ready, except that the straps still hung down at the sides,
but they were clearly superfluous; the officer did not need
to be strapped down. The condemned man, however,
noticing that the straps were undone and feeling that the
execution was incomplete if the straps were not fastened,
beckoned officiously to the soldier, and they ran to strap
the officer down. The officer had already stretched out a
foot to kick at the crank handle that would start the
scriber, but when he saw them coming he withdrew the
foot and allowed himself to be strapped down. Now, of
course, he could no longer reach the crank handle; neither
the soldier nor the condemned man would find it, and the
traveller was determined not to move. There was no need;
hardly was the last strap attached when the machine went
into operation; the bed vibrated, the needles danced over
the skin, the harrow swung to and fro. The traveller had
been staring at the sight for some time before he remembered that a wheel in the scriber ought to have been
grating; all was quiet, however, with not even the faintest
whirring to be heard.

Operating so quietly, the machine literally escaped the
traveller's attention. He looked across at the soldier and
the condemned man. The condemned man was the livelier
of the two, interested in everything about the machine,
bending down, stretching up, always with his index finger
extended to point something out to the soldier. The
traveller found this embarrassing. He was determined to
stay to the end, but he could not have put up with the sight
of those two for long. 'Go home,' he said. The soldier
might have been prepared to do so, but the condemned
man felt the order to be almost a punishment. Clasping his
hands together, he begged to be allowed to stay, and when
the traveller shook his head in adamant refusal he even

sank to his knees. Realizing that orders were useless here, the traveller was about to go over and chase the pair of them away when he became aware of a noise in the scriber. He looked up. Was that gear-wheel giving trouble after all? No, this was something else. Slowly the lid of the scriber rose higher and higher until it fell open completely. The cogs of a gear-wheel became visible, rising up, soon the whole wheel could be seen, it was as if some mighty force were squeezing the scriber, there was no room for this wheel, the wheel turned till it reached the edge of the scriber, tumbled down, rolled a little way in the sand, then fell over and lay still. But up in the scriber another was already emerging, many more followed, big ones, little ones, others virtually indistinguishable in size, the same thing happening to them all; surely the scriber must be empty now, you kept thinking, but then another, even more numerous cluster of them rose up, came tumbling down, rolled in the sand, and lay flat. Meanwhile the condemned man had forgotten all about the traveller's order; fascinated by the gear-wheels, he kept trying to catch one, urging the soldier to help him, but he drew his hand back in alarm each time because right behind came another wheel that, at least as it first started to roll, gave him a fright.

As for the traveller, he was deeply uneasy; the machine was obviously disintegrating; its easy action was an illusion; he felt he ought to be looking after the officer, now that the latter was no longer in a position to fend for himself. But while the fall of the gear-wheels had been occupying his whole attention he had neglected to keep an eye on the rest of the machine; now, the last gear-wheel having left the scriber, as he bent over the harrow he received another, even nastier surprise. The harrow was not inscribing, merely stabbing, and the bed, instead of turning the body over, merely thrust it, quivering, up at the needles. The traveller wanted to intervene, possibly to stop the whole process; this was not the torture the officer had wanted to achieve, this was plain murder. He reached out. But the harrow, with the body skewered on it, was

175

already canting up and over to one side, as it normally did only in the twelfth hour. Blood flowed in a hundred streams (unmixed with water, the water ducts too having failed this time). And now the last thing went wrong as well: the body failed to come off the long needles and, still gushing blood, hung above the pit without falling. The harrow tried to return to its original position, appeared to become aware that it was not yet free of its burden, and remained suspended over the pit. 'Come and help!' the traveller shouted to the soldier and the condemned man as he himself took hold of the officer's feet. He meant to push against the feet at his end, he wanted the others to go to the other side and take hold of the officer's head, and between them they would slowly lift him off the needles. The others, however, could not make up their minds to come; the condemned man actually turned away; the traveller had to go over to them and forcibly move them to the officer's head. In doing so he caught an almost involuntary glimpse of the face of the corpse. It was just as it had been in life, with no sign of the promised deliverance; what all the others had found in the machine, the officer had not found; his lips were pressed firmly together, his eyes were open and had the look of being alive, the expression in them was one of calm conviction, the tip of the great iron spike stuck out of his forehead.

As the traveller, with the soldier and the condemned man behind him, reached the first houses of the colony the soldier pointed to one and said, 'That's the tea-house.'

The ground floor of one of the buildings was occupied by a deep, low, cave-like room with smoke-blackened walls and ceiling. On the street side it was open along its whole width. There was little to distinguish the tea-house from the rest of the colony's buildings, which including the palatial quarters of the commandant were all in an advanced state of disrepair, yet on the traveller it had the effect of a reminder of the past, and he felt the power of an earlier age. He drew nearer, passed with his two attendants between the empty tables that stood in the street in front of the tea-house, and inhaled the cool, moist air coming from inside. 'The old man's buried here,' said the soldier. 'Chaplain wouldn't give him a plot in the cemetery. For a while they couldn't decide where to bury him, then in the end they buried him here. The officer won't have told you anything about that, because of course it's what he was most ashamed of. Once or twice he even tried to dig the old man up at night, but he always got chased away.' 'Where is the grave?' the traveller asked, unable to believe the soldier. Immediately the two of them, the soldier and the condemned man, ran ahead and pointed with outstretched hands to where the grave was. They led the traveller over to the rear wall, where customers were sitting at several of the tables. These were probably dockers, powerfully-built men with short, gleaming black beards. All sat jacketless, and their shirts were torn; they were poor, oppressed folk. As the traveller approached, some of them stood up, backed against the wall, and watched him expectantly. 'A foreigner,' went the whisper all around him, 'come to look at the grave.' They pushed one of the tables aside, and underneath there really was a gravestone. It was a simple stone and low enough to be concealed beneath a table. It bore an inscription in very small letters; the traveller had to kneel down to read it. It read: 'Here lies the old commandant. His followers, who now may bear no name, dug this grave for him and set up this stone. It is prophesied that the commandant will rise again after a certain number of years have elapsed and lead his followers out from this house to reconquer the colony. Wait in faith!' When the traveller, having read this, rose to his feet he saw the men standing around him and smiling as if they had read the inscription with him, found it ridiculous, and were inviting him to share their view. The traveller pretended not to have noticed, distributed a few coins among them, waited till the table had been pushed back over the grave, left the tea-house, and made his way to the harbour.

The soldier and the condemned man had come across

177

acquaintances in the tea-house who detained them. They must have quickly torn themselves away, however, because the traveller had only got as far as the middle of the long flight of stairs leading to the boats before they appeared in pursuit. Probably they wanted to make the traveller take them with him at the last moment. While he was negotiating with a boatman at the foot of the steps to take him out to the steamer, the other two came racing down the steps in silence, not daring to shout. But by the time they reached the bottom the traveller was already in the boat and the boatman was casting off. They could have leapt into the boat, but the traveller, picking up a heavy length of knotted rope from the floor of the boat and threatening them with it, prevented them from making the attempt.

A Country Doctor

for my father

(*Ein Landarzt*; these stories were written in the early part of 1917, except for *At the Door of the Law* and *A Dream*, which date from late 1914/early 1915; volume publication was by Kurt Wolff in late 1919.)

The new attorney

We have a new attorney, Dr Bucephalus. There is little in his outward appearance to recall the time when he was Alexander the Great's war-horse, though anyone familiar with the circumstances will spot things. Nevertheless, on the steps the other day I saw even a quite ingenous court usher, endowed with the expert eye of the humble racegoer, stare in amazement as the attorney, hoisting his legs high, strode up with each footfall ringing out on the marble.

On the whole the admission of Bucephalus has the authorities' approval. With remarkable understanding they say to themselves that, Bucephalus being in a difficult position with regard to the present-day social order, for that reason as well as on account of his historical importance he merits courtesy at the very least. Today—a fact no one can deny—there is no Alexander the Great. Plenty of people know how to kill; nor is there any shortage of the skill involved in hitting your friend with a spear hurled across the banqueting table; and there are many who, finding Macedonia too cramped, curse their father, Philip —but no one, no one is capable of leading the way to India. Even at that time the gates of India were beyond reach, but the king's sword pointed to where they were. Today the gates have been removed to a quite other, farther, and higher place; no one shows the way; many have swords, but only for waving about; and the eye that seeks to follow them becomes lost in confusion.

So perhaps it really is best to do as Bucephalus has done and immerse oneself in the statute books. Free, his flanks unburdened by the rider's loins, in quiet lamplight far from the din of Alexander's battles, he reads and turns the pages of our ancient codices.

A country doctor

I was in a quandary; I had an urgent journey to make; a dangerously-ill patient awaited me in a village ten miles away; dense snow flurries filled the distance between myself and him; I had a cart, a light one with large wheels, just right for our country lanes; wrapped in my fur coat, instrument case in hand, I was standing in the yard, all ready to go; but I had no horse, I had no horse. My own horse had lain down and died the night before, exhausted by this bitterly cold winter; my maid was now running round the village to obtain the loan of one; it was hopeless, though, I knew it, and with more and more snow falling on me, and myself becoming less and less mobile, I stood there in futile idleness. My maid appeared at the gate, alone, waving her lamp; of course—who was going to lend his horse for such a journey? Once again I paced across the yard; I could think of nothing I could do. In my worry and anguish I launched a kick at the flimsy door of the pigsty, which had been out of use for years. It flew open and swung to and fro on its hinges. Warmth emerged, and a smell like that of horses. A dim stable lantern swung from a cord inside. A man crouching in the low-roofed interior showed his frank, blue-eyed face. 'Shall I harness up?' he asked, crawling out on all fours. Not knowing what to say, I merely stooped down to see what else was in there. The maid was beside me. 'You never know what you've got tucked away in your own house,' she said, and we both laughed.

'Gee-up, brother, gee-up, sister!' the groom called, and one after the other two horses, powerful beasts with well-muscled flanks, forced their way out, legs tucked up to their bodies, lowering their shapely heads like camels, propelled by the sheer power of their twisting rumps and filling the doorway completely as they came. Next moment, there they stood on their long legs, bodies steaming thickly. 'Give him a hand,' I said, and the willing girl ran to help the groom with the cart harness. Hardly has she reached his side, however, when the groom embraces her and clamps his face to hers. She screams and comes running to me, the red imprint of two rows of teeth on her cheek. 'Brute,' I cry angrily, 'do you want me to take the whip to you?' But I remember immediately that he is a stranger, that I do not know where he comes from, and that he has volunteered his assistance where everyone else has let me down. As if he knows what I am thinking he does not take my threat amiss but, still busy with the horses, merely turns once in my direction. 'Get in,' he says, and indeed everything is ready. Aware that I have never ridden behind so fine a pair, I gaily climb in. 'I'll drive, though; you don't know the way,' I say. 'Of course,' he says. 'I'm not even coming; I'm staying with Rosy.' 'No,' screams Rosy, and with a just presentiment of the inevitability of her fate she goes running into the house; I hear the door chain rattle as she attaches it; I hear the bolt snap home; I see too how in the hall and as she races on through the rooms she turns out all the lights to make herself impossible to find. 'You come with me,' I tell the groom, 'or I'm not going, I don't care how urgent the trip is. I have no intention of handing the girl over to you as my fare.' 'Look alive there!' he says, clapping his hands together; the cart is whisked away like timber caught by the current; I just have time to hear the door of my house smash and splinter under the groom's assault before my eyes and ears are filled with a rushing that invades all my senses equally. But that too only for a moment, for as if my own gate led immediately into my patient's yard I find myself already there; the horses are waiting quietly; the snow has stopped falling; moonlight all around; the patient's parents come hurrying out of the house; his sister behind them; I am almost lifted from the cart; from their confused talk I can infer nothing; in the sick-room the air is barely breathable; the untended stove is smoking; I shall open the window; but first I want to see the patient. Thin, with no fever, neither cold nor warm, empty-eyed and

183

shirtless, the young man heaves himself up under the
quilt, clasps me round the neck, and whispers in my ear,
'Doctor, let me die.' I look about me; no one heard; the
parents are standing there, craning forward, waiting in
silence for my verdict; the sister has brought a chair for my
bag. I open the bag and search among my instruments; the
young man keeps reaching out towards me from the bed
to remind me of his request; I pick up a forceps, examine
it by the light of the candle, and put it back. 'Yes,' run my
sacrilegious thoughts, 'in cases like this the gods lend a
hand, send along the missing horse, add another for the
sake of speed, even go so far as to provide the groom—' At
this point I suddenly remember Rosy; what am I to do,
how shall I save her, how can I pull her out from under
that groom, ten miles from her and with ungovernable
horses in the shafts? These horses, who have now contrived to loosen the straps; push the windows—how, I
don't know—open from outside; stick a head each in
through them and, unperturbed by the family's screams,
are contemplating the patient. 'I'll be on my way again in a
moment,' I reflect, as if the horses were inviting me to
make a start, yet I allow the sister, who thinks me
overcome by the heat, to take my fur. I am offered a glass
of rum, and the old man claps me on the shoulder, this
sacrifice of his treasure justifying the familiarity. I shake
my head; in the narrow confines of the old man's mind I
would feel queasy; purely for this reason I decline the
drink. The mother, standing by the bed, lures me over to
it; I go and, as one of the horses whinnies noisily at the
ceiling, lay my head on the young man's chest, my wet
beard making him shiver. I find confirmed what I knew
already: the young man is in good health, with slightly
inadequate circulation, saturated with coffee by his anxious mother, but in good health and best kicked straight
out of bed. I am no Utopian, and I let him lie there. I am
employed by the local authority and do my duty to the full,
almost overdo it in fact. Poorly paid, I am nevertheless
generous and helpful to the poor. I must just look after
Rosy, then the young man can have his way and I, too,

want to die. What am I to do here in this endless winter!
My horse has perished, and no one in the village will lend
me his. I have to haul my pair out of the pigsty; had they
not happened to be horses I should have had to drive
sows. That's the way it is. And I nod to the family. They
know nothing about it, and if they did they would not
believe it. Writing out prescriptions is easy, but communicating with people beyond that is hard. That's the
end of my visit, then; once again I've been troubled
unnecessarily; well, I'm used to it; with the help of my
night bell the whole district makes a martyr of me; but that
I had to surrender Rosy as well this time, that lovely girl
who for years, almost without my being aware of her, has
been living in my house—this sacrifice is too great, and I
have somehow to justify it in my mind with stop-gap
subtleties lest I let fly at this family who with the best will in
the world cannot bring my Rosy back. But as I close my
bag and beckon for my fur, and the family stands there in
a body, the father sniffing at the glass of rum in his hand,
the mother, probably in disappointment at me—well, what
do people expect?—tearfully biting her lips, and the sister
waving a badly blood-stained handkerchief, I am prepared
in a way, under certain circumstances, to admit that the
young man may be ill after all. I go over to him, he smiles
at me as if I were bringing him perhaps the richest of rich
soups—ah, now both horses are whinnying; no doubt the
noise is ordained from on high with a view to facilitating
the examination—and I discover: yes, the young man is ill.
In his right side, in the pelvic region, a wound has opened
as large as the palm of a hand. Rosy in colour, many-
shaded, dark inside and lighter towards the edges, delicately textured, the blood gathered in blotches, gaping like
an open-cast mine. From a distance, that is. Seen from
close to, there is an added complication. It's a sight to
make anyone whistle under his breath. Worms of the
thickness and length of my little finger, rosy with their own
blood as well as being flecked with it, are fastened inside
the wound, wriggling their little white heads and many
legs towards the light. Poor lad, you're past helping. I have

185

found your great wound; this flower in your side is destroying you. The family is happy to see me doing something; the sister tells her mother, the mother the father, and the father several guests who tiptoe in, arms outstretched for balance, through the moonlight of the open door. 'Will you save me?' the young man whispers with a sob, blinded by the life in his wound. That's the way they are, the people in my district. Always asking the impossible of their doctor. They have lost the old faith; the priest sits at home and picks the vestments to pieces one by one; but the doctor, with his sensitive, surgical hand, is expected to do everything. Be that as it may: I didn't volunteer; use me for sacred ends and I'll submit even to that; what more can I wish for, an old country doctor bereft of my maid! And they come, the family and the village elders, and they strip me; a school choir with the teacher at its head stands outside the house and sings the simplest of tunes to the words:

'Strip him, then he will heal,
And if he does not, kill him!
He's only a doctor, only a doctor,
Only a doctor, that's all.'

Then I am stripped and, threading my fingers in my beard, I look calmly at the people with my head bent. My composure is complete, I am above them all and remain so, though little good it does me, because now they lift me up by my head and feet and carry me over to the bed. They lay me on the wall side, where the wound is. Then they all leave the room; the door is pulled to; the singing stops; clouds cover the moon; the bedclothes lie warmly about me; like shadows, the horses' heads sway to and fro in the window apertures. 'You know,' a voice says in my ear, 'I have very little confidence in you. You too were simply flung down somewhere; you didn't get here on your own two feet. Instead of helping me you take up room in my deathbed. I feel like scratching your eyes out.' 'Right you are,' I say, 'it's disgraceful. But then I am a doctor. What am I to do? Believe me, it isn't easy for me either.' 'You expect me to be satisfied with that excuse?

Oh, I'll have to be, I suppose. I'm always having to be satisfied with things. I was born with a beautiful wound; it's all I was equipped with.' 'Where you go wrong, my young friend,' I say, 'is in missing the wood for the trees. I have been in all the sickrooms the length and breadth of this district and I can assure you: your wound isn't so bad. Bitten at an acute angle with two blows of the axe. Lots of people offer their sides and hardly hear the axe in the forest, let alone the fact that it's coming nearer.' 'Is that really how it is, or are you deluding me in my fever?' 'That's how it is, you can take a public-health officer's word for it as you go.' And he took it and was still. Now, however, it was time to think of saving myself. The horses still stood loyally in their places; clothes, fur coat, and bag were gathered up in an instant; I did not want to waste time getting dressed; if the horses showed the same speed as on the outward journey, I should virtually be leaping straight from this bed into mine. Obediently one horse withdrew from the window; I tossed the bundle into the cart; my fur overshot, only catching on a hook by one sleeve. Near enough. I swung myself onto the horse's back. The reins dangling loose, one horse barely attached to the other, the cart following anyhow, and the fur being dragged through the snow behind. 'Look alive there!' I said, but it didn't work; with the slowness of old men we moved off into the snowy wilderness; for ages we could hear behind us the children's new but mistaken song: 'Be glad, ye patients, be glad; the doctor has joined you in bed!'

I shall never get home like this; my flourishing practice is lost; a successor is robbing me, but to no purpose since he cannot replace me; in my house the loathsome groom wreaks his havoc; Rosy is his victim; I refuse to imagine it. Naked, exposed to the frost of this most wretched of times, with an earthly cart and unearthly horses, I roam about, an old man. My fur coat is hanging from the back of the cart but I cannot reach it, and no one from the agile rabble of patients lifts a finger. Duped! Deceived! One response to a mis-ring of the night-bell—and there's no making amends.

In the gallery

Were some frail, tubercular trick rider on her swaying
mount to be driven round and round the ring before an
unflagging audience by her pitiless, whip-swinging boss
for months on end without interruption, whirling about
on the horse's back, blowing kisses, ducking and weaving
from the waist, and were this act together with the
continuous blare of the band and the roaring of the
ventilators to go on and on and on down the endless grey
avenues of the future, accompanied by the fade and swell
of the clapping of applauding hands that are really steam
hammers—perhaps then some young spectator in the
gallery would run down the long flight of steps between
the rows, burst into the ring, and call a: Halt! through the
fanfares of the constantly accommodating orchestra.

Given, however, that that is not the way it is; a lovely
lady in white and red comes flying in through curtains
proudly parted for her by liveried attendants; the ring-
master, devotedly seeking her glance, breathes his way
towards her in an animal crouch; anxiously lifts her onto
the dappled grey as if she were his darling granddaughter
off on a dangerous journey; cannot bring himself to crack
the whip; eventually, with an effort, resoundingly does so;
runs along beside the horse with his mouth agape; watches
eagle-eyed each of her leaps; can barely comprehend her
skill; shouts attempted warnings in English; furiously
exhorts the grooms with the hoops to take the greatest
care; heralds the climactic somersault by turning to the
band with arms upraised, asking for silence; and in the
end lifts the girl down from the trembling horse, kisses her
on both cheeks, and considers every ovation to be less than
her due; while she, with him supporting her, stretches up
on tiptoe, wreathed in dust, arms outspread and little head
thrown back in her desire to share this happiness with the
entire circus—given all that. the young man in the gallery,

laying his face on the balustrade and sinking into the final march as into a sombre dream, weeps without knowing it.

A leaf from the past

Much would seem to have been left undone as regards the defence of our fatherland. We never used to worry about it, we just went about our work, but recent events have been giving us cause for concern.

I own a shoemaker's shop in the square fronting the imperial palace. Hardly have I pulled my shutters up at first light when I see that the mouths of all the streets around the square are occupied by armed men. They are not our troops, though, but clearly nomads from the north. How they have done it I do not know, but they have pushed right through to the capital, which is a very long way indeed from the frontier. Anyway, there they are; there seem to be more of them each morning.

Being nomads, they sleep out of doors, for they abhor houses. They busy themselves honing swords, sharpening arrows, and doing exercises on horseback. They have turned this quiet square, which used to be kept scrupulously clean, into one enormous stable. We do occasionally try to get out in front of our shops and clear away at least the worst of the muck, but it happens less and less often because our efforts, besides being futile, involve the risk of our being trampled by their wild horses or cut with their whips.

One cannot talk to the nomads. They do not speak our language; indeed they hardly have one of their own. They communicate among themselves after the fashion of jackdaws. The cry of the jackdaw is constantly in one's ears. Our way of life and our institutions make no sense to them and are of no interest to them. Consequently they take the same negative attitude to any kind of sign language. You can dislocate your jaw and you can twist your wrists out of joint; they'll not have understood you and they never will. They frequently pull faces, turning up the whites of their eyes and foaming at the mouth, but it is

191

not with the intention of saying anything nor even to
inspire fright; they do it because that is their way. What
they need they take. Not that they can be said to use
violence. One steps aside when they grab and lets them
help themselves.

They have had many a choice item from my own stock,
though I cannot complain when I look at what has
happened to the butcher opposite, for example. Hardly
has he brought in his supplies when everything is torn
from his hands to be devoured by the nomads. Their
horses, too, eat meat; often a rider will be lying beside his
horse and both will be feeding off the same piece, one at
each end. The butcher is apprehensive and dare not stop
his deliveries. We understand that, though, and we pass
the hat round to support him. If the nomads no longer
had their meat, who knows what they might get up to; in
fact, who knows what they will get up to even having their
meat every day?

The butcher's latest idea was that he could at least save
himself the trouble of slaughtering, and one morning he
brought in a live bullock. He'd better not do that again. I
must have spent an hour lying flat on the floor at the very
back of my workshop with all my clothes and blankets and
pillows piled on top of me, purely in order not to hear the
bellowing as the nomads pounced on the bullock from all
sides and ripped out bits of its warm flesh with their teeth.
Not until long after silence had returned did I dare go out;
like topers around a wine barrel, they lay in an exhausted
circle around the bullock's remains.

That was when I thought I caught sight of the emperor
himself at one of the palace windows; he never comes to
these outer apartments normally, always keeping to the
innermost garden; but on this occasion—so at least it
seemed to me—there he stood at the window, with head
bowed, watching the goings-on outside his palace.

'How will things turn out?' we are all wondering. 'How
long will we suffer this burden and torment? The imperial
palace, having lured the nomads here, is incapable of
driving them away. The gate remains closed; the guard,

who used always to be marching in and out with a great deal of ceremony, stay inside behind barred windows. The salvation of the fatherland is in the hands of us artisans and tradespeople; we, however, are not up to such a task, nor have we ever pretended to be so. It is all a misunderstanding, and it will be the ruin of us.'

At the door of the law

Outside the law there stands a doorkeeper. A man from the country comes up to the doorkeeper and asks to be admitted to the law. But the doorkeeper says he cannot admit him at the moment. The man thinks about it and then asks whether in that case he will be allowed in later. 'Possibly,' says the doorkeeper, 'but not at the moment.' The door of the law standing open as always and the doorkeeper stepping aside, the man bends down to look through into the interior. The doorkeeper notices and says with a laugh, 'If you're that keen why don't you try to get in despite my ban? But remember: I am powerful. And I am only the lowest-ranking doorkeeper. From room to room there are other doorkeepers, each more powerful than the one before. The mere sight of the third one is already more than even I can stand.' The man from the country had not anticipated such difficulties; access to the law ought to be available to everyone at all times, he thinks, but after a closer look at the fur-coated doorkeeper, at his great pointed nose and his long, straggly, black Tartar beard, he decides that he will in fact wait until he receives permission to enter. The doorkeeper gives him a stool and lets him sit down to one side of the door. There he sits for days, for years on end. He makes many attempts to be let in and wearies the doorkeeper with his requests. The doorkeeper often starts interrogating him in a small way, asking him about his home and about many other things, but his questions are of the apathetic kind that high-ups ask, and he always finishes by repeating that he cannot let him in yet. The man, who had packed a good deal of equipment for the journey, invests everything, no matter how great its value, in attempts to bribe the doorkeeper. The latter accepts it all but says as he does so, 'I'm accepting this only lest you should think you'd left some stone unturned.' Throughout those many years the man observes the doorkeeper almost without interruption. He forgets about the other doorkeepers, and this first one seems to him the only obstacle to his entering the law. He curses his ill luck, recklessly and out loud in the early years, later, as he ages, only muttering under his breath. He grows childlike, and having in his years of studying the doorkeeper come to know even the fleas in the man's fur collar he pleads with the fleas, too, to help him by persuading the doorkeeper to change his mind. Eventually his sight begins to fail, and he does not know whether it is really growing darker around him or whether his eyes are deceiving him. He does, however, now discern in the darkness a brilliance that burst inextinguishably from the door of the law. He has not long to live. Before he dies, everything he has learnt in the entire time becomes concentrated in his head into a question that he has not asked the doorkeeper hitherto. He beckons him to approach, for his body is growing stiff and he can no longer get up. The doorkeeper has to bend right down to him, the difference in height between them having altered very much to the man's disadvantage. 'What do you want to know now?' the doorkeeper asks. 'You're insatiable.' 'Everybody seeks the law,' says the man, 'so how is it that in all these years no one but me has demanded admittance?' The doorkeeper sees that it is all over for the man, and to penetrate his growing deafness he shouts at him, 'No one else could gain admittance here because this entrance was meant for you alone. Now I'm going to close it.'

Jackals and Arabs

We were encamped at the oasis. My companions were
asleep. The tall, white figure of an Arab walked by me;
having seen to the camels, he was going to his sleeping-
place.

I lay back in the grass; I tried to sleep; I couldn't; a
distant jackal howled his lament; I sat up again. And what
had been so far away was suddenly quite close. A pack of
jackals milling round me; matt-gold eyes gleaming, van-
ishing; lean bodies ranged in nimble animation, as if at the
dictate of a whip.

One came from behind, pushed through under my arm,
pressing against me as if in need of my warmth, then stood
before me, almost eye to eye, and spoke:

'I am the oldest jackal in these parts. I am happy to be
still alive to welcome you. I had almost given up hope. You
see, we've been waiting for you for ages; my mother
waited, and her mother—in fact all their mothers, right
back to the mother of all jackals, believe me!'

'I'm surprised to hear that,' I said, forgetting to set light
to the pile of wood that lay to hand and so hold off the
jackals with its smoke. 'I'm most surprised to hear that. It's
quite by chance that I have come down from the far north
and am here on a short journey. What is it you want,
jackals?'

Evidently emboldened by this perhaps over-friendly
reception, they drew the circle tighter around me; they
were breathing fast and snarling.

'We know,' the oldest jackal began, 'that you are from
the north; hence our hopes. It is the home of the kind of
intelligence that, here among the Arabs, simply does not
exist. There's not one spark of intelligence to be struck
from their cold arrogance, take my word for it. They kill
animals to eat them; carrion they spurn.'

'Keep your voice down,' I said. 'There are Arabs

sleeping nearby.'

'You really are from foreign parts,' said the jackal, 'or you would know that never in all history has a jackal been afraid of an Arab. What, are we to fear them? Is it not bad enough that we should be outcasts among such people?'

'Possibly,' I said, 'possibly. I don't presume to pass judgement on matters so far removed from my own concerns; it seems to be a very ancient feud; a blood feud, probably; so it will probably take bloodshed to end it.'

'You are very wise,' the old jackal said; and they all began to breathe even faster; their lungs racing, though they were standing still; a sour smell, which at times was bearable only with clenched teeth, emanated from their open mouths. 'You are very wise; what you say is in accordance with our ancient law. So we shed their blood, and the feud is over.'

'Oh!' I said, more fiercely than I had intended, 'they will fight; they will mow you down in packs with their guns.'

'You misunderstand us,' he said, 'in the manner of men, which I see is not lost even in the far north. We shall not kill them. Not all the waters of the Nile could wash us clean. Why, we run at the mere sight of them alive, seeking the purer air of the desert, which is why it is our home.'

And all the jackals around me, who had meanwhile been joined by many more from farther off, lowered their heads between their forelegs and began to clean them with their paws; it was as if they were trying to conceal a loathing so appalling that it made me want to take a great leap out of their circle and escape.

'So what do you mean to do?' I inquired, trying to get up; but I could not move; two young animals had come up behind me and sunk their teeth into my robe and shirt; I had to remain seated. 'They're holding your train,' the old jackal explained earnestly, 'a mark of respect.' 'Well, tell them to let me go!' I shouted. I turned to them: 'Let go!' 'They will, of course,' said the old jackal, 'if you insist. Only it takes a little time, because they have bitten in deep, following our custom, and must ease their teeth apart slowly. Meanwhile, hear our plea.' 'Your behaviour has hardly put me in a receptive mood,' I said. 'Don't hold our clumsiness against us,' he said, and it was the first use he had made of the plaintive sound of his natural voice. 'We are poor beasts, we have only our teeth; for everything we want to do, good or bad, we have nothing but our teeth.' 'What do you want, then?' I asked, not much appeased.

'Master,' he cried out, and all the jackals howled; in the far, far distance it sounded to me like a tune. 'Master, you shall end the feud that divides the world. You are as the one our fathers prophesied would do this. We must have peace from the Arabs; air we can breathe; our outlook from horizon to horizon purged of their presence; not one cry of ram slaughtered by Arab; a quiet end for all animals; quietly let them lie for us to drink their blood and pick their bones clean. Purity, purity is all our desire,'—by now they were weeping and sobbing—'How, oh how do you suffer this life, oh noble soul, oh sweet and precious vitals? Filth is their white; filth is their black; their beards are an abomination; a glimpse of the corners of their eyes is enough to make one's stomach heave; and when they raise their arms their armpits are a gaping hell. Therefore, oh master, dear lord and master, lend us your all-powerful hands, lend us your all-powerful hands—take these scissors and cut their throats!' And at a jerk of his head a jackal came up with, on one fang, a small pair of sewing-scissors, coated with ancient rust.

'Hah, the scissors at last—right, that's enough!' cried the Arab in charge of our caravan, who had crept up on us from downwind and was now brandishing his colossal whip.

They hurriedly dispersed, but some way off they stopped and crouched close together, hundreds of animals so tight-packed and still as to look like a narrow pen wreathed with will-o'-the-wisps.

'Well, master, there's another spectacle for you,' said the Arab, laughing as heartily as the reticence of his race allowed. 'So you know what the animals are after?' I asked. 'Of course, master,' he said. 'It's common knowledge; for as long as there have been Arabs these scissors have wandered the desert, and they will continue to be with us until the end of time. Every European is offered them to do the great deed; every European is the very man whom they see as being called. They cherish a quite absurd hope, these animals; they are fools, complete fools. We love them for it; they are our dogs; handsomer than yours. Look—a camel died in the night; I've had it brought over.'

Four bearers arrived and dropped the great corpse in front of us. Almost before it hit the ground the jackals raised their cry. As if drawn irresistibly on individual ropes they approached with hesitant tread, bellies dragging the ground. They had forgotten the Arabs, forgotten their hatred; the all-smothering presence of the reeking carcass held them spellbound. Already one was at the throat, and his first bite found the artery. He was like a tiny, frenzied pump trying both determinedly and desperately to put out much too big a fire, every muscle in his body twitching and tugging under the skin. Soon they were all similarly engaged, piled up high on the carcass.

Suddenly the chief Arab's stinging whip was lashing at them this way and that. They lifted their heads; besotted and only half-aware; saw the Arabs standing there; caught a taste of the lash on their snouts; sprang back and retreated a little way. But by now the camel's blood lay in steaming pools; in several places its body had been ripped wide open. They could not resist; back they came; back went the whipper's arm; I checked it.

'You're right, master,' he said. 'It's their job—let them get on with it; anyway, it's time to move off. So you've seen them. Wonderful animals, eh? And how they hate us!'

A mine visit

The top engineers are down the mine with us today. The management has issued some directive or other for laying new tunnels, and the engineers have come to do the preliminary surveying. How young those people are, and already so different from one another! They have all developed independently, and their natures freely exhibit defined lines even in these early years.

One of them, dark-haired and vivacious, ran his eyes over everything.

A second, armed with a notebook, made notes as he went, looking about him, comparing, jotting things down.

A third walked stiffly upright with his hands in his pockets, so that everything about him was under tension; he maintained a dignified bearing; only his continual lip-chewing betrayed his impatient, irrepressible youth.

A fourth was explaining things—unasked—to the third; smaller than him, trotting along beside him like a petitioner, he appeared, with his forefinger perpetually in the air, to be reciting a litany on the subject of everything to be seen here.

A fifth, possibly the highest-ranking, kept company with no one; one minute he was in front, next minute he was bringing up the rear; the group took its step from him; he looked wan and frail; responsibility has hollowed out his eye-sockets; he repeatedly pressed a hand to his forehead in thought.

The sixth and seventh walked with a slight stoop, heads together, arm in arm, conversing intimately; were this not obviously our coal mine and our place of work in the deepest of its tunnels, one might have taken these gaunt, beardless gentlemen with their bulbous noses for young priests. One spent most of the time chuckling to himself with a cat-like purr; the other, also smiling, was the speaker and appeared to be beating time to his words with his free hand. How sure these two must be of their position, how much our mine must already owe to them, despite their youth, for them to be able, here, on so important an inspection carried out in the presence of their boss, coolly to concern themselves exclusively with their own affairs or at least with matters having no connection with the business in hand. Or could it perhaps be that, for all their laughter and lack of attentiveness, they were fully aware of all they needed to be aware of? One hardly likes to venture a firm opinion regarding such gentlemen.

On the other hand there is no doubt at all that the eighth had his mind incomparably more on the job than these two or indeed any of the others. He needed to touch everything and give it a tap with the little hammer he was forever taking out of his pocket and putting back there. Occasionally, disregarding his smart clothes, he knelt down in the dirt and tapped the floor; then, walking on, he would tap the walls as he passed or the ceiling above his head. Once he stretched out full-length on the floor and lay quite still; we were beginning to think something had happened to him; but then with a little jerk of his slim body he sprang to his feet: he had simply been making another check. We reckon we know our mine and its rock strata, but we cannot understand what that engineer kept on investigating in this way.

A ninth was pushing a kind of cart, rather like a child's perambulator, containing the measuring instruments. Extremely expensive equipment bedded in a thick layer of the finest cotton wool. Actually the attendant ought to have been pushing the cart, but it had not been entrusted to him; an engineer had had to step in, and one could see he did the job with pleasure. He was in all probability the youngest; he may not even understand all the instruments as yet, but his eyes were on them constantly, with the result that at times he was almost in danger of running the cart into a wall.

There was another engineer, however, walking alongside, who prevented this from happening. He evidently knew the instruments inside out and appeared to be their actual custodian. From time to time he took a piece of equipment out without stopping the cart, peered through it, screwed or unscrewed, shook or tapped it, held it to his ear and listened; and finally, with the person pushing usually coming to a halt, laid the tiny thing, which from a distance was barely visible, very carefully back in the cart. He tended to lord it a bit, this engineer, but solely on behalf of the equipment. Ten paces from the approaching cart we were expected to step aside at a wordless wave of his finger, even where there was no room to do so.

Behind these two gentlemen walked the attendant, with nothing to do. The gentlemen, understandably in view of their vast knowledge, have long since shed all pride, whereas the attendant has apparently gathered it all up in his person. With one hand behind his back and the other in front of him, stroking the gilt buttons or the fine cloth of his livery coat, he gave frequent nods to right and left as if we had saluted him and he were acknowledging our salute or as if he were assuming we had saluted him but could not, from his great height, verify whether we had done so. We did not salute him, of course, although one might almost have supposed, from his appearance, that there was something awesome about being office attendant to the mine management. When he had gone past we laughed, but since not even a clap of thunder could have caused him to turn round he retains a quality of incomprehensibility in our estimation.

Not much more work will be done today; the interruption went on for too long; a visit like that takes away all thought of work. One is far too tempted to gaze after the gentlemen into the darkness of the pilot tunnel down which they have all disappeared. In any case our shift is nearly finished; we shall not be seeing the gentlemen come back.

The next village

My grandfather used to say, 'Life is astonishingly short. As I look back on it now it becomes so telescoped in my mind that, for example, I have difficulty in understanding how a young man can come to a decision to ride to the next village without being afraid that—leaving possible misfortunes quite out of account—even the span of a normal, fortune-favoured existence will be wholly inadequate for the trip.'

A message from the emperor

The emperor—so the story goes—has sent you, his wretched subject, a shadow that has fled to almost vanishing-point remoteness from the imperial sun, the emperor has from his deathbed sent you, personally, a message. He made the messenger kneel at his bedside, and he whispered the message in his ear; so concerned was he about it that he had the man whisper it back to him. With a nod he confirmed that the recitation had been correct. And in the presence of the entire company assembled to witness his death—all walls that were in the way have been knocked down and on the broad, soaring sweep of the staircase the notables of the empire are forgathered in a circle—in the presence of all these people he has dispatched the messenger. The messenger is already on his way; a powerful, indefatigable man; stretching now this arm, now that arm before him, he forces a path for himself through the throng; whenever he encounters resistance he points to his breast, where the sun sign is; and he is making good progress, better than anyone else would. But the throng is so vast, their dwellings endless. Were he suddenly in open country, how he would fly, and it would doubtless not be long before you heard the majestic pounding of his fists on your door. Instead of that, how unavailing are his efforts; he is still pushing his way through the apartments of the innermost palace; he will never get beyond them; and if he did, nothing would be gained; he would have to fight his way down the stairs; and if he succeeded in doing that, nothing would be gained; he would still have the courtyards to cross; and beyond the courtyards the other, outer palace to penetrate; and more staircases and courtyards; and yet a third palace; and so on for millennium after millennium; and were he finally to burst from the outermost gate—but it can never, never happen—the capital would lie before him, the mid-point of the world, its lees piled high. No one gets through this far and certainly not with a message from a dead man. But you, you sit at your window and dream about it as evening comes.

The householder's concern

Some say the word Odradek is Slavonic in origin and seek to trace its derivation on that basis. Others believe it was originally German and was merely influenced by the Slavonic. The uncertainty surrounding both interpretations, however, suggests that perhaps neither is correct, particularly since neither of them furnishes a meaning for the word.*

No one, of course, would bother to pursue such researches were there not actually a creature called Odradek. It looks at first glance like a flat, star-shaped spool; it even appears to be wound with thread, or rather with a lot of old odds and ends of thread knotted together, some of them tangled together, and comprising a great variety of types and colours. But it is not just a spool, because projecting from the centre of the star is a little rod forming a cross-piece, with another little rod extending from it at right angles. By means of this latter rod on one side and one of the rays of the star on the other side, the whole structure is able to stand upright as if on two legs.

It is tempting to suppose that the thing once had some practical form and is now simply broken, but this does not appear to be the case; at least, nothing points to its being so; there are no stumps or fractures visible that might suggest anything of the kind; for all its seeming uselessness, the whole structure appears self-contained in its way. That, incidentally, is the most that can be said on the subject, because Odradek is quite exceptionally nimble and there is no catching him.

He stays by turns in the attic, on the stairs, in the

---

* Kafka made it up, and the critics are still divided as to what it stands for (*Tr.*)

corridors, and in the hall. Sometimes he disappears for months on end, having no doubt moved into other houses, but then inevitably he returns to our house. Sometimes, when one steps outside the door and he is leaning against the railings a little way down the steps, one feels like accosting him. One doesn't ask him any difficult questions, of course, but treats him—if only because of his diminutive size—like a child. 'What's your name?' one inquires. 'Odradek,' he says. 'And where do you live?' 'No fixed abode,' he replies with a laugh, but it is only the kind of laugh that can be produced without lungs. It sounds something like the rustle of fallen leaves. That is usually the end of the conversation. Incidentally, not even these answers are always forthcoming; often he is silent for long periods, like the wood he seems to consist of.

In vain I ask myself what will become of him. Will he ever die? Everything that dies has previously had some kind of goal, some kind of activity at which it has worn itself down; with Odradek this is not the case. Is he, for example, likely one day to go rolling down the stairs, trailing thread behind him, at the feet of my children and grandchildren? Clearly he does no one any harm; yet the idea of his outliving me, on top of everything else, is one I find almost painful to contemplate.

Eleven sons

I have eleven sons.

The first is very plain in appearance, but he is serious and intelligent; even so, while loving him as my child as I love all the others, I hold him in no great esteem. His thinking strikes me as too elementary. He looks neither to right nor left, nor does he look very far; he goes round and round within his limited circle of ideas or rather spins on his axis.

The second is handsome, slim, well-built; his on-guard position when fencing is a delight to see. He too is intelligent, but he is also a man of the world; he has seen a great deal, so that even our indigenous nature appears to be on more intimate terms with him than with those who stayed at home. Yet undoubtedly .this advantage is not wholly and not even in essence the product of his having travelled; rather it has to do with the boy's quality of inimitability, which is acknowledged by all who, for example, set out to emulate his almost savagely controlled multiple-somersault dive into water. Courage and aspiration last till the end of the springboard, but there, instead of taking off, the emulator sits down abruptly and raises apologetic arms.—Yet despite all this (I ought after all to rejoice over such a child) my relationship to him is not unclouded. His left eye is slightly smaller than his right and blinks a great deal; only a minor flaw, admittedly, making his face even jauntier than it would otherwise have been, and in the light of his unapproachably self-contained nature no one would single out that smaller, blinking eye for criticism. I, his father, do so. It is not of course the physical flaw that pains me but a minor irregularity in his mind that in some way corresponds to it, some poison wandering through his bloodstream, some inability to round off the structure—visible to me alone—of his life. On the other hand, of course, it is precisely this that makes him a true son of mine, for this flaw of his is at the same time the flaw of our whole family and has merely become obtrusive in this son.

The third son is also handsome, but it is not the kind of handsomeness I like. It is the handsomeness of the singer: the bold mouth; the dreamy eye; the head that needs a backcloth to have its effect; the hugely bulging chest; the hands that are quick to fly up and much too quick to fall; the legs that shilly-shally because they cannot take the strain. And that is not all: his tone lacks fullness; deceives momentarily; causes the connoisseur to prick up his ears; but soon runs short of breath.—Although on the whole there is every temptation to parade this son, I much prefer to keep him hidden. He does not push himself forward, though not for example because he knows his shortcomings but from sheer innocence. Also he feels out of place in our day; as if, while still belonging to my family, he belonged in addition to another that were forever lost to him, he is frequently out of sorts and nothing can cheer him up.

My fourth son is perhaps the easiest of all to get along with. A true child of his time, he is understood by everybody, standing on universally common ground, and everybody is inclined to nod assent to him. Possibly this general recognition lends his character a certain lightness, his movements a certain ease, his opinions a quality of nonchalance. Some of his statements one would like to repeat over and over again, but only some of them because, all in all, he suffers, again, from an excess of fluency. He is like someone who takes off magnificently, parts the air like a bird, yet still ends up in dreariness and dust, a nonentity. Thoughts like these mar the sight of this child for me.

The fifth son is kind and good; promised very much less than he has produced; used to be so insignificant that one literally felt alone in his presence; but has nevertheless achieved a certain standing. Asked how this happened, I would find it difficult to answer. Possibly innocence does still break through the tumult of the elements in this world

more easily than anything else, and he is certainly innocent. Possibly too innocent. Friendly towards everybody.
Possibly too friendly. I admit to feeling uncomfortable
when someone praises him to me. Surely it is cheapening
praise to praise so obviously praiseworthy a person as my
son.

My sixth son seems, at least at first sight, to be the most
pensive of them all. A misery and yet at the same time a
chatterbox. Consequently it is not easy to get the better of
him. If he is losing, he lapses into invincible sadness; if he
is on top, he stays there by chattering. Yet he is not
incapable of a kind of self-forgetting passion; in full
daylight he often fights his way down the avenues of
thought as in a dream. Without being ill—on the contrary,
he enjoys excellent health—he occasionally stumbles, particularly in the twilight, but he needs no help, does not fall.
Possibly his physical development is to blame for this
phenomenon in that he is much too tall for his age. This
makes him ugly overall, despite strikingly attractive details
such as his hands and feet, for example. His forehead is
ugly, too, both the skin and the bone structure having a
shrunken quality.

The seventh son is possibly more mine than any of the
others. The world does not appreciate him; it does not
understand his particular kind of wit. I do not overrate
him; he is slight enough, I know; were the world's only
failing its inability to appreciate him, it would still be
faultless. But within the family I would not be without this
son. He contributes both a restlessness and a respect for
tradition, and he blends the two, at least as I feel it, into an
incontestable whole. He himself, however, is the last
person to know what to do with that whole; he will never
set the wheel of the future spinning; yet this tendency of
his is so cheering, so hopeful; I wish he had children and
they had children of their own. Unfortunately my wish
does not look like being fulfilled. With a complacency that,
though I understand it, I find most undesirable, and that
is moreover in magnificent contrast to the opinion of those
around him, he loafs about on his own, taking no notice of

girls, yet will never lose his good humour.

My eighth son is my problem child, and I do not really know why. He looks at me like a stranger, while I feel a deep, fatherly attachment to him. Time has healed a great deal, but I used sometimes to start trembling at the very thought of him. He is going his own way; has broken off all contact with me; and will undoubtedly, with his hard head and small, athletic body—just his legs were very weak when he was a boy, but that may have corrected itself in the mean time—get by wherever he pleases. There have been many times when I felt like calling him back, asking how he was doing, why he cut himself off from his father in that way, and what he was basically up to, but he is so far away now and so much time has gone by, let things stay the way they are. I hear he is the only one of my sons to wear a full beard, which is not of course attractive on so short a man.

My ninth son is extremely elegant and has that look that is designed to charm women. So charming is it that I am occasionally seduced myself, aware though I am that literally all that is needed to efface that unearthly lustre is a wet sponge. But the odd thing about the boy is that he does not even set out to seduce; he would be happy to spend his whole life lying on the couch, squandering his gaze on the ceiling or, for preference, letting it rest beneath his eyelids. In this, his favourite position, he speaks with pleasure and not a little skill; tersely and vividly; only within narrow limits, though; if he oversteps those, which given their narrowness is inevitable, his speech becomes quite empty. One would signal him to stop if one had any hope of his sleep-filled eyes registering the gesture.

My tenth son is considered an insincere character. I wish neither wholly to deny such a failing nor wholly to confirm it. What is certain is that anyone who sees him approaching, clothed in a solemnity far beyond his years, in his invariably tightly-buttoned frock coat and his ancient but meticulously clean black hat, with his stiff features, his slightly protruding chin, his eyelids hanging heavily over his eyes, and with, occasionally, two fingers laid upon his lips—anyone who sees him approaching like that thinks: the man is an almighty hypocrite. But just listen to him speak! Sensibly; with deliberation; briefly and to the point; intercepting questions with mischievous vivacity; in astonishing, self-evident, delighted agreement with the world at large; an agreement that necessarily straightens his neck and lifts his head up higher. Many people who think themselves very clever and who, ostensibly for this reason, feel put off by his appearance have been powerfully attracted by what he says. But there are others who, indifferent to his appearance, nevertheless find what he says hypocritical. I as his father am reluctant to decide the matter here, though I must admit that those of the latter opinion are, at all events, more worthy of note than those holding the former.

My eleventh son is a delicate creature, probably the weakest of my sons; yet decpetive in his weakness; you see, he can be strong and determined at times, though even then it is his weakness that is somehow fundamental. Not that it is a weakness to be ashamed of but rather something that presents itself as weakness only on this earth of ours. Is not even readiness for take-off a kind of weakness, for example, consisting as it does in swaying and uncertainty and fluttering? My son exhibits something of the sort. Such qualities do not of course please a father; they are after all clearly bent on destroying the family. Sometimes he looks at me as if to say, 'I'll take you with me, father.' At such times I think: 'You're the last person I'd put my trust in.' And again his look seems to say, 'Well, as long as I'm the last, at least.'

Those are the eleven sons.

A case of fratricide

It has been proved that the murder happened as follows:

Around nine in the evening of that moonlit night Schmar, the murderer, positioned himself at the corner round which Wese, the victim, must come in passing from the street in which his office was situated into the street where he lived.

Cold night air, enough to chill anyone to the bone. Yet Schmar had on only a thin blue coat; and the skirt was even unbuttoned. He did not feel the cold; also he was in constant movement. The murder weapon, half bayonet, half kitchen knife, was in full view and he kept a firm grip on it. Held it up to the moonlight and examined it; the cutting edge gleamed; not enough for Schmar; he struck it against the brick pavement till it gave off sparks; perhaps had second thoughts; and to repair the damage drew it like a violin bow across the sole of his boot while standing on one leg, leaning forward, listening simultaneously to the ring of the knife on his boot and for any sound from the fateful side street.

Why did private-eye Pallas, who saw everything from his nearby second-floor window, permit all this? The enigmas of human nature! With his collar turned up, his dressing-gown belted round his ample body, he looked down on the scene and shook his head.

And five houses farther on, across the street from him at an angle, Frau Wese, wearing a fox fur over her night-gown, stood looking out for her husband, who was unusually late today.

At last the doorbell of Wese's office rings, too loudly for a doorbell, out over the city, upwards at the sky, and Wese, the industrious nightworker, emerges from the building, invisible from this street as yet, heralded only by the bell's signal; the pavement begins to register his quiet footsteps.

Pallas leans right out; he must not miss anything. Frau

213

Wese, reassured by the bell, rattles her window shut.
Schmar, however, kneels down; having no other parts
exposed at the moment, he presses only his face and hands
to the stones; with everyone else freezing, Schmar is aglow.

Right on the borderline between the two streets Wese
comes to a halt, with only his stick planted in the street
beyond for support. A whim. His attention has been
caught by the night sky, the dark blue and the gold. He
gazes at it, unsuspecting; unsuspecting, he lifts his hat and
smooths his hair; nothing up there shifts together to show
him the immediate future; everything remains in its
absurd, inscrutable place. Very reasonable, taken all
round, that Wese should walk on, but he walks into
Schmar's knife.

'Wese!' screams Schmar, standing on tiptoe, arm
upraised, knife pointing downwards, 'Wese! Julia waits in
vain!' And Schmar stabs him in the throat, once from the
right and again from the left, with a third stab deep in the
belly. Water rats, when you gut them, make the kind of
sound Wese made.

'Done,' says Schmar, and he hurls the knife—superfluous, bloody encumbrance—at the nearest house front.
'The bliss of murder! The release, the wings lent by the
pouring out of the other's blood! Wese, old man, friend of
my nights and boozing companion, away you seep in the
dark gutter. Why aren't you just a bladder filled with
blood, then I could sit on you and you'd disappear
altogether. All is not fulfilled, not every blossom cluster
opened out, your heavy remains lie here, already impervi-
ous to kicks; asking a wordless question, but what does it
mean?'

Pallas, choking all his rage into a confused mass in his
body, stands in the doorway of his house, the two leaves of
the door having sprung open. 'Schmar! Schmar! Saw
everything, missed nothing.' Pallas and Schmar examine
each other. Pallas is satisfied; Schmar fails to reach a
conclusion.

Frau Wese, a crowd on either side of her, comes
hurrying up; horror has put years on her face. The fur

flies open, she throws herself on Wese, her body in its nightgown is his, the fur closing over the couple like grass over a grave is for the crowd.

Schmar, stifling the last waves of nausea with an effort, his lips pressed to the shoulder of the policeman who nimbly leads him away.

A dream

Joseph K. was dreaming:

It was a fine day and K. felt like going for a walk. He had taken no more than a couple of steps, however, before he found himself in the cemetery. The paths there were extremely contrived and wound impracticably, but he went skimming along one such path as if descending a torrential stream in a single, unswerving glide. He fixed his eye on a freshly filled grave far ahead, beside which he wanted to stop. The mound of earth exerted what almost amounted to an attraction on him, and he felt he simply could not reach it quickly enough. At times, though, he could hardly see the grave, which was hidden from him by flags that furled and unfurled, slapping against one another with enormous force; the flag-bearers could not be seen, but it was as if there was great rejoicing there.

Still gazing into the distance, he suddenly saw the same mound of earth beside him near the path, in fact he had almost passed it. He quickly leapt into the grass. The path racing on under his take-off foot, he lost his balance and fell on one knee right in front of the mound of earth. Two men were standing behind the grave, holding a gravestone aloft between them; as soon as K. appeared they thrust the stone into the earth, where it stood as if set in concrete. Immediately a third man emerged from behind a bush, a man K. recognized at once as an artist. His only clothes were a pair of trousers and a half-unbuttoned shirt; he wore a velvet cap on his head; in his hand he was holding an ordinary pencil, with which he described figures in the air as he approached.

This pencil he proceeded to apply to the upper part of the stone; the stone was very tall, there was no need for him to bend down, but he did have to lean forward because the mound of earth, which he did not want to trample, lay between him and the stone. So he stood on tiptoe and supported himself with his left hand laid flat against the stone. By a particularly clever piece of manipulation he contrived, with this ordinary pencil, to produce letters of gold, writing, 'Here lies—' Each letter appeared cleanly and beautifully, deeply incised and with perfect gilding. Having written these two words, he looked back at K.; K., eager to see how the inscription went on, paid very little attention to the man but kept his eyes on the stone. Sure enough, the man made as if to continue writing, but he was unable to, there was something stopping him; he lowered the pencil and turned to look at K. once more. This time K. looked at the artist and saw that he was in a state of great embarrassment, though he could not say why. His earlier vivacity had disappeared completely. As a result, K. too fell victim to embarrassment; they exchanged helpless glances; there was an ugly misunderstanding in the air that neither was able to resolve. At this inopportune moment a little bell in the cemetery chapel began to toll, but the artist waved his upraised hand about and it stopped. After a pause it began again; very quietly this time, and breaking off at once without having been specifically requested to do so; it was as if it had merely wished to check its timbre. K., deeply saddened by the artist's situation, began to weep and went on sobbing for a long time, hands in front of his face. The artist waited until K. had recovered his composure and then decided, finding no alternative, to carry on writing. The first little stroke he made was for K. a great release, though the artist, in achieving it, clearly had to overcome enormous reluctance; nor was the writing so fine any more, seeming particularly to be lacking in gold, the line tracing a pale, uncertain course and the letter coming out very large. It was a J, and it was almost complete when the artist stamped furiously on the grave mound with one foot, sending the earth flying up in all directions. Finally K. understood what he meant; there was no time left for apologizing to him; using all his fingers, he dug away at the earth, which offered almost no resistance; everything appeared to have been made ready; a thin crust of earth had been thrown up purely for appearance's sake; immediately beneath it a large hole opened out with precipitous walls, and into this, a gentle current turning him over onto his back, K. sank. But as, at the bottom, his head still raised at the neck, he was already being received into the impenetrable depths, up above his name went racing over the stone with powerful flourishes.

Carried away by this sight, he woke up.

A report for an academy

Esteemed gentlemen of the academy,

You do me the honour of asking me to present a report to the academy concerning my previous existence as an ape.

Unfortunately I find myself unable to comply with your request as formulated. Nearly five years lie between me and apehood, not long, perhaps, in calendar terms, but an interminable time to canter through as I have done, accompanied along certain stretches of the way by some excellent people, pieces of advice, applause, and orchestral music, but basically alone because they all, in order to stay in the picture, kept well back from the barrier. This achievement would have been impossible had I sought wilfully to cling to my origins and to the memories of my youth. Wholesale abdication of my own will was the very first requirement I had set myself; I, a free ape, bowed to that yoke. This in turn, however, had the effect of increasingly cutting me off from my memories. If initially, had men so wished, it was open to me to return through the whole span of the sky's arch over the earth, as my evolution was whipped onward that gateway became steadily lower and narrower; I felt increasingly comfortable and enclosed in the world of men; the storm blowing after me out of my past abated; today it is no more than a breeze cooling my heels; and the distant hole through which it comes and through which I once came has grown so small that, even if I had the strength and the determination to go back that far, I should be obliged to strip the pelt from my body to get through. Speaking frankly, much as I prefer choosing metaphors for these things—speaking frankly: your own apehood, gentlemen, in so far as you have anything of the sort behind you, cannot be farther removed from you than mine from me. But everyone who walks this earth has an itchy heel: from the little chimpanzee to the great Achilles.

In the narrowest sense, however, I can perhaps answer
your question after all, and I am even delighted to do so.
The first thing I learnt was: how to shake hands; handshaking shows openness; today, at the climax of my career,
may that first handshake be followed up by frank and
candid speech. It will not tell the academy anything
essentially new, and it will fall far short of what has been
asked of me and what with the best will in the world I
cannot say—may it indicate nevertheless the general lines
along which one who was an ape entered the world of men
and has established himself there. Yet undoubtedly even
the slight contribution that follows would be beyond my
power to make were my confidence in myself anything less
than complete and my position on all the major variety
stages of the civilized world not by this time unshakably
assured.

I come from the Gold Coast. As to how I was caught, I
am dependent upon the reports of third parties. A big-
game expedition from the firm of Hagenbeck—and by the
way: the leader of the expedition and I have since emptied
many a bottle of good red wine together—was lying in wait
on the bank one evening as I and the rest of the troop ran
down to our watering-place. Shots were fired; I was the
only one hit; they got me twice.

Once in the cheek; not seriously, but it left a large bald
red scar that has earned me the repulsive, wholly inap-
propriate name—I mean it; an ape must have thought it
up—of Red Peter, as if the only difference between me
and the recently deceased, not unreputed trained ape
Peter had been the red mark on my cheek. This just in
passing.

The second shot hit me below the hip. This one was bad
and is to blame for the fact that I still have a slight limp
today. I read in a recent piece by one of the thousands of
windbags that go on about me in the papers: my ape-
nature is not yet wholly suppressed, the proof being that
when visitors come I delight in taking off my trousers to
show where the bullet went in. That fellow ought to have

every last finger of his writing hand shot off one by one. I can take off my trousers in front of anyone I want to, I can; no one will find anything there but a well-groomed pelt and the scar left by a—and let's have a specific word for a specific purpose, but let's hope it will not be misunderstood—the scar left by a wanton shot. Everything is open and above board; nothing need be kept hidden. When it's a question of the truth, every high-minded person drops the ultimate refinements. However, were that writer to take off his trousers when visitors came, that would be different, and I am prepared to see it as a mark of good sense that he does not do so. But then let him stay off my back with his delicate feelings!

After the shots I woke up—and here my own memories gradually take over—in a cage situated between decks on the Hagenbeck company steamer. It was no ordinary barred cage with four walls; instead it consisted of only three walls attached to a crate, the crate forming the fourth wall. The whole thing was too low for standing up and too narrow for sitting down. So I squatted with my knees tucked in—and trembling the whole time—and because at first I probably did not want to see anybody but only to be in darkness I faced towards the crate, with the bars behind me cutting into my flesh. It is considered a good thing to keep wild animals in this way during the initial period, and I cannot today, after my own experience, deny that from the human point of view this is indeed the case.

At the time, however, I did not think of that. For the first time in my life I had no way out; at least, straight ahead was no good; straight ahead of me were the solid wooden planks of the crate. There was admittedly a gap between the planks, which when I first spotted it I greeted with the blissful baying of ignorance, but the gap was nowhere near big enough even to push your tail through, and it would have taken more than an ape's strength to make it bigger.

Apparently—so they told me later—I made unusually little noise, from which they concluded that I was either about to pass away or, if I managed to survive the initial, critical period, would be excellent material for training. I survived that period. Muffled sobbing, painful flea-hunting, weary licking at a coconut, head-banging against the side of the crate, tongue-poking at anyone who came near—such were the first occupations of my new existence. All, however, performed with one feeling and one alone: no way out. What I felt then as an ape I can of course only describe today with human words, and they falsify the description, but although I can no longer quite attain the old ape truth it does at least lie in the direction I have indicated, of that there is no doubt.

I had always had so many ways out, you see, and now I had none. I was blocked. My freedom of movement could not have been more restricted had they nailed me down. Why was that? Scratch open the skin between your toes and you won't find the reason. Push yourself backwards against the bar till it nearly cuts you in two and you won't find the reason. I had no way out, yet I had to come up with one, because I could not go on living without it. Always having that crate in front of me—no, I would inevitably have perished. But a Hagenbeck ape's place is up against the crate—all right, so I stopped being an ape. A pellucid, beautiful train of thought, which I must somehow have dreamt up with my stomach, since apes think with their stomachs.

I am worried that people may not understand exactly what I mean by a way out. I use the phrase in its most ordinary and fullest sense. I deliberately do not say freedom. I do not mean that great feeling of freedom all around one. I may have known that as an ape, and I have met people who yearn for it. As for me, I neither demanded freedom then nor do I do so now. By the way: freedom is something that men all too often dupe themselves with. And as freedom is among the most sublime of feelings, so is the corresponding illusion among the most sublime. Often in variety theatres, before going on, I have watched artistes, perhaps a couple, busy on their trapezes up under the ceiling; hanging by their arms, swinging themselves up, soaring, catching each other, one holding the other by the hair with his teeth. 'That too is human freedom,' I thought, 'mastery in movement.' Oh, mockery of the sanctity of nature! No building would hold up under the laughter of the ape world at such a sight.

No, I did not want freedom. Only a way out; to right, to left, no matter where; I had no other request; and if the way out should be merely an illusion, the request being a small one, the illusion would be no greater. On, on! Anything but that standing still with arms upraised, pressed up against the side of a crate.

Now I see it all clearly: without enormous inner calm I could never have got away. Indeed, possibly I owe everything I have become to the calm that came over me after those first few days on the ship. And that calm I undoubtedly owe to the fellows on the ship.

They are good people, in spite of everything. Even now I recall with pleasure the sound of their heavy footsteps as it then echoed in my drowsy ears. They had a habit of taking everything extremely slowly. If one of them wanted to rub his eyes he would raise his hand like a great weight. Their jokes were crude but hearty. Their laughter was always mixed with a dangerous-sounding cough that, however, meant nothing. They always had something in their mouths to spit, and they did not mind where they spat it. They were always complaining that my fleas jumped over onto them; they never really held that against me, though; they knew, you see, that fleas flourish in my fur and that fleas jump; they accepted it. When they were off duty, sometimes some of them would sit in a semicircle round me; saying very little but cooing to one another; smoking their pipes as they stretched out on crates; slapping their knees as soon as I made the slightest movement; and every now and then one of them would take a stick and tickle me where I liked being tickled. If I were invited today to take a voyage on that ship I would certainly decline the invitation, but it is equally certain that it would not be only nasty memories of life between her decks that I might become lost in.

Above all, the calm I acquired amidst those people kept me from making any escape attempts. Looking back on it now, it is as if I had at least some idea that I must find a way out if I wanted to live but that that way out did not lie in flight. I forget whether flight was a possibility, but I believe it was; for an ape, flight should always be a possibility. With my teeth as they are now I have to be careful just cracking nuts, but at that time I would surely have succeeded eventually in biting through the padlock on the door. I did not do so. What would I have gained by it in any case? I would hardly have got my head outside before I was caught again and locked in an even worse cage; or I might have made it unnoticed to some of the other animals, say the giant pythons opposite, and expired in their embraces; or say I had managed to creep up on deck and jump overboard, I would have been rocked on the bosom of the ocean for a while and then would have drowned. Acts of despair. I did not work things out in as human a way as that, but under the influence of my environment I behaved as if I had.

I did not work things out but I did quietly observe. I watched those people walk up and down, always the same faces, the same movements, in fact it often seemed to me that there was only one of them. That person or those persons, I saw, went unmolested. I caught a glimpse of a lofty goal. No one promised me that if I became like them the bars would be opened. Promises like that, seemingly impossible of fulfilment, are not given. Make good the fulfilments, however, and the promises, too, will subsequently appear in the exact place where you had earlier looked for them in vain. Now there was nothing about those people as such that particularly tempted me. Had I been a devotee of the kind of freedom mentioned above I would undoubtedly have preferred the ocean to the way out that presented itself to me in their turbid gaze. Be that as it may, I had been observing them for a long time before such things occurred to me, in fact it was my accumulated observations that first gave me a push in the right direction.

It was so easy to imitate people. I could spit after only a few days. We used to spit in one another's faces, the difference being simply that I licked my face clean afterwards and they did not. I was soon smoking a pipe like an old man; if while doing so I pushed my thumb down the bowl, the whole crew roared approval; the only thing was, it took me a long time to grasp the difference between the pipe when empty and the pipe when full.

What gave me most trouble was the whisky bottle. I found the smell excruciating; I forced myself, summoning all my strength; but it was weeks before I was able to overcome my resistance. Curiously enough, people took these private struggles more seriously than anything else about me. I cannot tell people apart even in memory, but there was one man who kept coming back, by himself or with friends, at all hours of the day and night; planting himself in front of me with the bottle, he proceeded to instruct me. He could not understand me, wanted to solve the riddle of my existence. He slowly uncorked the bottle and then looked at me to see whether I was with him; I confess I always watched him with wildly over-enthusiastic attentiveness; no human teacher ever had a human pupil of the sort anywhere on this earth; having uncorked the bottle, he raised it to his mouth, with me following him with my gaze until I was looking right down his throat; he nodded, pleased with me, and put the bottle to his lips; I, in the ecstacy of dawning recognition, scratched myself all over at random, squealing as I did so; he was delighted, tipped the bottle, and took a swig; I then, in my desperate impatience to emulate him, fouled myself in my cage, which in turn gave him great satisfaction; whereupon, holding the bottle far away from him and with a sweeping movement returning it to his lips, he leant back with school-masterly exaggeration and drained it at a draught. I, exhausted with too much craving and incapable of following any more, sagged against the bars as he completed the theoretical side of my instruction by rubbing his stomach and grinning.

Now came the practical part. Was I not already too

wearied by the theory? Yes, I was. Such was my fate. Nevertheless I reached for the bottle as best I could when it was held out to me; uncorked it with trembling hands; and found that this success gradually gave me fresh strength; I lifted the bottle, my action almost indistinguishable from the original, put it to my lips, and—and hurled it with loathing, with loathing despite the fact that it was empty and contained nothing but the smell, hurled it with loathing to the floor. Much to my teacher's sorrow and even more to my own; neither he nor I was propitiated by my not forgetting, after I had thrown the bottle away, to give my stomach an exemplary rub and accompany the gesture with a grin.

All too frequently the lesson took this course. And to my teacher's great credit: he did not get cross with me; he may occasionally have held his burning pipe to my fur until it began to smoulder in some place I found hard to reach, but he always put it out again with his ample, generous hand; he did not get cross with me but saw that in the battle against apehood we were both on the same side and that I had the harder task.

So what a victory it was for him and for me when, one evening, before a large audience—it may have been a party, a gramophone was playing, an officer was strolling among the men—when, that evening, while no one was looking, I picked up a bottle of whisky that had inadvertently been left in front of my cage, methodically uncorked it to growing attention on the part of the assembled company, put it to my lips, and, without hesitation or grimaces, with the assurance of a professional, eyes goggling, throat gurgling, drank it well and truly dry; threw the bottle from me, not in despair this time but with conscious artistry; forgot, admittedly, to rub my stomach; but because I could not help myself, because I had the urge, because my senses were in a whirl, yelled a short, sharp 'Hello!', burst into human sound, with this cry joined mankind at one bound, and felt its echoing 'Listen, he said something!' spread like a caress over my whole ˙ked body.

I repeat: I was not tempted to imitate men; I did so because I was in search of a way out and for no other reason. Even that victory was small achievement. My voice failed again immediately afterwards; it did not come back for months; my aversion to the whisky bottle returned and was even greater than before. But my course had been set for me once and for all.

When on arrival in Hamburg I was handed over to my first trainer I soon spotted the two possibilities open to me: zoological gardens or variety. I did not hesitate. I said to myself: do your utmost to get into variety; that's the way out; the zoo is just another barred cage; fetch up there and you've had it.

And I learnt, gentlemen, I learnt. Oh, one learns when one has to; one learns if one wants a way out; one learns relentlessly. One stands over oneself with the whip; one lays one's back open at the least resistance. My ape nature rushed head-over-heels out of me and away, so that my first instructor himself became almost ape-like as a result and had before long to abandon my instruction and be admitted to a mental hospital. Fortunately he was soon discharged.

But I used a great many teachers and even a number of them simultaneously. When I was more confident of my abilities, with the public following my progress and my future beginning to look bright, I took on instructors myself, sat them down in five successive rooms, and learnt from all of them at the same time by leaping incessantly from room to room.

The progress I made! The beams of knowledge permeating the waking brain from all sides! I won't deny it: it was bliss. But I will own up to something else: I did not over-rate it, not even then, and how much less do I do so today. By dint of exertions the like of which have yet to be seen on this earth I acquired the average education of a European. In itself perhaps that would be nothing, yet it is something after all in that it got me out of the cage and gave me this particular way out, the human way out. There is an excellent expression denoting escape: to disappear in the undergrowth; that is what I did; I disappeared in the undergrowth. I had no alternative, always assuming that freedom was not an option.

Looking back over my development and where it has led me so far, I neither complain nor am I content. Hands in my trouser pockets, wine bottle on the table, I half lie, half sit in my rocking-chair and look out of the window. If I have visitors I receive them in the proper fashion. My manager sits in the outer room; if I ring he comes in and listens to what I have to say. Nearly every evening there is a performance, and I enjoy a success that would probably be difficult to surpass. Waiting for me when I get back late from banquets, scientific societies, or cosy at-homes is a small, semi-trained female chimpanzee and I have my way with her as an ape will. During the day I have no wish to see her; she has that mad look of the confused trained animal in her eye; only I can see it, and I cannot stand it.

On the whole I have undoubtedly achieved what I set out to achieve. Let no one say it was not worth the effort. Anyway, I am not interested in anyone's opinion; I am interested only in disseminating knowledge; I only report; to you, too, gentlemen of the academy, all I have done is to report.

A Fasting-artist

(*Ein Hungerkünstler*; the four stories were written between 1921 and 1924—*Josephine,* written in March 1924, was Kafka's last work—and published in volume form by Die Schmiede, Berlin, in 1924; Kafka read the proofs but died before the book came out.)

First sorrow

A trapeze artist—and this art, practised high up in the domes of the great variety theatres, is acknowledged to be one of the hardest within men's reach—had, at first purely out of a desire to improve but subsequently from the tyranny of habit as well, so organized his life that, for as long as he was working in the one establishment, he spent the whole time, day and night, on his trapeze. His very modest needs were all met by relays of servants who kept watch below and who raised and lowered everything required up above in specially constructed containers. His way of life occasioned no particular difficulties as far as those around him were concerned, except that, during the other numbers on the programme, it was slightly disturbing that he had stayed aloft—the fact could not be concealed—and that, although he usually remained motionless at such times, the odd gaze from the audience would stray in his direction. The management forgave him this, however, because he was an outstanding and irreplaceable artist. Also, of course, they appreciated that he did not live like that out of mischief and that it was in fact the only way in which he could keep himself in constant form and maintain his art at the level of perfection.

But in other respects too it was healthy up there, and when in the warmer weather the windows all around the dome were thrown open, and quantities of fresh air and sunlight invaded the dim interior, it was even delightful. There were limitations, admittedly, in terms of human intercourse, and it was only occasionally that an acrobat colleague would climb the rope ladder to join him and they would sit on the trapeze together, leaning on the safety ropes to right and left, chatting; or builders would be repairing the roof and would exchange a few words with him through an open window; or the fire officer, checking the emergency lighting in the upper balcony, would shout some deferential but virtually unintelligible comment across to him. Otherwise all about him was still; just occasionally some member of the theatre staff, wandering into the empty building in, say, the afternoon, would look thoughtfully up into the almost invisibly remote heights where the trapeze artist, with no means of knowing that he was observed, was practising his skills or resting.

The trapeze artist might have pursued this life undisturbed had it not been for the inevitable travelling from place to place, which he found most irksome. True, his manager saw to it that the trapeze artist was spared any unnecessary prolongation of his sufferings: for trips in towns they used racing cars, dashing, if possible at night or in the very early morning, through the deserted streets at top speed, though of course still too slowly for the languishing trapeze artist; in the train they took a whole compartment, where the trapeze artist, adopting a pathetic but at least partial substitute for his normal way of life, passed the journey up in the luggage rack; in the next theatre on their tour the trapeze was in place long before the trapeze artist's arrival and all the doors between them and the auditorium were opened wide and all the corridors cleared—yet even so the happiest moments in the manager's life were invariably those when the trapeze artist once more set foot on the rope ladder and in no time was back up there, swinging from his trapeze.

No matter how many successful trips the manager had behind him, each new one was a fresh ordeal for him, because apart from anything else they had an unmistakably damaging effect on the trapeze artist's nerves.

The two of them were *en route* again one day, the trapeze artist lying in the luggage rack and dreaming, the manager leaning in the window corner opposite, reading a book, when the trapeze artist quietly addressed him. The manager was at his service instantly. The trapeze artist said, biting his lips, that he must now have for his act not one trapeze as hitherto but always two trapezes; two trapezes facing each other. The manager was immediately agreeable. But the trapeze artist, as if intent on showing that in this case the manager's assent was as immaterial as, for example, his opposition would have been, said that from now on he would never again, not under any circumstances, do his act on only one trapeze. At the thought that there might nevertheless be such an occasion, he appeared to give a shudder. The manager, hesitant and watchful, reiterated his complete agreement that two trapezes were better than one and declared that this new arrangement had the further advantage of giving the act greater variety. At this the trapeze artist suddenly started to cry. Deeply shocked, the manager leapt to his feet and asked what was the matter, and when he received no answer he stepped up on the seat, stroked him, and pressed the trapeze artist's face to his own so that he too was bathed in the trapeze artist's tears. But it took much questioning and many blandishments before the trapeze artist sobbed, 'Only the one bar in my hands—how can I live like that!' After this it was easier for the manager to console the trapeze artist; he promised to send a telegram about the second trapeze to the next place on their tour as soon as they reached the next station; reproached himself for having let the trapeze artist work for so long on only one trapeze; and thanked him and gave him a big pat on the back for having at last pointed out what was wrong. In this way the manager was able to calm the trapeze artist down and eventually return to his corner. He himself was far from calm, however, and with a heavy heart he surreptitiously observed the trapeze artist over the top of his book. Once such thoughts had begun to torment him, could they ever altogether cease? Must they not become steadily worse? Were they not a threat to his very existence? Indeed, the manager now believed he could see how, in the apparently tranquil sleep in which the weeping had ended, the first lines were becoming etched in the trapeze artist's baby-smooth brow.

A little woman

There is this little woman; thin enough already, she is nevertheless tightly corseted; I always see her in the same dress, which is made of a yellowish-grey material—almost the colour of wood—with a number of tassels or button-like attachments dangling from it; she is invariably hatless, and her dull-blond hair, which she wears very loose, is smooth and not untidy. Corseted though she is, her movements are very supple; in fact she overdoes this slightly, delighting in placing her hands on her hips and all of a sudden twisting the upper part of her body sideways with amazing speed. Her hand impresses me in a way I can describe only by saying that I have yet to see another hand with the individual fingers so sharply defined in relation to one another as they are on hers. Yet there is nothing anatomically peculiar about her hand; it is a perfectly normal hand.

Now, this little woman is highly dissatisfied with me; she is continually finding fault with me, continually being wronged by me, I vex her at every turn; could one divide life up into the tiniest parts and judge each part separately, without a doubt each tiny part of my life would be a vexation to her. I have often wondered why it is I vex her so; possibly everything about me runs counter to her feeling for beauty, her sense of justice, her habits, her traditions, her hopes—such mutually incompatible natures exist; but why does she suffer so much as a result? There is no sort of relationship between us that would put her in the position of having to suffer at my hands. She need only decide to look upon me as a complete stranger—as indeed I am, nor would I oppose such a decision on her part but would welcome it enthusiastically—she need only decide to forget my existence, which after all I have never thrust upon her nor would I ever do so, and obviously all the suffering would be over. In saying this I take no account of myself and of the fact that her behaviour is of course also embarrassing to me; I take none because I fully appreciate that all my embarrassment is nothing in comparison with her suffering. At the same time, however, I am perfectly aware that this is no loving kind of suffering; she is not the slightest bit interested in actually reforming me, and in any case none of the things she finds fault with in me are of the sort that would ever interfere with my career. But nor is she concerned about my career; all she is concerned about is her purely private interest in avenging the torment I cause her and avoiding the torment I look like causing her in future. I did on one occasion try to point out to her how one might best put an end to this continual vexation, but in doing so I provoked such an outburst on her part that I shall not be repeating the attempt.

And also, if you like, I have a certain responsibility, because stranger though the little woman is to me, and notwithstanding the fact that the only relationship between us consists in the vexation I cause her, or rather in the vexation she allows me to cause her, I can hardly be indifferent to the way in which she clearly labours physically under that vexation. Now and then, and lately with increasing frequency, news reaches me of how she has once again started the day pale from lack of sleep, and with a splitting headache, virtually unfit for work; her relatives worry about her, puzzling as to the causes of her condition and up to now failing to identify them. I alone know them to be past and perpetually recurring vexation. Of course, I do not share her relatives' concern; she is strong and resilient; anyone capable of becoming so vexed can probably also get over the consequences; I even have a suspicion that—to some extent, at least—she only pretends to be suffering in order to direct public suspicion at me. Openly to admit how I torment her with my existence would be too much for her pride; invoking other people's help because of me she would see as self-abasement; it is sheer loathing, sustained loathing, that unremittingly drives her to occupy herself with me; she would be ashamed to expose so sordid an affair to public debate—ashamed. Yet it is also beyond her to maintain complete silence on a matter that continually oppresses her. So with a woman's cunning she attempts a compromise; silently, using only the outward signs of an inward sorrow, she seeks to bring her case before the court of public opinion. Possibly she even hopes that, if the public once takes a good look at me, the result will be a general public vexation with me that, given its enormous enforcement potential, will prosecute me with the utmost rigour of the law in a far more effective and expeditious manner than her comparatively feeble private vexation can achieve; that done, however, she will utter a sigh of relief and withdraw, turning her back on me. Well, if that really is what she hopes, she is making a big mistake. The public will not accept its role; the public will never find such boundless fault with me, no matter how closely it may scrutinize me. I am not so useless a person as she believes; I do not wish to boast, particularly not in this context; but, if I may not be distinguished by conspicuous usefulness, neither will I stand out by its absence. Only in her eyes, with their almost colourless gleam, am I so; she will never manage to convince anyone else. Does that mean I could be completely at my ease on this score? The answer is no; because if it really does become known that I literally make her ill by my behaviour, and one or two watchdogs, to wit the more assiduous among the newsmongers, are on the verge of discovering the fact or at least act as if they were on the verge of discovering it, and people come up to me and ask me why I torment the poor little woman with my incorrigibility and whether it is perhaps my intention to drive her to her death and when I shall have the sense and the simple human compassion to stop it—if people start asking me that, it will be difficult to answer them. Shall I confess to not placing much credence in her symptoms and so create the unpleasant impression that in order to escape blame I am accusing others, and in a pretty crude fashion, too? And could I, for example, go so far as to admit openly that, even if I believed she really was ill, I would not feel the slightest compassion because as I say the woman is a complete stranger to me and the relationship between us is entirely of her making and as such entirely one-sided? I am not trying to say that people would not believe me; they would neither believe me nor disbelieve me; they would not even reach the point at which that might become an issue; they would simply register the answer I had given with regard to a weak, sick woman, and that would do me no good. For here, however I answer, I shall be persistently thwarted by the world's inability, in a case like this, to avoid suspecting a love affair, although it is as clear as clear could be that no such relationship exists between us and that, if it did, it would be more likely to stem from my side than from hers, since I could indeed find it in me to admire the little woman for her trenchancy of judgement and tirelessness in pursuing the conse-quences were it not for the fact that those very virtues are a constant source of punishment to me. Be that as it may, on her side there is no suggestion of a friendly relationship towards me; in that she is straightforward and sincere; that is my last hope; not even if it fitted into her plan of campaign to foster belief in such a relationship towards me would she so far forget herself as to do anything of the kind. But the public, utterly insensitive in this respect, will stick to its view and invariably decide against me.

So in fact the only course left open to me would be to forestall the world's intervention by changing myself sufficiently to, I won't say eradicate the little woman's vexation, that is unthinkable, but at least modify it somewhat. And I have indeed frequently asked myself whether I was so satisfied with my current state as to have no wish to alter it, and whether it would not be possible to make certain changes to myself, even if I did so not out of any conviction of their necessity but purely in order to placate the woman. Moreover I honestly tried to, not without painstaking care; it even suited me, I almost enjoyed it; individual changes resulted, were plain to see, I did not even need to draw the woman's attention to them, she notices all that sort of thing sooner than I do myself, being alive to the merest expression of an intention in my manner; but success was not vouchsafed me. How could it have been? Her dissatisfaction with me is fundamental, I see that now; nothing could eradicate it, not even my own eradication; her rage at the news of, say, my suicide would be ungovernable. Now, I cannot imagine that she, sharp-witted woman that she is, does not see this as well as I do, and I refer not only to the futility of her efforts but also to my innocence, my inability, even with the best will in the world, to meet her demands. Of course she sees it, but being a fighter she forgets it in the heat of battle, and it is my unfortunate nature, which, however, I am not at liberty to alter since it is simply given me, to want, when I see a person run amok, to whisper a word of warning in his ear. We shall never understand each other like this, of course. I shall go on stepping out of the house into, say, the bliss of early morning and seeing that careworn face—careworn on my account—the sullenly protruding lips, the searching look, which knows in advance what it will find, sweeping over me and, even at its most fleeting, missing nothing, the bitter smile boring into the girlish cheeks, the agonized glance directed skyward, the hands laid on the hips to steady herself, and then, as the indignation comes out, the blanching and trembling.

Recently—for the first time ever, as I realized to my amazement at the time—I dropped one or two hints regarding this affair to a close friend of mine, just a few casual words in passing, playing down the importance of the whole thing, slight though this basically is to me as far as the outside world is concerned, to a point some little way below the truth. Oddly enough my friend did not, even so, disregard my remarks; indeed, he volunteered the view that the importance of the affair was in fact much greater; he would talk about nothing else, and he refused to be shifted from this position. But what was even odder was that he did after all underestimate the affair in one crucial respect in that he earnestly advised me to go away for a while. No counsel could be more unwise; the situation looks simple enough, anyone can understand it who examines it at close quarters, but it is still not so simple that it would be wholly or even in essence resolved by my going away. On the contrary, that is something I have to guard against doing; if there is any plan at all that I should follow, it is surely to contain the affair within its present narrow limits, which do not as yet include the outside world; in other words, to sit tight and not permit any major, conspicuous changes as a result of this affair, which means among other things avoiding talking to anybody about it, not on the grounds that it is some kind of dangerous secret but because it is a minor, purely personal, and therefore altogether tolerable matter and ought to remain so. In this my friend's remarks were not after all without their usefulness; they taught me nothing new, but they confirmed me in my basic opinion.

As indeed more considered reflection shows it generally to be the case that such changes as the situation appears to have undergone in the course of time are changes not in the circumstances of the affair but simply in the evolution of my attitude towards it, that attitude becoming to some extent calmer, more manly, getting closer to the heart of the matter, but also to some extent taking on a slightly nervous quality under the influence—which there is no overcoming—of recurrent emotional upsets, however petty these may be.

I am becoming calmer about the affair in that I believe I recognize that a decision, however imminent it may seem at times, will probably not come quite yet; one is much inclined, particularly in one's younger years, grossly to overestimate the speed at which decisions do come; whenever my little judge, grown faint at the sight of me, sank sideways into her chair, one hand clutching the backrest for support, the other fumbling at her corset, and tears of anger and despair rolled down her cheeks, I used invariably to think that the moment of decision had arrived and that I was about to be called upon to justify myself. But not a bit of it, no decision, no justification, women are always feeling queasy, the world has too little time to attend to every case. So what in fact has happened in all those years? Simply that such cases have recurred, with greater or lesser degrees of severity, and that they now add up to a larger total. And that people hang about in the vicinity, keen to intervene if ever they found a way of doing so, but they find none; hitherto they have relied exclusively on their sense of smell, and that, though it keeps those exercising it extremely busy, on its own serves no other purpose. But actually it was always like that; there were always these loafers about, breathing good air, and they always excused their proximity in some smart-alec way, their favourite excuse being kinship; they were always sniffing around, their noses had a permanent twitch, but all any of this has led to is that they are still there. The only difference consists in my having gradually come to recognize them, to tell their faces apart; I used to think that they were gradually gathering from all over the place, that the matter was assuming ever greater proportions, and that this would in itself force the issue; today it is my belief that that has all been so since time immemorial and has very little if anything to do with the approach of the decision. And anyway, why do I use such a big word as decision? If it should ever—certainly not tomorrow or the next day and probably never—reach the point where the public, which as I shall never tire of repeating is not competent in this matter, does nevertheless take it up, I shall not, admittedly, survive the proceedings unscathed, but allowance will surely be made for the fact that I am not unknown to the public, having always lived in the public eye, trustingly and in a manner worthy of trust, and that therefore this suffering little woman, who appeared on the scene subsequently, and whom, be it said in passing, anyone but myself would perhaps long ago have recognized as a leech and, soundlessly as far as the public was concerned, crushed beneath his boot, that this woman could at worst contribute no more than a small, ugly flourish to the diploma in which the public long ago declared me to be an estimable member of itself. That is how things stand today; I have, in other words, little cause for concern.

That some of my calm has in fact given way to concern over the years has nothing at all to do with the importance of the matter as such; one simply cannot abide being a constant source of vexation to somebody, even when one is in no doubt as to the groundlessness of that vexation; one becomes uneasy, one begins, as it were in a purely physical way, to watch for decisions, even when one has the sense not to place too much faith in their coming. To some extent, though, it is simply a sign of advancing age; everything sits well on the young; unlovely details disappear in the inexhaustibly welling strength of youth; if a young man has a slightly watchful look, no one takes it amiss, no one even notices it, not even he himself, but what is left in old age are remains, each is needed, none is ever renewed, each one is under constant observation, and the watchful look of an aging man is a very obviously watchful look and not difficult to detect. Only here again there is no real, material deterioration.

Whichever way I look at it, then, it is apparent every time, and I stand by this, that if I keep this little matter even just lightly concealed with my hand I shall be free to continue, undisturbed by the world, living my life as hitherto for a very long time to come, despite all the woman's ranting.

A fasting-artist

Interest in fasting as an art has declined very considerably in recent decades. Whereas it used to be well worth staging major performances in this discipline on an entrepreneurial basis, nowadays that is quite impossible. Times have changed. Then the whole city used to be involved in what the fasting-artist was doing; public participation increased from day to day of his fast; everybody wanted to see the fasting-artist at least once daily; during the later stages season-ticket holders used to sit in front of the little barred cage all day long; there was viewing at night, too, with flares to enhance the effect; on fine days the cage was carried out into the open, when it was particularly for the children's benefit that the fasting-artist was exhibited; whereas for grown-ups he was often no more than a joke with which they went along for the sake of fashion, the children used to gaze in open-mouthed wonder, for safety's sake holding one another by the hand, at the pale figure who, dressed in a black bathing-suit, ribs protruding hugely, spurned even a chair to sit in a heap of straw, and who sometimes, nodding politely, answered questions with a strained smile and even stretched his arm out between the bars for people to feel how thin he was. At other times, however, withdrew into himself completely, took no notice of anyone, not even of something so important to him as the stroke of the clock, which was the only piece of furniture in the cage, but simply stared straight ahead of him through half-closed eyes and took occasional sips from a tiny glass of water in order to wet his lips.

Apart from the spectators, who came and went, there were also permanent guards there, men chosen by the public—curiously enough they were usually butchers —who, operating in shifts of three, had the job of keeping watch on the fasting-artist day and night lest, for example, he should in some mysterious fashion contrive after all to take food. This was purely a formality, though, introduced to reassure the masses. Initiates knew perfectly well that during his fast the fasting-artist would never, under any circumstances, even under coercion, have eaten the least little thing; the dignity of his art forbade it. Of course, not all the guards were capable of understanding this, and it happened sometimes that a night shift was extremely lax about the way it kept watch, the men deliberately retiring to a remote corner and settling down to a game of cards, clearly with the intention of letting the fasting-artist enjoy a little refreshment, which it was their opinion he was able to procure from some secret source. Nothing caused the fasting-artist greater torment than guards of this sort; they made his life a misery; they made fasting appallingly difficult for him; sometimes he would overcome his weakness and sing during these night shifts, keeping it up for as long as he could in order to show the people how unjustly they suspected him. Not that it helped; they only marvelled at his skill in managing to eat even while singing. He much preferred the guards who sat down close to the bars and who, not satisfied with the auditorium's dim night lighting, kept him in the beams of the electric torches with which they had been issued by his manager. The glare did not bother him, he was unable to sleep in any case, and he could doze a little in any light and at any time, even in the crowded, noisy auditorium. He was quite prepared, given such guards, to spend the night entirely without sleep; he was prepared to joke with them, tell them stories from his much-travelled past, and listen in turn to their stories, all purely in order to keep them awake, in order to be able to demonstrate to them over and over again that he had nothing edible in the cage and that he was fasting as none of them would be capable of doing. His happiest times, though, were when morning came and they were brought, at his expense, a lavish breakfast on which they fell with the appetite of healthy men after a hard night's vigil. True, there were even some who insisted on seeing this breakfast in terms of exercising undue influence on the guards, but that was really going too far, and when asked whether they would be willing to take on the night shift purely for the job's sake, without any breakfast, they made off in a hurry, though they took their suspicions with them.

These and other suspicions, however, were an inseparable concomitant of the whole business of fasting. No one, you see, was able to stand guard over the fasting-artist continuously, day and night, for all that time, so no one could ever know at first hand whether his fast really had been continuous and complete; only the fasting-artist himself could know that, in other words only he could at the same time be a wholly satisfied spectator of his own fast. But then there was another reason why he was never satisfied: it may not even have been his fasting that had made him so extremely thin that many people had regretfully to miss his performances, the sight of him being too much for them; he may have become so thin purely out of dissatisfaction with himself. For he alone knew—not even any of the initiates knew this—how easy fasting was. It was the easiest thing in the world. He told people so, too, but they did not believe him, attributing his claim to modesty at best but more often to publicity-seeking, some even calling him a fraud who found fasting easy only because he had found an easy way of doing it and who, on top of that, had the effrontery to hint as much. All this he had to put up with, in fact over the years he had grown accustomed to it, but disappointment kept on gnawing away at him inside, and not once, on conclusion of a fast—this much had to be said for him—had he left the cage voluntarily. The manager had set a maximum fasting period of forty days; he never let a fast go beyond that, not even in big cities, and for a very good reason. Experience had shown that for about forty days, by steadily intensifying your publicity, you could fan a city's interest higher and higher, but then the audience folded and you began to record a substantial drop in popularity; there were of course minor discrepancies in this respect as between different cities and different countries, but forty days was regarded as the maximum. On the fortieth day, then, with an enthusiastic crowd filling the arena and a military band playing, the doors of the flower-garlanded cage were opened, two doctors entered the cage to carry out the necessary measurements on the fasting-artist, the results were announced to the audience through a megaphone, and finally two young ladies, delighted that the lot had fallen to them, came and tried to lead the fasting-artist out of the cage and down a couple of steps to a small table laid with a meal that had been selected in strict accordance with dietary principles. And at that point the fasting-artist always put up some resistance. He placed his skinny arms willingly enough in the ladies' helpfully outstretched hands as they bent over him, but he refused to stand up. Why, after forty days, stop now? He could have kept going for a long time, indefinitely long; why stop now when he was on his best fasting form, no, had not even reached his best fasting form? Why did they want to rob him of the glory of fasting even longer, the glory not only of becoming the greatest fasting-artist of all time, which he probably was already, but of surpassing even himself to reach inconceivable heights, for he felt his fasting potential to be unlimited. Why did this crowd that professed to admire him so much have so little patience with him; it he could keep up his fasting, why were they not prepared to keep it up too? Also he was tired, it was comfortable sitting in the straw, and they now expected him to drag himself to his feet and go and consume food, the mere thought of which provoked feelings of nausea to which he refrained with an effort from giving expression out of respect for the ladies. He looked up into the eyes of these ladies who seemed so friendly but were in reality so cruel, and he shook a head grown too heavy for its feeble neck. Then, however, events always took the same course. The manager came; silently, since the band made speech impossible, he raised his arms over the fasting-artist as if calling upon heaven to look down at its handiwork crouching in the straw, at this pitiable martyr, which incidentally the fasting-artist was, only in quite another sense; grasped the fasting-artist round his thin waist, seeking by an exaggerated carefulness of manner to suggest how frail an object he was dealing with; and handed him over—not without covertly giving him a little shake, so that the fasting-artist's legs and torso lolled about in an uncoordinated fashion—to the now deathly-pale ladies. The fasting-artist suffered all this in silence; his head lay on his chest as if it had rolled there and for no apparent reason come to rest; his body showed cavernous hollows; his legs, with the instinct of self-preservation, pressed themselves together at the knee while at the same time shuffling along in such a way as to suggest that this was not the real ground, they were still looking for that; and the whole weight of his body, which was not of course very great, lay upon one of the ladies who, casting about for help, her breath coming in gasps—this was not what she had imagined her honorary office would involve— tried at first to crane her neck as far as it would go in order at least to prevent her face from coming into contact with the fasting-artist, and subsequently, failing in this and finding that her more fortunate companion did not come to her aid but contented herself with bearing tremblingly before her the little bundle of bones that was the fasting-artist's other hand, burst into tears amid the delighted laughter of the audience and had to be relieved by an attendant who had been placed in readiness well before. Then came the meal, with the manager spooning a little food into the almost comatose fasting-artist, chatting gaily the while in order to divert attention from the fasting-artist's condition; after that there was even a toast to the audience, allegedly proposed by the fasting-artist in a whispered communication to the manager; the band sanctioned each piece of business with a tremendous flourish, everybody dispersed, and no one had any right to feel dissatisfied with what he had seen; no one, that is, except the fasting-artist, and him alone.

He lived in this way, with regular, brief rest periods, for many years, an apparently brilliant success, held in universal esteem, yet spending most of the time in a mood of gloom that was made gloomier still by people's inability to take it seriously. How was one to cheer the man up? What more did he want? And, when some kind-hearted soul did take pity on him and tried to explain that his sadness was probably a by-product of his fasting, it sometimes happened, particularly if the current fast was well-advanced, that the fasting-artist would reply with a furious tantrum and to everyone's alarm begin rattling the bars of his cage like an animal. For fits of this kind, however, the manager had a punishment he was not loath to impose. He apologized to the assembled audience on the fasting-artist's behalf, admitting that only the irritability engendered by fasting and not immediately comprehensible to the well-fed could in any way excuse such behaviour; went on, while on the subject, to speak of the fasting-artist's claim, which also called for some explanation, that he was capable of fasting for much longer than he did; praised the high aspiration, excellent intentions, and enormous self-denial that were undoubtedly implicit in that claim; then, however, sought to refute the claim by the simple enough means of producing photographs, which were at the same time on sale, that showed the fasting-artist on the fortieth day of a fast, lying in bed almost dead of exhaustion. This distortion of the truth, familiar though it was to the fasting-artist, always exasperated him afresh. What was the effect of premature termination of his fast was here being represented as its cause! There was no combating that kind of stupidity; it was all-embracing. Up to that point he always clung to the bars, listening eagerly and in good faith to what the manager had to say, but when the photographs came out he invariably relaxed his grip and with a sigh sank back into the straw, whereupon the audience, reassured, was once more able to approach and view him.

When witnesses of such scenes looked back on them a year or two later, they were often puzzled by their own behaviour. For by then the change already referred to had taken place. It happened almost overnight; there may have been deeper reasons, but who was interested in discovering them; anyway, the fasting-artist, accustomed to adulation, suddenly found himself abandoned by the pleasure-seeking masses, who elected to pour into other shows. His manager went chasing round half Europe with him one more time to see whether the old interest was not still to be found here and there; all to no avail; as if by some process of collusion, what amounted almost to a distaste for exhibition fasting had set in everywhere. In reality, of course, it cannot have supervened so abruptly, and indeed, thinking back, one began to recall a number of premonitory symptoms that at the time, in the euphoria of success, had been insufficiently noted and inadequately dealt with, but by then it was too late to do anything about them. Of course, fasting was bound to make a comeback one day, like everything else, but that was no consolation to the living. What was the fasting-artist to do now? A man who had been cheered by thousands could not appear as a mere sideshow at village fairs, and as far as taking up another profession was concerned the fasting-artist was not only too old but above all too fanatically dedicated to fasting. So, discharging his manager and associate in a quite unique career, he signed on with a big circus; consideration for his own feelings prompted him to leave the terms of the contract unread.

A big circus with its vast numbers of people, animals, and items of equipment forever balancing and supplementing one another can find a use for anybody at any time, even a fasting-artist—if suitably modest in his requirements, of course—on top of which, in this particular instance it was not only the fasting-artist himself who was being engaged but also his long-famous name; indeed, it being a peculiarity of this art that a practitioner's skills do not diminish with advancing age, one could not even say that this was a case of a superannuated artist, past his prime, seeking refuge in a leisurely circus job; on the contrary, the fasting-artist declared—and there was every reason to believe him—that he was fasting as well as ever, in fact he even claimed that, if they let him have his way—as they had no hesitation in promising to do—the day was yet to come when he would really give the world something to wonder at, although in view of the mood of the time, which in his enthusiasm the fasting-artist was prone to overlook, this claim of his provoked no more than a smile from the experts.

Deep down, however, even the fasting-artist retained his sense of proportion, accepting as perfectly natural the fact that he and his cage were not, for example, given star billing and put in the centre of the ring but were placed outside in what was nevertheless a most accessible position in the vicinity of the stables. Large, brightly-painted signs surrounded the cage, announcing what was to be seen there. When during the intervals the audience thronged towards the stables to see the animals it was almost inevitable that they passed the fasting-artist and that people stopped for a moment; they might have stayed with him longer had not the passageway been a narrow one and the pressure of those coming along behind, for whom this constituted an inexplicable hold-up on the way to their desired goal, ruled out a more extended and leisurely look. This was also the reason why the fasting-artist, though he looked forward eagerly to these visits as justifying his existence, also trembled at the prospect of them. At first he had hardly been able to wait for interval time; he had feasted his eyes on the advancing throng —only to bow all too soon, since even the most stubborn, almost deliberate self-deception was not proof against the lessons of experience, to the conviction that, every single time, at least as far as intentions were concerned, it was yet another lot *en route* to the stables. Moreover that view of them from a distance was always the most beautiful in memory. Because as soon as they drew level with him his ears were assailed by the shouting and scolding of the two factions that formed and re-formed continually: those on the one hand—for the fasting-artist they were soon the more embarrassing faction of the two—who wished to contemplate him at their ease, not out of any appreciation of what he was doing but out of a spiteful whim, and those who for the moment hankered only after the stables. Once the main body had gone by there came the stragglers, but they, with nothing to prevent them from lingering for as long as they liked, strode rapidly past, almost without a sideways glance, in order to be in time to see the animals. And it was an all-too-infrequent treat when a father chanced along with his children, pointed to the fasting-artist, explained in detail what was involved here, and told them of similar but incomparably more magnificent performances that he had attended years before, and when the children, although as a result of their inadequate preparation both academically and at the hands of life they still stood there uncomprehending—what was fasting to them?—nevertheless revealed in the brightness of their inquisitive eyes a glimpse of fresh, more generous times to come. Possibly it was true, the fasting-artist used then to say to himself sometimes: everything would be that little bit better were his pitch not quite so close to the stables. It made the choice too easy for people, to say nothing of the fact that the smells emanating from the stables, the animals' restlessness during the night, the carrying past of pieces of raw meat for the carnivores, and the cries at feeding-time were all deeply offensive to him and weighed permanently on his mind. To lodge a complaint with the management, however, was more than he dared; after all, it was the animals he had to thank for the vast number of visitors, among whom there might just be the odd one for him, and there was no knowing where he would be hidden away if he attempted to remind them of his existence and consequently of the fact that, when all was said and done, he was no more than an obstacle on the way to the stables.

A minor obstacle, admittedly, and growing smaller all the time. People became accustomed to the strangeness, in this day and age, of anyone's seeking to claim attention for a fasting-artist, and with that his fate was sealed. Fast as he might—and he did so as only he knew how—nothing could save him now; people passed him by. You try explaining fasting to someone! Unless a person feels it he can never be made to understand it. The beautiful signs became soiled and illegible, they were torn down, and no one thought to replace them; the little board showing the number of days fasted, which had at first been kept scrupulously up to date, had for a long time now indicated the same figure, even this small task having become a burden to the staff after the first few weeks; and so, although the fasting-artist fasted on, just as he had once dreamt of doing, and even succeeded without difficulty in accomplishing precisely what he had then said he would accomplish, no one was counting the days, no one, not even the fasting-artist himself, knew the scale of his achievement to date, and his heart grew heavy. And when, as happened at one point, a passing idler stopped in front of the cage, ridiculed the old figure, and spoke of fraud, it was in a sense the stupidest lie that indifference and innate malice could contrive since it was not the fasting-artist who was cheating, he was doing an honest job, it was the world that was cheating him of his reward.

Many more days went by, however, and there came an end to that, too. A foreman, noticing the cage one day, asked the attendants why a perfectly good cage was allowed to stand around unused, full of rotten straw; no one knew the answer until one man, his memory jogged by the little board with the numbers on it, recalled the fasting-artist. They turned the straw over with sticks and found the fasting-artist underneath. 'You still fasting, mate?' the foreman asked. 'Aren't you ever going to stop?' 'Forgive me,' the fasting-artist whispered, addressing them all, though only the foreman, with his ear to the bars, could hear. 'Of course,' the foreman said, putting a finger to his temple to indicate to his men what sort of state the fasting-artist was in. 'Of course we forgive you.' 'I always wanted you to admire my fasting,' the fasting-artist said. 'And so we do,' the foreman said obligingly. 'But you shouldn't admire it,' the fasting-artist said. 'Well, all right, we don't,' said the foreman, 'but why shouldn't we?' 'Because I have to fast, I can't help it,' the fasting-artist said. 'Well, I'm blowed,' said the foreman, 'and why can't you help it?' 'Because,' the fasting-artist began, lifting his head a little and, with lips pursed as if for a kiss, speaking right into the foreman's ear lest anything be lost, 'because I've never been able to find the kind of nourishment I like. If I had found it, believe you me, I'd not have made this fuss but would have eaten my fill the same as you and everyone else.' Those were his last words, but his shattered gaze retained the firm if no longer proud conviction that he was fasting yet.

'All right, deal with this mess!' the foreman said, and they buried the fasting-artist together with the straw. Into the cage they now put a young panther. It was a palpable relief even to the most stolid to see this savage animal thrashing about in the cage that had been bleakly lifeless for so long. He lacked nothing. The food he liked was brought to him by his keepers without a second thought; even freedom he did not appear to miss; that noble body, endowed almost to bursting-point with all it required, seemed to carry its very freedom around with it—somewhere in the teeth, apparently; and sheer delight at being alive made such a torch of the beast's breath that the spectators had difficulty in holding their ground against it. With a conscious effort, however, they crowded round the cage and, once there, would not budge.

Josephine the singer, or The mouse people

Our singer is called Josephine. Anyone who has not heard her does not know the power of song. There is no one her singing does not enthral, which, given that as a species we are not fond of music, is saying a great deal. Peace and quiet are our favourite music; our life is hard, and even when we have for once tried to shake off our everyday cares we can no longer rise to things as far removed from our normal lives as music is. Yet we have no great regrets; we do not even get that far; in our view a certain practical cunning, which of course we also desperately need, constitutes our chief asset, and the smile that goes with it we use to console ourselves for everything, as we would even if—though this does not happen—we were to crave the happiness that music possibly provides. Josephine is the sole exception; she loves music, and she knows how to put it across; she is the only one; with her passing, music will disappear from our lives—who knows for how long?

I have often wondered what it is about this music. We are totally unmusical, after all; how is it that we understand Josephine's singing or rather, since Josephine denies that we understand it, at least think we do? The simplest answer would be that her singing is too beautiful for even the most stolid to resist, yet this answer fails to satisfy. If it were really so, her singing would give one once and for all the feeling of something out of the ordinary, the feeling that there issued from that throat something we have never heard before and do not even possess the ability to hear, something that only this one individual, Josephine, and no one else, makes us capable of hearing. That is not, however, my own view of the case; I do not feel that, nor have I observed anything like it in others. Among ourselves, in confidence, we freely admit that Josephine's singing, *qua* singing, represents nothing out of the ordinary.

So is it in fact singing at all? We may be unmusical but we have our traditions of song; singing was not unknown to our people in the olden days; it is mentioned in legend, and there are even songs that have come down to us, though of course no one can sing them any more. We have some idea of what singing is, then, and strictly speaking that idea does not tally with what Josephine does. So is this in fact singing? Isn't it perhaps, after all, simply squeaking? And squeaking is something we all know about; it's what you might call the special skill of our people, or rather not even a skill so much as a typical sign of life. We all squeak, though of course no one thinks of passing it off as art; we squeak without paying any attention to the fact, indeed without being aware of it, and there are many among us who do not even realize that squeaking is one of our distinguishing characteristics. So if it were true that Josephine does not sing but only squeaks and, as it seems to me at least, perhaps barely transcends the scope of normal squeaking at that—in fact she may not even possess the strength required for the kind of normal squeaking that a common labourer can keep up all day long, on top of doing his job—if all that were true, then although it would dispose of Josephine's claim to artistic status it would make the riddle of her enormous influence more puzzling than before.

You see, what she produces is not just squeaking. If one stands a long way away from her and listens, or, even better, if one puts oneself to the tes on this point and, with Josephine singing, say, beneath other voices, sets oneself the task of picking out her voice, one will invariably identify no more than a commonplace squeak, which if it stands out at all does so by its delicacy and lack of force. But when one is standing in front of her it is not just a squeak; to understand her art it is necessary not only to hear her but also to see her. Even if it were only our everyday squeaking, there is already something special about a person making a formal appearance in order to do merely what is normal. Cracking open a nut can hardly be called art; consequently no one is going to assemble an audience, stand up in front of it, and seek to entertain it by cracking nuts. If he does so none the less, and if he succeeds in his purpose, there has to be more involved than mere nutcracking. Or it is only nutcracking that is involved but it turns out that we have been overlooking this art, being past masters of it, and that it has taken this new nutcracker to show us what it is really about, the point being that the effect might even be enhanced if the person concerned were a marginally less competent cracker of nuts than most of us.

Perhaps it is like that with Josephine's singing; we admire in her what we would not dream of admiring in ourselves; here, incidentally, she is in complete agreement with us. I was present on one occasion when—as often happens, of course—someone directed her attention to our habit, as a people, of squeaking; it was most discreetly done, but it was too much for Josephine. I have never seen a haughtier, more disdainful smile than the one she gave then; she who is outwardly the very epitome of delicacy, strikingly delicate even among a people so blessed with such females as is our own, looked then almost coarse; she must, by the way, given her enormous sensitivity, immediately have become aware of this herself, for she pulled herself together. Anyway, the fact is that she denies any connection between her art and squeaking. For those who are of the opposite opinion she has nothing but scorn and probably unacknowledged hatred. Nor is this common vanity; the opposition, to which I half belong myself, certainly admires her no less than the majority does; Josephine, however, wants not simply to be admired but to be admired in precisely the way she has laid down; admiration alone means nothing to her. And sitting in front of her one understands her; one does one's opposing only from a distance; sitting in front of her, one knows: what she is squeaking is no mere squeak.

Since squeaking is one of the things we do habitually and without thinking, one might have supposed that in

Josephine's audience too there would be some squeaking; we feel good, listening to her art, and when we feel good we squeak. Her audience, however, does not squeak; there is no audience so quiet as one of mice, and we might already be enjoying the longed-for peace from which our own squeaking, if nothing else, shuts us out, so silent do we remain. Is it her singing that fascinates us or is it rather the solemn silence enveloping that feeble little voice? On one occasion some silly baggage did in all innocence start to squeak while Josephine was singing. And, do you know, it was just exactly what we were hearing from Josephine; from the front came her squeaking, quite timid still despite all her experience, and from the audience this child-like squeak of self-forgetfulness; no one could have told them apart; yet we all hissed and squeaked the intruder down, though in fact there was no need, for even had we not done so she would undoubtedly have crawled away in fear and shame; meanwhile Josephine, quite beside herself, launched into her triumphal squeak with arms outflung and neck stretched as far as it would go.

But she is always like that; every little thing, every chance occurrence, every hint of intractability, a creaking floorboard, a gnashing of teeth, a blown light-bulb, is grist to her mill when it comes to heightening the effect of her singing; in her view, you see, she is singing to deaf ears; there is no shortage of enthusiasm and applause, but what she calls true understanding is something she long ago learned to do without. So all disturbances are highly opportune as far as she is concerned; every external factor that stands in the way of the purity of her singing and is defeated almost or indeed entirely without a struggle, simply as a result of that confrontation, has its part to play in rousing the crowd and teaching it perhaps not understanding but respect and a sense of foreboding.

And if she uses little things in this way, what doesn't she do with big things! Our life is a very troubled one, every day bringing surprises, alarms, hopes, and fears of a sort that the individual could not possibly cope with did he not at all times, day and night, have the support of his comrades; even so it is often extremely difficult; sometimes as many as a thousand shoulders tremble beneath a burden originally intended for one alone. Then Josephine sees her time as having come. Up she gets on the instant, the delicate creature, quivering alarmingly, particularly below the bosom, looking as if she had invested her whole strength in her song, as if every part of her not directly of service to her singing had had all the strength, almost all the life potential stripped from it, as if she were naked, exposed, wholly given over to the protection of beneficent spirits, as if, having withdrawn from herself completely in order to inhabit her song, she might be carried off by a mere breath of cold air. But it is precisely this sort of spectacle that prompts us would-be opponents to say to ourselves, 'She can't even squeak; look what a dreadful struggle it is for her to get out not a song—let's not talk about singing—but even anything approaching our ordinary squeak.' And so it seems to us, yet this impression, though unavoidable, is as I was saying a transient, even a fleeting one. Soon even we are immersed in the crowd's emotion as, warm body to warm body, all listen with bated breath.

And to gather us round her, we being a people almost constantly on the move, dashing hither and thither after goals that are often none too clear, all Josephine usually needs to do is to throw her head back, half open her mouth, and turn up her eyes—in other words, take up the stance that shows she intends to sing. She can do it wherever she likes, the place need not be visible from far off, any sequestered corner picked out at random, the choice of a momentary whim, will do just as well. The news that she wishes to sing spreads immediately, and soon they come streaming in. Just occasionally, though, there is some difficulty; Josephine likes best to sing in stirring times, when of course all kinds of problems and emergencies compel us to adopt all manner of remedies and we cannot, with the best will in the world, gather as quickly as Josephine would like us to, so that she may perhaps be standing there for some little while, holding her big pose, without a sufficient number of listeners—then of course she gets very angry, stamping her feet, swearing in a most unladylike way, and even biting. Yet even this sort of behaviour does her reputation no harm; rather than try to restrain her extravagant demands, one endeavours to meet them; messengers are sent out to bring in more listeners; she is not told that this is happening; a cordon is set up on the roads around with sentries to beckon fresh arrivals to hurry; all this being kept up until eventually a reasonable number has assembled.

What makes our people go to such lengths for Josephine? The question is no easier to answer than the one about Josephine's singing, with which it is in fact connected. One could cancel it out by completely fusing it with the second question if, for example, we could be said as a people to be unconditionally devoted to Josephine because of her singing. This is not, however, the case; unconditional devotion is virtually unknown among us; a people that loves above all else a harmless enough cunning, goes in for childish whisperings, and practises an innocent enough sort of gossip involving no more than the lips—a people like that is quite incapable of devoting itself unconditionally, and Josephine probably feels that herself; that is what she fights with all the might of her feeble throat.

One must not of course take these sweeping judgements too far; as a people we are devoted to Josephine, certainly we are, only not unconditionally. For example, we could never laugh at Josephine. Let's face it: there are plenty of things about Josephine that invite laughter; and laughter as such is something that is never far from our mood; amidst all the miseries of our existence we've always got time for a bit of a laugh, as it were; but we never laugh at Josephine. I sometimes have the impression that the people as a community sees its relationship to Josephine in terms of this frail, vulnerable, somehow exceptional creature—exceptional for her singing, it thinks—in terms of this creature having been entrusted to its care, nobody knows quite why, but that appears to be the fact of the matter. Now, one does not laugh at what has been entrusted to one; to do so would be a breach of duty; the ultimate in spite that the most spiteful among us vent on Josephine is when they sometimes say, 'We don't feel like laughing once Josephine appears.'

So the community looks after Josephine as a father will adopt a child that, perhaps pleadingly, perhaps peremptorily, holds out its little hand to him. One might have thought that as a people we were not up to such fatherly duties, though actually, at least in this case, we discharge them in exemplary fashion; no individual could do what in this respect the community as a whole can do. Of course, the difference in strength between community and individual is so enormous that the former needs only to draw the candidate for protection into the warmth of its nearness for him to be protected quite adequately. No one dare mention such things to Josephine, however, because she pooh-poohs them. 'A squeak for your protection,' she says. 'You said it,' we think. And, anyway, there is really no repudiation in her rebelling; it is in the nature of children to rebel, it is their way of expressing gratitude; and it is in the nature of fathers to take no notice.

Yet there is something else involved here, something that is more difficult to explain in terms of this relationship between the people and Josephine. Josephine, you see, takes the opposite view; she thinks that it is she who protects us. In a grave political and economic situation her singing supposedly constitutes nothing less than our salvation; if it does not banish misfortune, at least it gives us the strength to bear it. She does not say so, either directly or indirectly, she does not talk much at all, she is silent compared with us chatterboxes, but it flashes from her eyes, and on her closed lips—not many of us are able to keep our mouths shut; she can—the same message is legible. Whenever there is bad news—and on some days it comes pouring in, including false and partly-false reports—she immediately stands up, whereas most of the time she spends lying tiredly on the floor, she stands up and cranes her neck and tries to embrace her whole flock with her gaze as the shepherd does before a storm. Granted, children make similar claims in their wild, undisciplined way, but Josephine does so with slightly more justification than they. Of course she does not save us, nor does she give us strength; it is easy to pose as the saviour of a people that, used to suffering, unsparing of itself, quick to make up its mind, no stranger to death, only seeming to be anxious in the atmosphere of recklessness in which it lives the whole time, and on top of that as prolific as it is bold—it is easy, I say, to present oneself after the event as the saviour of this people that has always somehow saved itself, be it at the cost of sacrifices that make the historian—generally speaking, the study of history is something we neglect completely—blanch with horror. Nevertheless it is true that in emergencies we do listen to Josephine's voice more attentively than at other times. The threats hanging over us make us quieter, more self-effacing, more submissive to Josephine's commands; we come together gladly, we press up against one another gladly, especially for an occasion so far removed from the agonising main issue; it is as if we were drinking a quick—oh yes, haste is necessary; Josephine too often forgets that—a quick cup of peace together before going into battle. It is not so much a song recital as a public assembly—one, moreover, at which, with the exception of the faint squeaking up at the front, absolute silence reigns; the moment is much too solemn to spend in chattering.

Such a relationship, however, could never satisfy Josephine. For all her edgy discontentment with the fact that her position has never been made entirely clear, Josephine is so blinded by her own self-confidence as to fail to see certain things and can be persuaded without too much difficulty to overlook a great deal more, a bevy of flatterers being permanently occupied in pursuit of this goal, which is after all in everyone's interests—but just to sing on the side, unheeded, in one corner of a public assembly, just for that, though in fact it would be no small thing, she would certainly not sacrifice her singing.

But she has no need to, because her art does not go

unheeded. Although we are basically preoccupied with quite other things and the silence is by no means exclusively due to the singing, many of those present not even looking up but burying their faces in their neighbours' fur so that up at the front Josephine appears to be going to great pains for nothing, nevertheless—and there is no denying this—something of her squeaking does undoubtedly get through to us. That squeaking, that sound where everyone else is enjoined to silence, comes across almost like a message from the community to the individual; Josephine's reedy squeak in the midst of difficult decisions is almost like the wretched existence led by our people amid the tumult of a hostile world. This is Josephine asserting herself; this nothing voice, this negative achievement asserts itself and finds a way through to us; it is good to remember that. Should a true exponent of the art of singing ever emerge from among us, we would certainly not put up with him at such a time but would by common consent reject such a performance as absurd. May Josephine be preserved from ever finding out that the fact that we listen to her tells against her singing. She probably suspects as much—why, otherwise, would she deny so passionately that we do listen to her?—but she always sings or rather squeaks herself out of her suspicion.

That apart, though, there would still be some consolation for her in the fact that we really do, in a manner of speaking, listen to her in probably much the same way as one listens to a true singer; she affects us in ways that a true singer would seek in vain to do and that are granted solely and precisely to her poverty of resources. The likelihood is that this has to do mainly with our way of life.

Among us there is no such thing as youth and only the briefest period of childhood. Demands are always being made to the effect that children should be granted special liberties, a special indulgence, that their right to a little freedom from care, a little giddy romping around, a little play, that this right should be recognized and steps taken to implement it; such demands are made and have almost everyone's approval, there is nothing one could approve of more, but nor is there anything that, in the reality of our lives, is less likely ever to be conceded; the demands are approved, attempts are made to meet them, but before long everything is back as it was. The fact is, our life is such that a child, as soon as it is a little mobile and can make some sense of its surroundings, has to fend for itself just like an adult; the territories throughout which economic considerations force us to live dispersed are too extensive, our enemies are too many, the dangers placed in our way wherever we turn are too incalculable—we cannot shield our children from the struggle for existence; if we did, it would mean their premature demise. On top of these distressing reasons there is of course a more edifying one: the prolificacy of our race. Generation—and they are all numerous—follows on the heels of generation, leaving the children no time to be children. Other peoples may take great care of their children, they may build schools for their little ones, and the children may stream out of those schools daily, the people-to-be, yet with them it is always the same children that emerge, day after day, over long periods of time. We have no schools, but out of ourselves as a people emerge at almost negligible intervals the countless hordes of our children, merrily chirping or peeping, those that cannot squeak yet, rolling along or being bowled along by the pressure behind, those that cannot run yet, clumsily, swarmingly sweeping everything along with them, those that cannot see yet—ah, the children! And not, as in those schools, the same children, oh no, new ones, new ones every time, a never-ending, uninterrupted stream, with each child scarce appearing before it has ceased to be a child, the new child-faces already pressing behind it, indistinguishable in their numbers and haste, pink-cheeked with happiness. Of course, beautiful as this may be, and much as others may rightly envy us for it, it does mean that we are unable to give our children a proper childhood. And that is not without its consequences. A certain abiding and ineradicable childishness pervades us as a people; in diametrical opposition to our best side, which is our infallibly practical good sense, we sometimes behave with outright silliness, and it is the kind of silliness that characterizes children's behaviour: giddy, extravagant, recklessly generous—and all for the sake, often, of a little fun. And although our delight in this cannot of course have the full force of a child's delight, a little of that nevertheless lives on. Among those who have always profited from this childishness of ours is Josephine.

We are not only childish, however; there is a sense in which we are also prematurely old, childhood and adulthood taking a different course with us than among other peoples. We have no youth, we go straight into adulthood, and we are then adult for too long; as a result a certain weariness and hopelessness cut a wide swath through the basically tenacious and determinedly hopeful nature of our people. That probably has something to do with our non-musicality as well; we are too old for music, its surging excitement does not suit our gravity, we wearily decline it; we have retreated into squeaking; a bit of a squeak now and again is what we need. Who knows, there might be some among us with a gift for music; if there were, however, the character of their fellows would inevitably suppress the gift before it developed. Josephine on the other hand can squeak or sing or whatever she likes to call it to her heart's content; that does not bother us, in fact it suits us, we can take a lot of that; if there should be any musical content involved, it is reduced to the merest trifle; a certain musical tradition is respected, but without it being the least bit burdensome to us.

But, given this disposition of ours, there is something else that Josephine brings us. At her concerts, particularly in time of crisis, it is only the very young who are interested in the singer as such, only they who watch astonished as she puckers her lips, expels the air between her dainty front teeth, and, faint with admiration for the sound she is herself producing, uses that very sinking to whip herself up to new and, to her, ever more incomprehensible heights of achievement; the majority—this can be seen quite clearly—retreat into themselves. Here in

263

these brief interludes between battles an entire people dreams; it is as if the individual's limbs relaxed, as if, putting off his restlessness, he could lie down in the great warm bed of the people and for once stretch out as he pleased. And into these dreams comes, every now and then, the sound of Josephine's squeaking; she says it purls in, we say it comes pounding in; be that as it may, this is its place as nowhere else, indeed as music scarcely ever finds its appointed moment. Something of our poor, short-lived childhood is there, something of a lost happiness we shall never see again, but also something of our busy present existence and its unfathomable yet persistent and quite inextinguishable element of gaiety. And all this is certainly not proclaimed in booming tones but in delicately confidential, sometimes slightly hoarse whispers. Of course it is squeaking. How should it be anything else? Squeaking is the language of our people; it is only that some squeak their whole life through without knowing it, whereas here squeaking is freed from all the trammels of everyday life and so, for a short while, sets us free too. Oh no, we would not miss those performances for anything.

But from there to Josephine's assertion—that at such times she gives us fresh strength and so on and so forth—is a very big step. For ordinary folk, that is; not for Josephine's flatterers. 'How could it be otherwise?' they say with quite shameless audacity. 'How else do you explain the huge attendances, particularly under the immediate threat of danger, attendances that have even, on more than one occasion, precluded adequate and timely measures to repel that very danger?' Now this last point is unfortunately true, though it hardly constitutes one of Josephine's claims to fame, particularly if we add that, when such assemblies have been unexpectedly broken up by the enemy and many of our number have met their deaths as a result, Josephine, who was to blame for the whole thing, whose squeaking, indeed, may have been what attracted the enemy, was always in possession of the safest place and invariably contrived, under the protection of her escort, very quietly and quickly to be the first one away. When all is said and done, however, everybody knows about this too, and still they come running as soon as Josephine takes it into her head to get up and sing, wherever that may be. From which one might conclude that Josephine was virtually above the law, that she can do as she likes, even if it puts the community at risk, and all will be forgiven her. In which case Josephine's pretensions would also be quite understandable; indeed one might almost see in this freedom bestowed on her by the people, in this extraordinary gift given to no one else and actually running counter to our laws, an admission to the effect that the people does not understand Josephine, as she says, but that it views her art with impotent wonder, does not feel worthy of it, hopes by a positively desperate effort to make up for thus wronging Josephine, and, as her art lies beyond its comprehension, places her person and her desires likewise beyond its command. Well, not a bit of it; possibly in matters of detail the people does surrender to Josephine too readily, but, as it surrenders unconditionally to no one, neither does it do so to her.

For some time now, possibly since the start of her artistic career, Josephine has been fighting to be let off all work because of her singing; in other words she wants the worrying about her daily bread and everything else that goes with our struggle for existence taken from her and—one assumes—transferred to the community as a whole. Anyone easily roused to enthusiasm—and there were those who were—might have concluded merely from the strangeness of this request, from the state of mind capable of framing such a request, that it was inherently justified. As a people, however, we drew different conclusions and calmly turned the request down. Nor did we go to great lengths to refute the argument behind it. Josephine pointed out, for example, that the strain of working impaired her voice, that although the strain of working was minimal when compared with that of singing it still made it impossible for her to take sufficient rest after singing to refresh herself before singing again, and that she must therefore face total exhaustion while yet being unable, in the circumstances, ever to give of her best. We listened to her and took no notice of what she said. Though as a people we are easily moved, sometimes there is no moving us at all. This rejection is sometimes so harsh that even Josephine hesitates; she seems to accept it, works as she should, sings to the best of her ability, but never for very long before, summoning fresh strength—and for this she appears to have an unlimited supply—she takes up the fight once more.

It goes without saying, of course, that Josephine does not actually aspire to what she is asking for, not in so many words. She is sensible, she is not work-shy, that being something altogether unknown among us, and she would undoubtedly, even after her request had been granted, live no differently than before; work would in no way hinder her singing, though nor would her singing become any more beautiful—no, what she aspires to is simply public recognition for her art, recognition that shall be unambiguous, timeless, and far exceeding anything known hitherto. While almost everything else seems to be within her grasp, however, this persistently eludes her. She ought perhaps from the outset to have aimed her attack in a different direction, possibly she has seen the mistake herself by now, but now she can no longer retreat; retreating would mean being untrue to herself; now she must stand or fall by her request.

If she did have enemies, as she maintains, they could follow the fight as amused onlookers without needing to lift a finger themselves. But she has no enemies; there are those who take exception to her for one reason or another, but this battle amuses nobody—if only because the people is here presenting its cold, judicial side, an aspect of it that one otherwise very rarely sees. And while the individual may consent to that approach in this particular case, the idea that the community may one day proceed in like manner against himself rules out any possibility of his doing so gladly. No, the point about this rejection, rather as with the request, is not the rejection itself but the fact that the community can so impenetrably shut itself off from one of its members and do so the more impenetrably for the fact that in every other respect it looks after that selfsame member with fatherly, indeed, more than fatherly, with humble concern.

Were an individual involved here rather than the community, one might suppose that the man had given in to Josephine the whole time in response to a continuous, burning desire to bring the giving-in to an end at last; he had made superhuman concessions in the firm belief that the business of making concessions would nevertheless find its proper level; in fact he had made more than necessary, purely in order to speed up the process, to spoil Josephine and make her want more and more until she did eventually come out with this last request; then, of course, he had briefly, having prepared his move well in advance, countered with the ultimate refusal. Well, that is most certainly not the way things stand; the people has no need of such ruses; what is more, its admiration for Josephine is sincere and proven, and indeed Josephine's request is so exorbitant that any uninhibited child could have told her the outcome; nevertheless, in Josephine's view of the situation such suppositions may conceivably play a part, giving the pain of rejection a bitter edge.

But even if she does entertain such suppositions she has not let them deter her from the fight. Recently this has even been increasing in intensity; whereas before she fought with words alone, now she has begun to use other methods that in her opinion are more effective and in our opinion constitute more of a danger to herself.

There are those who believe that Josephine is becoming so importunate because she feels she is growing old and her voice is showing signs of weakening, so that it seems to her high time she launched her final campaign for recognition. I do not believe this is true. Josephine would not be Josephine if it were. For her there is no growing old and no weakening of her voice. When she asks for something it is not outward circumstances that move her to do so but inner consistency. She is after the highest crown not because it happens to be hanging a little lower at

267

the moment but because it is the highest; if she could, she would hang it even higher.

This contempt for external difficulties has not, however, prevented her from using the most unworthy methods. Her rights are, as far as she is concerned, beyond doubt; so what does it matter how she achieves them, particularly since in this world, as it presents itself to her, it is the worthy methods that inevitably fail? That may even be why she has removed the fight for her rights from the domain of her singing to pursue it in another that means little to her. Her followers have circulated statements by her according to which she feels quite capable of singing in such a way as would afford true pleasure to all sections of the community, including the most secret opposition, true pleasure not in the people's sense, for they claim always to have experienced such pleasure when Josephine sings, but in the sense of Josephine's desire. But—she adds—since she can neither fake the superior nor flatter the commonplace, things must stay as they are. It is different with her fight to be let off work; that too is about her singing, but there she is not fighting directly with the precious weapon of her singing, so that any method she chooses will do.

For example, the rumour was put about that, if her request was not granted, Josephine intended to shorten her coloratura. I know nothing about coloratura and have never been aware of anything of the kind in her singing. But Josephine was going to shorten her coloratura—not, for the time being, to cut them out completely; simply to shorten them. They say she carried out her threat, though I noticed no difference from her previous performances. The people as a whole listened as usual without commenting on the coloratura, and the handling of Josephine's request did not change either. Josephine, incidentally, as well as being extremely graceful in her person, is sometimes undeniably so in her thinking, too. For example, after that concert she announced, as if her decision regarding the coloratura had been too hard on the community or too abrupt, that she would soon be singing the coloratura again in their entirety. After the next concert, however, she thought better of it; this time it was really over with the full coloratura, and they would not be back until a decision had been made in Josephine's favour. The people simply ignored all these announcements, decisions, and counter-decisions as an adult absentmindedly ignores the chattering of a child, wishing the child well, basically, but from a distance.

But Josephine was not giving in. Recently, for example, she claimed to have hurt her foot at work, which made standing as she sang very difficult for her; since she could only sing standing up, she would now have to shorten the songs themselves. Although she started walking with a limp and had her followers support her, no one believed the injury was real. Even if you allow for the exceptional sensitivity of her tiny frame, we are a people born to toil, and Josephine is one of us; if as a people we were all to start limping at every little scratch, there might never be an end to it. But though she had herself carried about like a cripple, though she even, in this pitiful condition, appeared more frequently than usual, the people still listened to her singing with undiminished gratitude and delight, and about the performances being shorter we made no great fuss.

She could not limp all the time, so she invented something else; she pretended to be tired, or in a bad mood, or feeling faint. As well as a concert we now got a pantomime. Behind Josephine we could see her escort, pleading with her and beseeching her to sing. She would have loved to, but she could not. They comforted her, they cajoled her, they virtually carried her to the place where it had already been decided she should sing. Finally, weeping enigmatic tears, she gave in, but as she mustered what were clearly her last reserves of will-power to sing, with her whole body slumped and her arms not outspread as usual but hanging limply at her sides, giving the impression that they were perhaps slightly too short—just as she was about to strike up, no, it was no good, an involuntary jerk of her head denoted as much, and she collapsed before our eyes. But then up she got again, pulled herself together, and sang, as I believe, not much differently than usual, though perhaps an ear for the finer nuances might have picked out that marginally extra quality of excitement, which of course could only help matters. And when she finished she was in fact less tired than when she had begun, and with a firm tread, if her mincing scuttle can be referred to in such terms, she walked off, refusing all assistance from her followers, eyeing the crowd coldly as, awed, it parted to let her through.

That was the situation until a short while ago; the latest thing is that, on one occasion when she was expected to sing, she was nowhere to be found. Not only her followers have been looking for her, many others have offered their services in the search, but to no avail; Josephine has disappeared, she does not want to sing, does not even want to be asked to sing; this time she has deserted us completely.

It is curious how badly she has miscalculated, our clever Josephine—so badly that one must assume she has not calculated at all but is simply being driven on by her destiny, which in our world can only be a most unhappy one. She is deliberately declining to sing, herself destroying the power that she has acquired over our hearts and minds. How was she ever able to acquire that power if she knows those minds so poorly? She hides herself away and does not sing, but the people, showing no disappointment, an imperious, self-sufficient mass that can literally, despite appearances to the contrary, only give presents, never receive them, not even from Josephine, this people quietly goes its way.

Josephine, however, can only go downhill. It will not be long now before her last squeak sounds and falls silent. She is a minor episode in the unending history of our people, and the people will get over its loss. Not that it will be easy for us; how will assemblies be possible in complete silence? Though, of course, were they not silent even with Josephine there? Was her actual squeaking appreciably louder and more lively than the memory of it will be? Was it in fact, even in her lifetime, any more than a memory? Is it not rather that the people in its wisdom valued Josephine's singing so highly precisely because it had this kind of lasting quality?

So possibly we shall not be missing anything very much, while Josephine on the other hand, released from all earthly afflictions, though in her view these are the privilege of the elect, will happily vanish amid the countless throng of the heroes of our people and soon, since we do not go in for history, enjoy the even greater release of being forgotten like all her brethren.

Born in Prague in 1883, Franz Kafka was the author of three novels, *The Trial* (1925), *The Castle* (1926), and the unfinished *America* (1927), published posthumously. He is, however, best known for his short stories, of which 'The Metamorphosis' (1915), and 'The Judgement' (1913), are the most famous. Franz Kafka died in 1924.